DEVIL BY THE TAIL

A GARNICK & PASCHAL MYSTERY

Jeanne Matthews

D. X. VAROS

Published by:
D. X. Varos, Ltd
7665 E. Eastman Ave. #B101
Denver, CO 80231

Book cover design and layout by, Ellie Bockert Augsburger of Creative Digital Studios.
www.CreativeDigitalStudios.com
Cover design features:
Beautiful woman, portrait in retro style. The girl wearing black vintage dress in the winter's park By Leka / Adobe Stock
decoration with golden lights By Gstudio / Adobe Stock
Wiktoriańska ulica By Unholy Vault Designs / Adobe Stock
Nature fog by Glebstock / Adobe Stock
Falling real snowflakes, heavy snow by salman2 / Adobe Stock

ISBN
978-1-941072-97-4 (paperback)
978-1-941072-98-1 (ebook)

"The morning papers had heralded the melancholy and mysterious murder through the city...thousands of persons had already marveled over the boldness and success, the silence and suddenness with which the deed was done, leaving not a clue by which to trace the perpetrator. The public mind was busy with conjectures as to the motive for the crime – and it is not in the nature of a daily paper to neglect such opportunities for turning an honest penny." *The Dead Letter, An American Romance,* by Metta Fuller Victor writing under the pen name Seeley Register, 1866.

CHAPTER 1

The man slapped the *Cairo Daily Democrat* onto Quinn Sinclair's desk and stabbed a finger at the headline. **Man Chokes Wife to Death and Escapes**. "I didn't do it."

He stood more than six feet tall and glared down at her with wary, hostile eyes. His hands were rough and powerful looking and he flexed them repeatedly, as if he didn't know what to do with them.

"What is your name, sir?"

"Ned Handish." He stabbed the headline again. "It's a load of muck is what it is."

Quinn spared a moment to consider the aptness of his name and the fierceness of his denial. "Won't you take a chair while I read, Mr. Handish?"

"Where's your boss man? Shouldn't he be the one to hear my story?"

"Mr. Garnick stepped out to lunch." Quinn concealed her irritation. She and Garnick were equal partners in the detective agency. "I'll just obtain the preliminary facts, sir, and Mr. Garnick will assess the case when he returns."

Handish folded his long limbs into the client chair and she commenced reading.

The orgy of crime continues and this reporter's pen must hasten to keep pace with the bloody track of the monster.

She noted the date of the paper – January 3, 1867. It was now mid-July. The accused monster sitting across from her had been at large for six months.

Ned Handish murdered his wife yesterday morning at the boarding house of Mr. Sullivan, on Nineteenth Street, by choking her to death. The murderer and his wife were comparatively little known in this city. He was irregular in his habits and mysterious in his movements. He had worked at the Cairo Docks, but it was conjectured by those who knew him that his real business was counterfeiting.

Quinn frowned. The new agency wanted clients, but she expected them to pay in legal U.S. tender.

On the night of the crime, members of the Sullivan family overheard quarreling between Handish and his wife, their difference appearing to be that he wanted to take a boat upriver to Mound City and she did not.

A loud pop startled her and she jumped. Handish had clapped a mosquito between his big hands. He wiped a spot of blood off onto his trousers. Those paws looked as if they could crush a human skull, let alone a windpipe. Quinn wasn't afraid. She kept a loaded derringer in her desk drawer and had no compunction about using it if need be. Still and all, she wouldn't mind seeing Garnick drift back to the office.

Handish said, "You need to put cheesecloth over these windows."

"I'll mention it to Mr. Garnick. Would you like a fan?"

He gave the offer the back of his hand and she resumed reading.

It was supposed that she and Handish had sat together quarreling into the night while he nursed his murderous anger and devised his fiendish resolves. Later, when the world slept and there was no eye to see but that of the doomed and hapless victim and Him who sees all, he sprang with the ferocity of a wild beast at her throat and

2

never loosened his fatal grip till the murderous work was completed."

"If I'd of done it," said Handish, "I'd have headed south downriver, not north."

That didn't seem to Quinn the most solid of defenses, but it spoke a certain ornery logic. He had managed to evade the law until now. Why come forward and introduce himself unless he really was innocent?

He cracked his knuckles. "Florrie had a fancy man. What I want is, I want your boss man to find him and clear my name with those jackasses down in Alexander County."

Quinn laid the newspaper aside and regarded her prospective client with a mixture of fascination and mistrust. He looked to be about forty years old and judging from his weathered skin and callused hands, a lot of those years had been spent outside doing manual labor. The stink wafting through the windows from the befouled Chicago River didn't quite cover the odor of rank sweat that enveloped him. "Florrie was your wife?"

"I put it to her, let's go see this fly-by-night you've been trifling with. Let's see which one of us you want to stay with. She acted all ruffled and insulted, said I could go eat horse apples if I thought so low of her. I said she could eat 'em herself since she never served a decent meal no how. I left her spitting mad and went to Hathaway's Tavern to get drunk."

"You didn't choke her before you left?"

He leapt out of his chair, face contorted, fists clenched. "I said I didn't do it."

Without taking her eyes off him, she opened her desk drawer and placed her hand over the derringer. "I beg you not to distress yourself, Mr. Handish. These are the same questions you'd be asked by a defense lawyer, should you ever be charged."

"Ah, nuts." He plunked back down, cracked his knuckles, and stared into his lap.

3

Quinn slid her hand off the gun but left the drawer open. "Was there no one in the tavern who could confirm your whereabouts at the time of the murder?"

"All blind drunk, if the lazy lawman down there took the trouble to ask."

"What is the name of the man you say Florrie fancied?"

"Jack Stram. He's the one that done it. Tell your boss just find him, he don't have to do nothing else. I'll beat a confession out of the twister."

Garnick walked in as Handish was speaking. "Those are strong words, sir. I can see you're het up to settle accounts." He tossed his hat onto his desk and lobbed a mischievous glance at Quinn. "Afternoon, Miz Paschal. Do the introductions if you will, please."

Quinn was still getting used to her alias, a name lifted from a novel she'd read. Her maiden name, McClellan, was too Irish to attract clients in anti-Irish Chicago, and her married name couldn't be used until her claim against her deceased husband's parents for her widow's dower had been resolved. She had adopted the name Mrs. Paschal for business purposes but she couldn't deny a small, transgressive thrill. Having an alias made her feel bohemian and raffish. She said, "Mr. Garnick, this is Mr. Ned Handish. He wishes to employ the agency to search out a man he believes killed his wife in Cairo."

Garnick held out his right hand. "How-do, Mr. Handish. I'm sorry for your loss."

Handish hove to his feet and gave Garnick's maimed hand a quick pump. "It wasn't no loss. Florrie needed killing but it wasn't me. Like I told your secretary, it was a rounder name of Jack Stram. He's here in Chicago. When you find him, I'm gonna kick his teeth down his throat."

Quinn said, "If it's your intention to do violence, we can't accept the job, Mr. Handish. We have a reputation to uphold and you wouldn't want to give Mr. Stram grounds to have you arrested for assault, would you?"

4

Handish scowled. "You let her talk up like that?"

"Miz Paschal is a graduate of the Pinkerton Detective Agency," said Garnick. "She knows all the latest methods. And as for the teeth kicking, best we leave it to the police. It's legal when they do it." He pulled a chair next to Quinn's desk and gestured for Handish to sit again. "Let's hear your story."

Handish repeated the gist of the news article with Quinn supplying a detail here and there. She said, "You must have lived only a short time in Cairo to be so little known and mysterious. Where had you lived previously, Mr. Handish?"

He glowered. "Here and there. Florrie came from Moline."

"Where'd she meet Stram?" asked Garnick.

"I don't know. Next time they meet, it'll be in hell."

"I'm guessing you've done a fair amount of looking before you came here," said Garnick. "What makes you think Stram's in Chicago?"

"A female pal of Florrie's told me. She's seen him at Cap Hyman's card house and some of the skinning places around Randolph and Clark."

The detectives didn't need to inquire what Florrie's pal did for a living. Any woman who walked inside Cap Hyman's gambling den of her own free will had to be a prostitute.

"Well," said Garnick, "I reckon we can take on your case."

"How much?"

"Our standard fee for locating an individual is twenty dollars, cash in advance. Delivering him to the coppers could cost extra, depending on how cooperative he is."

Handish pulled a roll of bills out of his pocket, peeled off a single bill, and dropped it onto Quinn's desk. "I'll be back next week. If you've found him, that's good enough. I wouldn't give you a button to drag his sorry carcass to the coppers." He rubbed his palms down the front of his breeches and turned toward the door.

"Wait," called Quinn. "What does he look like?"

He cracked his knuckles and squinched his eyes as if calling Stram's features to mind required some effort. "Towheaded. Lanky. Likes to fiddle with a spent bullet on the end of his watch chain."

"Clean shaven or bearded?"

"Horseshoe mustache."

"And Florrie's pal," said Quinn. "What's her name and where can we find her?"

"She ain't around anymore." He shot Quinn a surly look and strode out the door.

"Disagreeable sort of a bub," said Garnick. "I'd bet there's a wanted poster with his face on it in police stations all across town. If we're in luck, they'll nab him before he comes back."

"Poor Florrie," said Quinn. "She can't have led a happy life. And what do you suppose he meant about her pal not being around anymore?

"She prob'ly decamped for parts unknown quick as she could get away."

"Let's hope so. Here, you'd better take a closer look at this twenty. According to the newspaper, Handish also dabbles in counterfeiting."

Garnick held it up to the light. "It looks genuine enough. Let's go to the bank and pick out the teller with the feeblest eyes."

"Tomorrow's soon enough. Mr. Micah Winthrop will be stopping by for a visit later this afternoon."

"That shyster invents a fresh excuse every few days to waste your time. How long's he been hypnotizing you with his legal mumbo jumbo?"

"Only since the end of March. He's keeping me apprised of his progress negotiating with my former in-laws. He says that because Thom and I had no children, I may be entitled to one-half of his estate."

"He's been apprising you for nigh-on four months and you ain't, you haven't received a dime. It don't take a mastermind to see he's either swindling you or courting you. All his smooth talk and superior airs give me the pip."

Garnick swept a film of dust off his desk with the sleeve of his shirt and moped. Two years soldiering in the Confederate Army and another two as a prisoner of war in the disease-infested confines of Chicago's Camp Douglas had left him lean, wry, and susceptible to fevers and ague. He had missing fingers on his right hand from frostbite and a dashing, blade-thin scar across his left brow. Quinn suspected he hid less well-healed scars inside, but he had a dry sense of humor and on most days, he was tolerant and easygoing. She put today's peevishness down to the heat and a dearth of cases. That was about to change.

"It so happens Mr. Winthrop is bringing us a case. A big one."

"A big one, eh? What do you reckon it is? Somebody's elephant gone missing?"

Quinn wasn't unconscious of recent changes in Garnick – his prickliness whenever Winthrop stopped by, the speculative way he looked at her when he didn't think she was paying attention, a spruce trim of his previously devil-may-care dark hair and a subtle aura of Florida Water. He'd even begun minding his grammar.

They'd met six months ago, the day after her father was murdered, when there wasn't one person in the world she could trust. Garnick had become that one person. He helped her get through her ordeal and solve the murder. They felt a spontaneous natural liking for each other and emboldened by their success, decided to join forces to form Garnick & Paschal. Theirs was an unlikely affinity. Her husband died fighting to save the Union. Garnick's wife died while he was interned at Camp Douglas. Quinn wondered what she had been like and whether he still missed her. Sometimes she wondered what it would be like to kiss him.

Her husband's kisses had been earnest and eager but stirred no reciprocal feeling. The only other man she'd kissed had left her breathless and craving more. To her chagrin, he turned out to be an accomplished liar with an ulterior motive. There had been no second kiss. Still, it had kindled an immodest desire for further experimentation. Over the last few weeks, she'd been thinking a lot about Garnick, whose way of walking and moving radiated a kind of virile competence. Like he was ready for anything. Like he'd be good at it.

Of course kissing carried risks. If a woman liked it too well, it led to a dilemma. She had to choose between marriage and life as a chattel, or unsanctified carnal relations and life as a social pariah. Twenty-two now and independent for the first time, Quinn had no wish to remarry and she was too guarded, or perhaps too romantic to become a Free Lover. However restrictive the bonds of marriage, intimacy outside of marriage was a spider's web of complications and consequences, the most worrisome being an unblessed addition to the population. For now, wondering was the better part of valor. Besides, whatever lay behind Garnick's speculative looks, he hadn't broached the subject of kissing. Not yet anyway.

She said, "Winthrop has been engaged to represent Elfie Jackson and he wants us to help him investigate."

"The girl who burned down the Kadinger place and killed him and his daughter?"

"That's right. Some charitable members of the First Unitarian Church are paying for the girl's defense. Winthrop wants us to find out if there's anyone else who could have done it. He calls it 'reasonable doubt.'"

"Shouldn't be hard. There's men in this town who'd set fire to their own mama for the next shot of red-eye." He took his revolver out of his desk, broke open the chamber and began loading it. "I'll leave you to yak with Lawyer Winthrop. He'll want to apprise you about the Jackson case without me crowding in."

"But you need to be here. To hear the facts and ask questions."

"You're the one good at thinking up questions. Good at ginning up business, too. Keep telling Winthrop what a wizard he is and maybe he'll shower us with cases."

"I don't curry favor, Garnick. But if Winthrop chooses to give us business, I will certainly welcome it and be nice."

"I'll be nice as pie, but I ain't got the energy for it today." He raked a hand through his hair, tousling it in the old familiar way, and strapped the gun under his belt. "I reckon I'll mosey over to Randolph Street, see if I can pick up the spoor of Jack Stram."

"Be careful," she said to his back.

CHAPTER 2

Micah Winthrop ambled into the office at three o'clock sharp. Tall and broad shouldered with hair as yellow as Indian grass, he exuded robust health, four-square respectability, and the clean, medicinal scent of wintergreen toilet soap. He wore a starched blue linen suit and appeared impervious to the heat.

"Good afternoon, Mr. Winthrop." Quinn finished pasting a label on the file she'd created for Ned Handish, deposited it in her desk, and greeted the lawyer with a smile. "It's good of you to come out in this heat to consult with me."

"Not at all. I trust the day finds you well, Mrs. Sinclair. Or should I use your *moniker*?"

"You make me sound quite scandalous."

"A shade unconventional." His brow corrugated, as if the distinction was problematic. "It would be different if you sought publicity, but you've kept your little hobby discreet. You are being extremely considerate of your late husband's family by not employing the Sinclair name in your business. I hope you won't think me forward when I say your deportment has been the epitome of gentility and good form."

"Thank you, Mr. Winthrop." It was not as charming a speech as he seemed to think it was. "Have the Sinclairs made any offer of settlement?"

"Not yet. Their attorney advises me that your father-in-law is disposed to put the matter to rest, but his wife—"

"Let me guess. *In*disposed?"

"Adamantly."

Quinn had hoped the lawyer could negotiate a fair settlement by simply citing the law. She should have known better. The Sinclairs had disapproved of her from the start and when their son died without leaving a will, they set about to obstruct all efforts on her part to acquire a share of his estate. "My mother-in-law is and always will be opposed to anything that could conceivably make my life easy. Do please sit down, Mr. Winthrop. Will you have a glass of fizzy water? Orange and lemon, or I have cider."

"Thank you, no." He ensconced himself in the client chair, plucked at the smart creases in his trousers, squared his shoulders, and placed a leather portfolio on Quinn's desk. "Business before pleasure."

Quinn didn't see how a glass of seltzer could hinder their discussion, but she followed his lead and sat down. "Is there no way to force the Sinclairs to sell the hundred acres Thom owned in DuPage County?"

"Unfortunately," said Winthrop, "Your husband's name does not appear on the deed their attorney showed me."

"But it does! I've seen it."

"Do you think the document could have been tampered with?"

"Geneva Sinclair hates me, but I can't believe she'd stoop to forgery."

Winthrop steepled his fingers under his chin and contemplated the ceiling. "I know you don't want to further antagonize the Sinclairs, but I think it's time I file a lawsuit. The elder Mrs. Sinclair impresses me as a woman who wouldn't enjoy being summoned to court to testify before a jury and suffer the indignity of having her veracity questioned."

"She'd rather be flayed alive."

"Then with your permission, I'll draw up the complaint tomorrow." He opened the portfolio. "Now shall I tell you what I'd like you to do in the Elfie Jackson case?"

"Yes. And thank you for trusting me, this agency, with the investigation. I know you could have gone to the Pinkertons, but I'm sure we can do the job as well if not better and you'll find the cost of our time less dear."

"Actually, I had in mind a barter arrangement."

"Barter?"

"That's right. I'll conduct your lawsuit at no cost and you conduct a search for character witnesses for Miss Jackson, if there are any. No need for cash to change hands."

Quinn stifled a spurt of exasperation. She had paid him a fifty-dollar retainer just two months ago. "Won't my fifty dollars cover the filing of the lawsuit?"

"I've had three lengthy meetings with your mother-in-law and the Sinclairs' attorney already, and two cable exchanges with your father-in-law in France."

"Even so, that's a very lot of money for three meetings and no results. I've been counting on that money to hire a receptionist and buy a horse and buggy. Can't you just write Geneva a letter saying I'm going to sue and see if she relents?"

"As you've said, the lady is resistant. She and her attorney will delay as long as they can. Of course if you prefer, I can submit a bill for additional communications and pleadings. Another fifty should see us through the initial phase."

"No. We'll barter." Quinn made a mental note. Garnick & Paschal's fee for three witness interviews, regardless how long or how short, would total no less than fifty dollars, possibly more. "Tell me about Elfie Jackson."

"Age twenty, intelligent enough in a rustic way, but no schooling to speak of. She cohabited with Burk Bayer in Rock Island for about two years. He worked in one of Mr. Frederick Weyerhaeuser's sawmills. Last spring

13

Weyerhaeuser dispatched him to Chicago to procure logs coming in by schooner from Michigan and Wisconsin. Elfie followed. The two continued as before until Bayer informed her he was leaving to marry Miss Delphine Kadinger."

"How did Bayer meet the lady?"

"Kadinger buys and sells finished lumber. He runs a couple of steam barges, which Bayer enlisted. Kadinger subsequently invited him to his home."

"Did the fact of Bayer's cohabitation with Elfie, even if it was never solemnized by clergy, not constitute marriage?"

"It would if there were mutual agreement. Elfie believes they are man and wife, although she asserts no breach of promise to marry, which would be legally enforceable. Bayer claims she was just a live-in cook and laundress, well paid for her services."

"And Delphine believed him?"

Winthrop shook his head. "How an intelligent, cultured girl like Delphine could fall prey to a mongrel like that boggles the mind. I've heard it said she was wayward, but Kadinger should have taken steps to protect his only daughter from such a cad."

"How long from the time Bayer jilted Elfie to the time of the wedding?"

He pulled a sheet of densely notated stationery from his portfolio and scanned it. "Approximately six weeks. Bayer moved out of the house he and Elfie had shared in mid-April. He took a room in the Tremont House where he lived until the day of the wedding on June first. Elfie went to the hotel once or twice to try and dissuade him."

"Obviously to no avail," said Quinn.

"If she was as hysterical on those occasions as she was when I saw her, she would have caused quite a disturbance." He went back to his notes. "The newlyweds made the Kadinger family mansion at the north end of Wabash their temporary residence while a new house in Hyde Park Township was being built. On the night of July fifth, while

14

Bayer was away on business in Rock Island, the house caught fire. Both Delphine and her father perished. The only survivor was a housemaid named Rhetta Slayne. The evidence pointed to incendiarism and the police concluded that Elfie was the culprit."

"Why?" asked Quinn.

"Jealousy, of course. Have you not been reading the *Chicago Tribune*?"

"I don't read the *Tribune*. I don't like..." she almost said the way it reviles the Irish, but Winthrop didn't know she was Irish and it served no good purpose to test his liberality. "I don't like their style."

"Nor do I." He flourished a page of newsprint and for the second time today, an emphatic finger jabbed at an offending article. "Read this."

Elfie Jackson could not foresee the betrayal that awaited her in Chicago any more than the barbarian witch Medea could foresee Jason's breach of faith when she debarked in Corinth. Cast aside by the man who'd promised to marry her and forced to watch in helpless fury as he married another, Elfie so nearly duplicated Medea's ghastly vengeance that the sorceress might well be a phantom in her delirious brain."

It read like a sensation novel. Quinn wondered if all newspaper reporters entertained literary ambitions. "Who is this Medea? What did she do and what does it have to do with the Jackson case?"

"Medea was...it's hard to explain. If you knew anything about Greek mythology, you'd understand."

Quinn knew the names of the Greek gods and goddesses, the Romans, too. She'd had six years at St. Xavier Academy for Women and this prig made her feel as if she'd failed some test of basic literacy. "Did Medea set somebody's house on fire?"

"I take it you didn't attend *Médée*, the play at the Opera House in January?"

"No."

"It would be helpful if you go to Booksellers Row tomorrow and see if you can find a book on Greek mythology. Suffice it to say, half the city's eligible jurors and their wives were in the audience at the Opera House for that performance. They know about Medea and it bodes ill for Elfie Jackson."

"A myth won't matter if we can establish an alibi for her at the time of the arson."

"If she has one, he'll have been a buyer of bawdy services." Winthrop crimped his mouth. "Where's that scrofulous scamp Garnick? He'll be able go into the brothel where the police found Elfie living and talk to the hookers without arousing suspicion."

Quinn bristled. "Mr. Garnick is my partner and friend. If you are implying that he is in any way morally degenerate, or a frequenter of brothels, I must ask you to apologize."

Winthrop's straw-colored eyebrows skewed up. "I merely assume he is the more suitable one to inquire whether Miss Jackson had a liaison on the night of the fire."

"Maybe he is," said Quinn. "Garnick and I will discuss the matter and decide which of us is likely to get more information from the women."

"Surely you're not thinking of going to a bawdy house yourself?"

"I will if I think it useful. Where is it?"

"One-fifty-five North Fifth Avenue."

"Annie Stafford's place," said Quinn. "She's notorious."

"With good reason. Her house is a cesspit of harlotry. My sources tell me it's a rabbit warren of women offering..." he broke off, the word trapped behind pinched lips.

"Horizontal refreshment," said Quinn, enjoying his scandalized expression. She was tempted to ask the names of his sources. His prudishness irked her, although to be fair, he had been hired by an alliance of Christian ladies whose sensibilities regarding brothels must give him pause.

16

She said, "I'm a detective, Mr. Winthrop. If I were too delicate to make inquiries in disreputable places or too frightened to venture into the criminals' territory, I would not have entered the profession. Besides, the women may feel more comfortable talking with another woman."

"Very well. If you must." He appeared to resign himself. "The prominence of the Kadingers makes it a difficult case at best and Elfie's stay in a brothel makes it all the more difficult. Whatever you do, be discrete."

"Of course. And do you think you can set up a visit for us with Miss Jackson in her jail cell?"

"There's no reason for you to meet her in person. She's half out of her mind. I was at pains to coax a coherent word out of her."

Quinn didn't press. Garnick played cards with a police captain who almost always owed him money and didn't mind paying with favors instead of greenbacks. He could get them in to see Elfie. "Did anyone have a grievance against Mr. Kadinger?"

"Rolf Kadinger was a hard businessman, exacting and tight with a dollar. He was sued twice in the last year, once by an Irish saw filer named Murphy who alleged Kadinger cheated him out of his wages, and once by a builder, Mosley, who claimed Kadinger shorted him on a shipment of lumber. You can probably find others who didn't like the man's politics or the wages he paid."

"What about the housemaid who got out of the house alive? Rhetta Slayne."

He referred to his notes. "The fire fighters questioned her. She was distraught, coughing from smoke inhalation and crying for her mother. She told them who was still in the house and they sent her on her way."

"Maybe now that some time has passed she'll recall more about that night. What's her address?"

"She lived with the Kadingers. Didn't say where her mother lived and the firemen didn't ask."

"The police haven't tried to locate her? How do they know she didn't start the blaze by accident and run away because she felt guilty?"

"That will be something for you to pursue. The more suspicion we can spread around, the better. Loggers, servants, strumpets, if there's a plausible culprit other than Elfie. A jury will presume the killer was someone of that ilk. Talk to as many people as you can find who'll give her a good character. Something exculpatory may turn up. We have ten days until the trial." He replaced his notes in his portfolio and smiled. "When it's over, I shall take you to dinner at John Wright's restaurant to celebrate."

After he'd gone, Quinn massaged the tightness in her jaws. If Garnick thought her in danger of succumbing to Winthrop's charms, he couldn't be more wrong. The man's arrogance made her face ache. Barter! For mercy's sake. He had money, a goodly amount of it hers. From the look of him, he was probably one of those shirkers who paid some starving Irish immigrant to go to the war in his stead. She'd like to tell him to go boil his shirt, but she'd always been able to hold herself in. She would bide her time. One of these days when she didn't need his business, she'd put a flea in his ear.

She picked up her pen and began to record her notes for the Elfie Jackson file. Maintaining a detailed file for each case was one of the more constructive lessons she'd learned from the Pinkertons. She wrote down the names of people to be interviewed and their connection to the defendant. Elfie topped the list. Besides the girls at the brothel, there was the maid Rhetta Slayne, the men who sued Rolf Kadinger, and the hotel manager at the Tremont. Maybe he could tell her something about Elfie's set-to with Bayer and whether the girl had made threats of any kind.

She fanned away a mosquito humming next to her ear and thought about Burk Bayer. The man had uncanny good luck. Not only was he the heir to his wife's fortune, he'd been conveniently elsewhere at the time of the fire. She appended his name to her list and lastly, the unknown *Tribune* reporter who'd made a feast of the similarities between Elfie and that mythical witch.

Like Medea, Elfie's fidelity to the man she called "husband" was her be-all and end-all. Alas! Having dwelled in Annie Stafford's den of iniquity amongst the most dissolute daughters of sin in this city, her flesh must now be defiled and her soul deformed beyond even the enormity of murder.

What a stinkard. Was he infatuated with his own rhetoric or did he have other reasons to write so unfavorably about Elfie?

CHAPTER 3

From the office window, Quinn watched Garnick drive around the corner and park his rig, a modified buckboard with a makeshift enclosure for the passenger seat and an awning that sloped like a shanty roof. When she first met him, he was hiring out as a hackney driver. He still took fares when there was no detecting to do, which had been most days since they opened the agency in April. It was both inconvenient and annoying that Winthrop wanted to barter, but if she and Garnick did an exceptionally good job, maybe the lawyer really would shower them with cases and refer others to the agency.

Garnick jumped down and rewarded his big sway-backed horse, Leonidas, with an apple.

Quinn tucked her witness list into her reticule and went to meet him. "Any luck tracing Jack Stram?"

"Naw. He's drawn the bottom pair a few times at Cap Hyman's over the last month. None too sporting about it, from what I heard. The last time he visited, Cap's lieutenants assisted him into the street, hind end first."

"As it turns out, Cap's bride figures in our other case."

"Gentle Annie? How's that?"

"The police found Elfie Jackson living in her brothel."

His eyes glinted with amusement. "When it comes to gambling and prostitution, Chicago's still a small town. A lot of our local vice has consolidated since Cap and Annie tied the knot and Roger Plant retired from sin and moved to the country."

"So it would seem. I don't know if Elfie was working or just hiding out with someone she knew. Tomorrow morning before everyone's gotten drunk and gone hunting for love, I think I'll pay Mrs. Hyman a visit and make inquiries."

He looked doubtful but didn't argue. "Hair-trigger Block should be quiet early in the day but take your derringer. And when you put your questions to Annie, best not get over-audacious. Whoever it was dubbed her "Gentle" had a right ironic turn of mind."

"I'll be careful, and while I'm there I'll ask if she's seen Jack Stram. With Florrie gone, he may be seeking a new companion and Annie's brothel is probably the closest to her husband's gambling establishment."

"I'm sure Cap and his boys recommend Annie, 'specially to the sports who've been wily enough to win a buck in spite of Cap's stacked decks and loaded dice. Out of one pocket, into the other. It's all in the family."

Quinn wanted to keep an open mind, but she hoped Elfie wasn't one of the girls who sold her favors for a dollar. "Let's head over to the Tremont. Elfie went there to see Burk Bayer after he threw her over and they may have had an altercation. I'd like to find out if anyone heard what they said. I'll give you the rest of the story on the way."

The late afternoon streets bustled with traffic, everyone seemingly inured to the putrid exhalations that hovered over the city. The day scavengers paid by the Board of Health to cart away the night soil couldn't remove it fast enough and the heat and humidity exacerbated the stench. She held a handkerchief over her nose and they drove along in silence. It wasn't just the smell that inhibited her from speaking. She was ashamed to admit that Winthrop had proposed barter. She should have conferred with Garnick before she agreed to the deal.

22

He said, "This air makes me queasy. Those corpses His Honor ordered dug up out of their graves are sure taking their revenge. I hope the unholy smell is whiffing up the mayor's hateful snout, same as the rest of us."

Quinn didn't want to think how much of the fetor emanated from City Cemetery, where Mayor Rice had directed that thousands of bodies of Confederate prisoners of war be disinterred and hauled away for burial in a mass grave. The operation provoked a good deal of bitterness from Garnick. She said, "It must have been hard seeing so much death all around you. How did you keep your spirits up?"

"By reflecting on how lucky I was not to be on a battlefield somewheres where I'd be obliged to kill boys I had no call to kill or else be killed by one of them. Anyways, all in all I reckon the Yanks didn't treat us Southrons any worse than we deserved. A few Samaritans in blue even shared their whisky with us on paydays. It was heartwarming the way those sweethearts got fuddled after only a few swigs and they were lousy card players." He sawed a finger across his chin and gave Quinn one of his speculative looks. "You were a prisoner, or as good as. Fine grub and silken sheets in your in-laws' house, but you didn't have the wherewithal to leave. They had you under their thumb and you couldn't say or do what you wanted. How'd you keep *your* spirits up?"

"You can wall people in, but I learned you can also wall them out. I walled Geneva out. Most days I was scarcely aware of her." She glanced at her locket watch and plunged ahead with her admission. "Winthrop wants to trade his legal expertise for our detective services. It's a sharp deal, more to his advantage than ours. Investigating an arson and murder is sure to take a lot more time than haggling with the Sinclairs and I don't trust him to make the trade come out equal, but I said yes. I should have talked it over with you but I didn't and I'm sorry, Garnick."

He didn't say anything. He seemed disinclined even to look at her. Did he feel slighted? Taken for granted? Put upon? She'd rather he rub it in that he'd warned her Winthrop was a slick operator.

After a minute she said, "If you don't want to have any truck with the man, I'll understand. We can work the Handish and Jackson cases separately."

He still didn't look at her. "Till we can afford a second horse and rig for you, going separate would be kind of limiting."

"I can ride the horse-car or hire a hackney, Garnick. You're not obligated."

"I am if we're to keep on as partners."

Was there an intimation that "keeping on" was conditional and, if so, on what? She dabbed at the perspiration trickling out of her hair and down her neck. Maybe her overheated imagination had mistaken his tone. His morning at Cap Hyman's couldn't have been pleasant. Combined with the stench of disinterment and Winthrop's stinginess, he had reason to feel frustrated. "What do you want to do, Garnick?"

"The paper says the trial's coming up in ten days. Handish's twenty will tide us over till then and we can sort out whether Winthrop set fair terms when it's over. Go on and tell me about Elfie Jackson."

By the time she'd finished her summary and ticked off the names of potential witnesses to be questioned, he seemed to have forgotten his aggravation and become engrossed in the case. He said, "You didn't name Burk Bayer."

"I doubt if he'd be willing to speak to us."

"Maybe. But what if Bayer wasn't as fond of the Kadinger girl as a husband oughta have been. What if he was only fond of her money? With her dead, he stands to inherit a boodle."

"He does," she said, "and I think he was probably a bigamist when he married her. But he was out of town."

"He could've hired it done," said Garnick.

"True. I'll ask Winthrop, but I think it's illegal for a married woman to make a will of her own. When Delphine Kadinger married him, Bayer would have assumed absolute ownership of her property and if she was her father's sole heir, the entire estate would pass to Bayer."

"It might be interesting to have a look at Rolf Kadinger's will," said Garnick. "Kadinger's lawyer would know the particulars, and maybe even his business clerk."

"Good idea."

Garnick pulled up in front of the Tremont House at the corner of Lake and Dearborn. Its sedate brick façade belied its colorful history. Abraham Lincoln had launched his campaign for the Senate from the balcony in 1858. In 1860, when the Republican Convention nominated him for the presidency, the hotel served as Party headquarters. There were plenty of less savory episodes, too. In 1862, a heavily intoxicated Cap Hyman roared into the lobby and took all of the guests hostage.

Garnick hitched Leonidas to a post and gave her a hand off the bench. She said, "I'll have a chat with the manager and you can talk to the men at the front desk." Belatedly, she realized how high-handed that sounded. "Or you could talk to the manager and I'll—"

"His name's Enoch Bean, a pernickety little strutter. Treats the hotel like it's his private estate. Him and me had a few squabbles when I was driving the hackney. He thought I hogged the parking place in front of the door and steered fares away from the other drivers, which I did whenever I could. You'd best question Bean, yourself. I'll have a go at the doormen and porters. Most of 'em know me."

They climbed the stairs to the front entrance and right away Garnick was hailed by a ruddy faced fellow in a bell-boy's jacket. "Looking for a passenger, Garnick?"

Quinn left them to converse and approached the front desk. "I'd like to see Mr. Bean if he is available."

"Are you a guest of the hotel, madam? If there's a problem I can take care of, there's no need to trouble Mr. Bean."

She presented the Garnick & Paschal business card. "I'm Detective Paschal. I have questions about one of your previous guests, Mr. Burk Bayer."

"Oh."

"You remember Mr. Bayer?"

"Of course I do. Him *and* his bride. They had their wedding party right here in the hotel dining room. Over a hundred guests. It's a heartbreak what happened to the lady. She was a dainty little thing, sweet as could be to all the waiters even after—"

"After what?"

"Nothing. The biscuits and ham didn't get served like they were supposed to be."

"Do you recall Miss Elfie Jackson? I believe she visited Mr. Bayer prior to his marriage?"

A mask of caution dropped over his face. "You'd better talk to Mr. Bean. He doesn't like his staff gossiping. You'll find him in his office. Room One, second floor."

Quinn thanked him and proceeded up the stairs. A man stood in the hallway outside Room One browbeating a chambermaid in a hissing whisper. He had a military bearing, salt-and-pepper hair oiled flat across his scalp, and a stunted sprout of a chin beard. "It is the second time a guest has come to me to report the articles on her dressing table had been disturbed."

"But I was only dusting, Mr. Bean."

"Shh! Keep your voice down."

"But I not take nothing." The maid's voice quavered.

"If there were the least suspicion of theft, you'd be gone already and in police custody. I give you warning. A third complaint and you'll be dismissed immediately."

"Yes sir, Mr. Bean." She scuttled away, head bowed.

Bean saw Quinn and his manner became deferential. "I beg your pardon, madam. I hope you weren't disquieted by that incident. We hold our personnel to a high standard and must occasionally issue reprimands. Is there something I can do to make your stay with us more pleasant?"

"I'm not a guest, sir. My name is Detective Paschal."

"What?" Deference turned to pique.

She foisted a card on him. "I've come to ask your recollections of Mr. Burk Bayer. I believe Miss Elfie Jackson visited Mr. Bayer when he was a guest of the hotel, did she not?"

"Shh!" He flashed a nervous look down the hall and motioned her into his office. "In here."

She stepped inside. He followed and closed the door behind him. "Who are you?"

"As I said, I'm a detective."

"I've no time for tittle-tattle. Be serious."

"I'm as serious as a summons to court, sir."

His eyes narrowed. "That is out of the question."

"I'm making inquiries on behalf of Miss Elfie Jackson's attorney. You would be wise to answer my questions here today or the attorney will compel you to answer his questions in public court."

"That's outrageous. This is the most prestigious hotel in the city. My guests have a right to their privacy. I will not tarnish anyone's reputation or the reputation of the Tremont House by appearing in court."

"Then you have no choice but to talk to me," she said, giving the words an extra bite in recompense for his treatment of the maid. "I believe Miss Jackson visited Mr. Bayer during his residence at the Tremont House. Did you or any of your employees hear anything of their conversation?"

"The entire fourth floor heard. The woman wailed and pounded on Bayer's door until he came out into the hall. I heard the commotion from the lobby. The deskman and I ran upstairs and tried to intervene, but she couldn't be hushed."

"What did she say?"

"'What'll I do, Burk? Where will I go?'"

"And how did Mr. Bayer respond?"

"'Back to Rock Island,' he said, and stuffed a wad of money into her hand. She flung it in his face and screamed. Doors opened up and down the hall. It was appalling."

"What did Bayer do?"

"There was nothing he *could* do. He was plainly embarrassed. He tried to quiet her, but she was crazed. Screaming. 'I'm not a pile of logs you can ship off like common freight. I gave you everything.'"

"How did Bayer respond to that?"

"Nothing loud or profane. Something like, 'Elfie, you mean less to me than a pile of logs.' He turned to go back inside his room, but she dove at him, clawing and cursing. Her language was shocking. Bayer retreated inside his room and my deskman forced the door closed behind him. Two men escorted her out the building and thereafter, the staff kept a close eye with orders to bar her from returning."

"During the scuffle, did she threaten to harm Mr. Bayer or his fiancée and her father?"

"Great Scot! She burned them alive, didn't she?"

"Somebody did, Mr. Bean. Did Miss Jackson say anything to threaten them in your hearing?"

"No."

"Did she try to return?"

"Not to my knowledge." He sniffed and tugged at his little tuft of chin hair. "However I do not think an attorney with any hope of keeping that creature off the gallows will wish to hear my recital of her behavior at the Tremont."

Burk Bayer's cold-blooded words sparked in Quinn an instinctive sympathy for Elfie. Any woman would have been furious at such callous disregard. Elfie may have reacted badly. That didn't mean she stewed for a month and took out her hatred on a woman she didn't know. She may well have pitied Delphine Kadinger.

"Have I answered all of your questions?"

Enoch Bean's condescension strained her ability to keep her own behavior seemly. "For now," she said. "I appreciate your candor, Mr. Bean. I know you are loath to tarnish anyone's reputation."

She left him tugging at his goatee and went back to the lobby to look for Garnick. She found him in conversation with a portly gentleman in a stovepipe hat, frock coat, and striped extenuations. Garnick introduced him as Mr. Edmund Allbright, a banker.

"I used to drive Mr. Allbright and his partners around town to meetings with their investors."

"A lot of investors in a panic today, Garnick. A rumor's flying that the city will default on those bonds it issued to pay for the new Water-Works. Corruption, misappropriation, ineptitude, the whole ball of wax. I'm off to counsel an anxious bondholder now. Pleasure to meet you, Mrs. Sinclair. Be sure to warn the elder Mrs. Sinclair against those bonds." He tipped his hat and took his leave.

Quinn said, "He's seems like a friendly fellow."

"He is. He asked what I'd been doing since I gave up driving. I allowed as how the two of us had gone into the detection line, working to solve the Kadinger murders. His ears pricked up and we got to jawing. Turns out his daughter Josabeth was a bridesmaid at the Kadinger girl's wedding and the Allbright family were guests at the after party here at the Tremont."

"Did he recall anything unusual that happened?"

"There was a fire in the hotel kitchen during the party. It caused some hollering and flapping around, but the staff got it put out in a hurry. Bean didn't want the fire brigade called in. Kadinger laughed about it at the time. In hindsight, Allbright opines it was a bad omen."

CHAPTER 4

As Garnick drove her home to her rooming house on East Ohio Street, Quinn lapsed into a pensive mood. "I didn't have a bridesmaid. There were no attendants at my wedding, only Thom and me, my brother Rune, and a tipsy Unitarian minister with the hiccups. "Do you take this – hic! – man to have and to – hic! –hold?" I was seventeen. It seems forever ago."

"How long did you and Thom know each other before you married?"

"About a year. We were secret friends, Rune and Thom and I. His family was Protestant and in my father's way of thinking, Protestants were an abomination. Thom's family felt the same about Irish Catholics."

"With all that, how'd you come to find yourselves in front of a minister?"

"My father had flown into one of his rages and knocked me silly. I vowed that would never, ever happen again. Rune gave me what money he had and I took the train to New York City. I had no idea what to do or how to support myself after I arrived. Mostly I walked around and gaped at the sights. After a week, I wired Thom. I knew he'd come after me."

"He loved you?"

"Yes. Thom was an idealist. I was a fair-haired maiden, persecuted and in need of a savior. He arrived like a knight on a white charger, took me to the theater, took me sailing on the Hudson River and horseback riding in Central Park. I was dazzled, I guess. I'd spent all Rune's money and had no place to go. When he asked me to marry him, it was an easy decision."

"He sounds like a fine gentleman and never a boresome moment. You must have believed you'd be happy."

"I suppose I did. I thought by becoming Mrs. Thomas Sinclair I wouldn't have to be Irish anymore."

Her father had been a member of the revolutionary Fenian Brotherhood, dedicated to winning independence for Ireland. He hated the English, hated the Protestants, and hated the politics of Abraham Lincoln. His fanatical devotion to "the old country" confounded Quinn's understanding. She yearned to belong to the new country, to blend in, to cease being separate and despised. Unlike the recent influx of unschooled and impoverished immigrants, her family was educated and had a comfortable living. They could have passed if her father hadn't been so pigheaded and confrontational.

"The best soldiers on both sides of the war were Irish," said Garnick. "The fightingest spirit and the funniest stories. Your husband had no problem with you being Irish, did he?"

"No, but his mother did. She was mortified that her beloved only son had demeaned the family name by yoking himself to common Irish trash. She made a longsuffering best of it while he was alive. After he died, having left no will or made any provision for me, she turned into a tyrant. I was stranded. I couldn't go home and hadn't the means to go elsewhere. If that Pinkerton job hadn't come along when it did, I'd have gone right round the bend." She blew out a sardonic breath. "As the saying goes, marry in haste and repent at leisure."

"It's that bloody war that scotched your chances," said Garnick, waxing pensive himself. "I'd give my eyes never to have put on a uniform."

32

"Because you fought on the wrong side?"

"There's that. No way to justify going to war to keep people in chains. At first I had some notion of loyalty to my neck of the woods, allegiance to kith and kin like the states' rights firebrands preached. But the more time goes by, the less reason a man can conjure up for the killing and sorrow he's caused. What I repent at leisure? I made at least two widows like you before the Yanks stopped me."

Quinn would have liked to tell Garnick that not all widows grieved. She didn't. She twisted her wedding ring and tried to visualize Thom's face, but it was nebulous, like an image in sepia.

A herd of hogs on their way to the stockyards trotted briskly down the middle of the street and coursed past them. Garnick geed Leonidas to the verge to wait. As the hogs passed, a tumult of grunts and squeals and dust engulfed the hack. Quinn took out a handkerchief and covered her nose and mouth.

Garnick crooked his elbow across his face. "These dog days have got everybody perturbed, even the pigs. Dust, drought, fevers, knifings. A few streaks of dry lightning last night, but no rain. We need a thunderstorm to cool things off and clear the air."

When the noise and dust receded, Garnick flicked the reins and they started off again. "Maybe if Thom had come home from the war and y'all had moved far off by yourselves and away from your families, you'd have been happy."

"Maybe if I'd had a bridesmaid to confide in, she'd have talked me out of getting married in the first place. I wonder if Delphine confided in Josabeth Allbright about her romance with Bayer before the wedding or worried out loud about any problems he might've had."

"You mean problems besides Elfie?"

"Mr. Bayer strikes me as a man with no more conscience than a cat. It wouldn't surprise me if his past is littered with broken hearts and angry women. Quite possibly a few angry men, as well. Bayer himself may have been the arsonist's target."

"If," said Garnick, "the arson was intended to kill anyone. It might've been just some random meanery gone wrong."

A shot exploded out of nowhere. Leonidas let out a terrified whinny and reared. The carriage tipped onto its rear wheels and Quinn slipped to the floor, her skirt billowing around her ears. The carriage lurched forward. She didn't know how, but Garnick was on the ground, running beside her, still holding onto the reins and calling "whoa" and "easy boy" over and over again.

A second shot splintered the carriage back and tore into the seat where she'd been sitting. The carriage surged and stopped, surged and stopped.

Somebody yelled, "Stop them hogs! Cut 'em off!"

Crouched on the floor, Quinn peered out through a blizzard of dust. The hogs had turned and stampeded in all directions, chased by shouting drovers. Pedestrians scattered. Horses shrieked. Was there another shot? From somewhere, she heard glass shattering. Finally Garnick gained control of his big horse, the carriage slowed and came to rest next to the curb.

He stuck his head in the window, a stricken look on his face. "Are you hurt?"

"Just scared."

His eyes riveted on the bullet hole. "Stay low. The shooter may not be done."

"Did you see him?"

"No. The shots came from above, maybe one of those windows in the mercantile over yonder."

She looked, but the windows were dark and empty. Practically every man in Chicago carried a gun, but the streets in this part of town weren't known for being dangerous. They weren't known for stampeding hogs either.

"Some reckless drunk, you think? Somebody trying to cause a stampede?"

"Maybe."

"Moses' horns! You don't think he was aiming at *us*, do you?"

"It crossed my mind."

A few minutes went by and Quinn pushed herself back up on the seat, shying away from the hole where the bullet had lodged. The drovers began to get the hogs rounded up and the racket subsided.

Garnick climbed back onto the driver's bench. "I might have made a mistake giving out our calling card when I was nosing around after Stram this morning. Could be this is his way of telling me he ain't desirous to make my acquaintance."

Quinn's heart thudded and her hands shook. Only this morning she'd boasted to Winthrop how brave she was. She took a deep breath and anger displaced fear. She said, "If we find out it was Stram that shot at us, I will reconsider Mr. Handish's suggestion about kicking his teeth down his throat."

***

She slept with the derringer under her pillow and woke at six to the complaints of a jay outside her window. Happily, the boarding house had invested in wire cloth for the windows to keep out flies and mosquitos, so the night had passed in relative comfort. However the sun was already beating through the lace curtains and left no doubt that it was going to be another scorcher.

The aroma of Mrs. Mills' coffee roused her to a pleasant state of alertness. Her landlady had a percolating machine, which meant fewer grounds to pick out of one's teeth, and she was a fine baker, as well. Quinn looked forward to her morning slice of Sallie Lunn or apple crumb pie. But it was the feeling of waking up free and independent, accountable to nobody but herself that gave her the most satisfaction. If she could make a success of the detective agency, it would go a long way toward making up for those years she languished in her mother-in-law's elegant tomb of a house. She donned a modest gray dress she'd worn during her half-mourning, braided her russet mane, and pinned it under a prim spoon bonnet. She didn't want to be mistaken for a nymph of the pavement as she walked in a neighborhood teeming with brothels. She didn't discount Winthrop's admonition, or Garnick's advice to beware of Gentle Annie. Last summer Annie took a horsewhip to her faithless lover, Cap Hyman, and flogged him through the streets, a ferocious show of love that persuaded him to ask her hand in marriage. In spite of the madam's legendary antics, or perhaps because of them, Quinn looked forward to the adventure.

At the breakfast table, her fellow boarders, Miss Gilbertine Nearest and Miss Ida Franks, were sharing a morning newspaper. Miss Franks, a thin, tight-lipped spinster in her late twenties, was an assistant telegraph clerk for Western Union and rarely uttered a complete sentence. Quinn attributed her terse speaking style to long days of nothing but di-di, dah-dah, and dit-dit. Miss Nearest could not have been more different in either appearance or disposition. Broad-hipped and brimming with enthusiasms, she spoke in long paragraphs replete with obscure facts and uplifting moral sentiments. She was a retired missionary and nurse who had accompanied Florence Nightingale to Egypt and Greece in 1849 and 1850. Quinn poured herself a cup of coffee and joined them.

"The pastry is excellent this morning, Mrs. Sinclair, but the news is harrowing," began Miss Nearest. "A Methodist missionary and seven Christian converts cooked and eaten by cannibals on some Fijian island. Viti Levu. A lone guide survived to tell the grisly tale. Those godless savages bashed

36

the Reverend in the head with a rock, roasted him, and fed him to their chief."

"With forks," added Miss Franks.

"Yes, yes. And closer to home, sanitation workers found two badly decayed human bodies near the new water intake crib in Lake Michigan. Can you believe it? The engineering marvel that promised us clean drinking water and no live fish in our drinking goblets and now we must take care not to imbibe the remains of dead men."

"Horrifying," said Miss Franks.

Miss Nearest tapped the newspaper. "Here's an interesting item. That spiritualist woman who's been giving lectures on the blessings of magnetic healing has declared herself a Free Lover. Victoria Woodhull is her name. She says men are allowed all manner of sexual license and no law should infringe a woman's natural right to love whomever she chooses and change her mind every day if it pleases her."

"The brass," said Miss Franks.

"She's divorced, but living with...who is it now?" Miss Nearest straightened a fold in the paper for a clearer view. "Colonel James Blood. It says here that he's in Chicago seeking a divorce. If he isn't yet divorced—"

"Bigamy," pronounced Miss Franks.

"So it would seem," said Miss Nearest. "If they were legally married, why wouldn't she call herself Mrs. Blood?"

"Why shouldn't she be able to call herself whatever she chooses?" asked Quinn.

"You are being flippant, Mrs. Sinclair," said Miss Nearest. "A married woman always takes her husband's surname. She and her husband are considered one."

"And the 'one' is the man," shot Quinn. "I rather admire this Victoria Woodhull's brass. You ladies were wise never to marry. You haven't had to live under the law of coverture, which means that a wife has no separate existence apart

37

from her husband. She has no individual rights, no property rights, no say in what he does or how she's treated."

"I quite agree that married women should be allowed more of a voice in matters affecting the home," said Miss Nearest, "especially with regard to the process by which the population is increased."

"Gilbertine!" Miss Franks was aghast.

"Now, now Ida. We mustn't be old-maidish," said Miss Nearest. "I'm sure Mrs. Sinclair was only repeating what some of those radical spiritualists have been saying. As a widow, she is as far removed from such concerns as you and I."

Quinn hid her irritation behind her coffee cup. It was no joy to be included in the same category as these eternally celibate old biddies. And what would they think if she told them she had a *nom de guerre,* investigated murder, and carried a loaded gun in her pocket? They'd demand that Mrs. Mills send her packing. She switched to a different topic. "You've been to Greece, Miss Nearest. Do you know the Medea myth?"

"I saw the Euripides play in Athens with dear Florence, a special performance in English, and Miss Franks and I attended the adaptation at Crosby's a few months ago with that Italian tragedienne, Adelaide Ristori. I will tell you this, Ristori's interpretation of the Medea character could not have been more surprising. Instead of a cold, cunning murderess, she portrayed the sorceress as Jason's victim, abandoned in a foreign land without recourse. A few bleeding hearts may have shed a tear. Not I. Her crimes were atrocious, did you not think so, Miss Franks?"

"Wicked," said Miss Franks. "Like that Elfie Jackson."

"Elfie Jackson isn't a sorceress," said Quinn, reflexively defensive. "I'd be surprised if she can read or write."

Miss Nearest helped herself to another wedge of cake. "Ignorance is fertile soil for savagery, Mrs. Sinclair, as attested by the cannibals of Viti Levu. But I should think

38

Miss Jackson's ignorance is irrelevant, consumed as she was by jealousy and hate. As the poet said, 'Heaven has no rage like love to hatred turned, nor hell a fury like a woman scorned.' Who was the poet, Ida?"

"Congreve."

"Yes, Congreve. He could well have been describing Medea. If you wish, I shall lend you my copy of the play, Mrs. Sinclair. We can have a nice, long discussion about it when you return this evening from visiting your invalid brother in the hospital. It's a very great kindness for you to spend so much time with him every day."

Quinn regretted the need to tell such a lie, but it wasn't her fault people were so close-minded. She patted the derringer nestling in her pocket, bid the ladies good day, and set off to Annie Stafford's brothel.

CHAPTER 5

Every seat on the horse-car was occupied save one, next to a
sprawling, unkempt laborer who gave off an odor of
fermented cabbage. Quinn squeezed herself into the space,
shrinking as far away from the smell as possible, and
brooded. If most of her gender held the same view as the
boarding house ladies, it was just as well that only men were
permitted to serve on juries. Of course she would try her best
to discover exculpatory evidence but failing that, she hoped
Elfie had a pretty face. Last year a jury acquitted a woman
named Mollie Cosgriff of shooting her lover dead in Seneca
Wright's saloon. Her lawyer pleaded temporary emotional
insanity, which may have influenced the verdict, but the
jurors couldn't have been oblivious to the accused's comely
shape.

Quinn left the car on Randolph and crossed the street
to avoid passing in front of the saloon. Most of the buildings
on this side were dormitories housing the overflow of single
men who flocked to the city to work in the slaughterhouses,
lumberyards, rail and shipyards, and the new industries
located to the south along the Calumet River. The presence
of so many restive, untethered men with money in their
pockets had given rise to a proliferation of gambling houses
and brothels to take it away from them. She kept her eyes

down and pretended not to hear the lewd calls coming from the saloon.

A burly man with a head start on his drinking stumbled out of a doorway and bumped her. "Hey, *fraulein*, you want have some beers *mit* Horst, *ja?*" He caught hold of her arm, but she snatched it away and hurried on.

She turned onto 5th Avenue and saw the "Why Not?" signs painted on the window shades. This was Annie's place, but the idea of the "Why Not?" signs had been stolen from Roger Plant, whose squalid "Under the Willows" brothel still operated despite his retirement. Quinn checked behind her to see if anyone was looking and dashed through the red door with the number 155 in flaking gold leaf. The small vestibule was dark and dingy, the air thick with stale tobacco smoke, lamp oil, and rancid cologne. A narrow, steep stairwell led upward toward light and the sounds of bickering.

"You'd get more trade if you do the French. Annie says she'll give you an extra dollar off your keep."

"I don't care if she gives me ten, it's disgusting."

Quinn hiked up her skirt and climbed, topping out in a room with peeling red-and-gold papered walls, a crystal chandelier, and a row of red velvet settees. The bickerers faced off across a high pedestal table held aloft by a chipped marble nude. The woman who refused to do the French sneered and stalked off down a dim hallway. The man, hulking and beetle-browed, gave Quinn a churlish look. "Annie ain't hiring."

"I'm not here to apply for work. I'm a detective."

"And I'm U.S. Grant."

"Will you please tell Mrs. Hyman I'd like a word?"

He guffawed. "She'll chew you up and spit you out."

She handed him a business card. "It's important."

He gave it and her an appraising look and sauntered off, presumably to inform the madam. Quinn stood in a dark corner, afraid a customer would walk up the stairs and misapprehend her reason for being there. A miasma of cloying perfume and rampant lust pervaded the room. She thought about the kinds of transactions that took place here every day. How self-cheapening it must be to sell one's body to strangers, over and over again. She suppressed a shudder of revulsion. Was it only this morning she'd defended Victoria Woodhull's assertion of a woman's right to the same sexual license as a man? Standing here, she was as sanctimonious and judgmental as the boarding house biddies.

"What can I do for you, honey?"

She turned in the direction of a high-pitched, scratchy voice and met the round button eye of a large green parrot. She crossed the room and stared into its brass cage. The bird lifted a foot off its perch as if in salute. "What can I do for you, honey?"

"What's your name?" asked Quinn.

"His name's Romeo," came a voice from behind like rolling thunder. "Mine's Annie."

She was enormous. Tightly corseted in a low-cut canary yellow dress, she resembled a belted balloon, the upper bulge near to bursting. Her hair was flame red, her eyes small and shrewd, and she emitted an aggressive fragrance of otto of roses. She thumped the business card. "Which one are you, Paschal or Garnick?"

"I'm Paschal. Mrs. Paschal."

"Mrs., eh? Your old man must be a broad-minded cuss to let you sashay around in this part of town all by your lonesome."

"He was killed in the war."

"Well, cheer up. There's plenty of live ones and all much the same but for the size of their wallets." Her laugh rumbled and her vast bosom jiggled. She installed herself on a settee and filled it, arm to arm. "Take a seat, honey, and speak your piece."

43

Quinn alighted on the edge of a facing settee. "My agency is trying to locate a man named Jack Stram. He gambled at your husband's place recently. Have you or any of your...your renters met him?"

"I'm sorry to say I have. He came in drunk a while ago after Cap threw him out. Cap's cursed with a tender heart. He let the cur slink off. Stram hadn't been here ten minutes before he punched one of my girls. He's one jasper should've been squashed in the cradle. Whoever it was paid you to find him, I'll lay odds it wasn't a woman."

"Do you know where Stram is staying or where he went when he left here?"

"To the hospital, I guess. He was bloody as a stuck pig when he left here. There was a write-up about the fracas in the *Tribune*. Little snooper showed up saying he wanted to print my side so folks wouldn't take me for a heathen. I said better a heathen than a Holy Roller that comes oozing in here of a Saturday night and leaves his wife at home to darn his socks. Damn if the paper didn't quote me."

"Does the woman Stram visited know where he lives?"

"You'd have to ask her. Name's Jemelle Clary."

"Is she here?"

"No more. Stram knocked out one of her front teeth and I had to give her the boot. Stupid heifer. I expect my girls to know how to dodge a fist and control their customers. She's a waste of space now till her mouth heals."

"Where did she go?"

"Lou Harper took her in over at the Mansion on Monroe. Lou's a soft touch and Jemelle's a fair earner, or was. A few of her regulars still come in asking for her."

"On another matter," said Quinn, holding back a sarcastic retort, "I'm interested in another girl who stayed here for a while. Elfie Jackson."

"The fire bug."

"Alleged fire bug. Can you tell me anything that might cast doubt on her guilt? Did she perhaps have a...a visitor on

44

the night of the fire? That would have been on Friday, the fifth of July."

Annie's laugh erupted like a cannon.

Quinn flinched. "What do you find so hilarious, Mrs. Hyman?"

"Your mealy-mouthed delicacy, for one thing. *Renter. Visitor.* I ain't bashful about running a whorehouse. Most of our 'visitors' are paying customers. My girls make four times the money they'd make in a factory and my cut of their earnings makes me rich enough to tell the do-gooders and reformers to go to hell."

"I meant no offense," said Quinn.

"It's nothing to me if you did."

"I'll be blunt then. Did Elfie have a paying customer on the night of the arson?"

Annie snorted. "That hellcat would gut any man who tried to touch her. She was here for a few weeks, slept on a pallet in Jemelle's cubby, but Elfie never worked for me. She near about kept Jemelle from working. I don't care if a girl pulls a knife if a jasper gets rough with her, but Elfie took a swipe at a customer who brushed up against her accidental like. I got onto her for interfering with the flow of business, told her to keep out of the way or clear out."

"Why did Jemelle let her stay if she interfered with business? Were they friends?"

"They knew each other from Rock Island, or so they said."

"Did Elfie have any friends besides Jemelle or talk to any of the other girls?"

"I'm no mother hen. Long as they do an honest day's work and don't hold out on me, who they gab with is their own affair."

"You say Elfie didn't work. Can you tell me if she was here on the night of the fire?"

"I don't take a head count every night. Maybe Jemelle would know."

Annie was no mother hen, but those shrewd little eyes of hers suggested she noticed more than she let on. If Jemelle had known Elfie in Rock Island, it stood to reason she would also know Elfie's lover. "Did Mr. Burk Bayer ever visit Jemelle or Elfie?"

The big woman levitated off the settee with surprising lightness and loomed over Quinn like a giant yellow moth. "Enough of this blabber. Me and the mayor and the city council, we get on just fine if you know what I mean. Everybody feeds at the trough. Everybody goes home happy. But Kadinger was a bigwig with bigwig friends. His murder's got the council running scared, spouting off about restoring morals and purging corruption. I don't want sparks off that fire Elfie Jackson set blowing back my way."

"What makes you so sure Elfie set the fire?" asked Quinn.

"I don't know who set it. All I know, that girl's a Jonah, bad luck to one and all. I was glad when the coppers dragged her out of here in cuffs and I'll be glad to see the back of you, Detective Paschal."

Quinn stood and met Annie's menacing stare without blinking. "Then I shall take my leave."

"You do that, honey, and if I catch you snooping around here again, I'll boot your meddlesome bottom into the next county."

"I daresay you would not find booting my bottom as easy an undertaking as you imagine, Mrs. Hyman."

Annie let out a growling laugh. "Well, ain't you the bold one."

"Good day to you," said Quinn and flounced past her down the stairs. Without a rawhide whip, the old harridan didn't scare her, but the heavy atmosphere of lust and debauchery and pungent perfume had brought on a headache. Was it true the city council and the mayor were involved with a house of prostitution? It was common knowledge the police accepted bribes in exchange for keeping clear of the area. Did Annie also pay off the mayor and his council? She had been cooperative until Quinn dropped the name Burk Bayer. Was it Bayer's connection to Kadinger that agitated her or was she hiding something? At least she'd provided one valuable lead – Jemelle Clary. Was it odd that Jemelle had become the main link to both Jack Stram and Elfie?

Thoughts churning, she emerged into the bright sunshine and leaned her back against the door. Her head felt like a smithy's forge and the hammer struck the anvil every second. She closed her eyes. She needed to talk with Jemelle as soon as possible, but the thought of calling in at another brothel right away made her faintly nauseous. She decided to go home, bathe her face and neck in cool water, and eat some lunch. She couldn't interview Jemelle or anyone else until this headache eased. If she felt better in the afternoon, she would return to the office and ask Garnick to drive her to Lou Harper's Mansion.

She opened her eyes. A flash of light and an explosive whoof made her cringe.

"Perfect!"

She turned in the direction of the shout and a photographer came into focus. He stood barely as tall as his camera, a smoking tray held high in one hand like a trophy.

"What are you doing?"

"That's obvious, isn't it?"

"But you've no right."

"It's a public street. I can take any image I want." A bramble bush of black hair added to his height, but his severely bowed legs subtracted in equal measure.

"Not without permission. I demand you give me that plate."

"Not going to happen, missy." He lowered the tray and poked his head under the dark camera cloth. When his face reappeared, he wore a triumphant grin. "You stood still just

47

long enough. My chemicals are the best money can buy. None faster. This will be a beaut. What's your name?"

"None of your business. What's yours?"

"Fen Megarian, star news maker of the *Chicago Tribune.*"

"You're going to publish that picture in the paper?"

"I wouldn't worry if I were you. It'll fetch you more customers." He folded his tri-pod, balanced the bulky camera across one shoulder, and swaggered off down the street.

An ominous feeling tickled up Quinn's spine. She looked behind at what had been the backdrop of the photograph. The "Why Not?" sign blazoned almost directly above her head.

CHAPTER 6

Quinn stripped off her dress, which had absorbed the smells of the brothel, and dumped herself onto the bed. The smithy inside her head continued to hammer. She kneaded her temples. Why had that insolent little gnome wanted a picture of Annie Stafford's whorehouse? The newspaper rarely published photos. It relied on the manipulation of the written word to stir up fusses and sell newspapers. Could Fen Megarian be the same person who concocted the article comparing Elfie to a mythological witch? Was he looking to smear her further with a concoction about the poor girl's descent into prostitution?

But it wasn't Elfie's image he'd captured. It was hers. Jesus, Joseph, and Mary. Winthrop would have a conniption if he saw her face under the "Why Not?" sign. And how would she explain such a photograph to her housemates?

"Mrs. Sinclair, are you there?"

Miss Nearest. Quinn groaned, but whatever Megarian meant to do with the image, no one in this house could have seen it yet. "Yes, I'm here."

"I've brought you a cup of my special willow bark and peppermint tea."

On her return from Annie's, Quinn had torn through the house like a tempest, waving off concerned queries and flying pell-mell to her room. They must have thought she was dying. She couldn't snub them or rebuff their kindness. She pulled on a wrapper and opened the door.

"This will bring you 'round in two shakes of a sheep's tail." Miss Nearest marched into the room and set a tray on the bedside table. "The ancient Egyptians used willow bark for all their aches and pains. In my years as a nurse, I've seen it work wonders."

Quinn feigned a smile. "Thank you. It smells invigorating."

"Capital, as our English cousins are wont to say. You'll also find the Medea drama you asked about under the cup and doily. Since our talk this morning, I've been reviewing the supernatural elements in the play. Fate, don't you know, the overwhelming power beyond mortal control. As in life, the things we think will happen do not. The gods bring matters to surprising ends. As an example ..."

It was late afternoon by the time Quinn escaped Miss Nearest's disquisition, put on a fresh dress, and made her way back to the office. The windows were open and the room abuzz with mosquitos. Garnick sat with his feet propped on his desk. Micah Winthrop paced back and forth, head down, as if counting knotholes in the floor. The heat had finally penetrated his crisp exterior. The back of his coat was wrinkled, his cravat askew, and his yellow hair damp.

She dispensed with hello. "Is something wrong, Mr. Winthrop?"

He looked up, his face an angry red. "She knifed one of the guards."

"Elfie?"

"Yes, Elfie.

"Is he dead?"

"Nothing grievous," said Garnick. "She took a small fillet out of his side."

Winthrop rounded on him. "It's grievous to my case. That girl is mad. Abe Lincoln himself couldn't defend her now."

"From what's told about old Abe," said Garnick, "he was a stickler for facts. He might've asked the guard how she came to get ahold of his knife."

"It belonged to the guard?" asked Quinn.

"Immaterial," snapped Winthrop. "She's proved herself capable of face-to-face murder. The prosecutor will have no trouble convincing a jury she lit a fire in the dead of night with no one around to see."

The accumulation of stories about Elfie's wildness disabused Quinn of the idea that she was a helpless waif. They didn't alter her conviction that the girl was a convenient scapegoat. She said, "It's possible the guard tried to take advantage of her and she was only defending herself."

Winthrop's forehead ridged like a washboard. "She lured Sergeant Fogerty into her cell, moaning that she was sick. When his back was turned, she shoved him and grabbed the knife."

"Must be a strapping girl," observed Garnick. "Fogerty's built like a Hereford steer."

Winthrop gave him a sour look and turned to Quinn. "Have you come up with anyone who can swear Elfie was someplace else or with someone else on the night of the fire?"

"I have."

"You've found an alibi witness?"

"Yes."

"Who?"

"Jemelle Clary." The lie popped out spontaneously. Since becoming a detective, she'd come to count on the efficacy of a confident lie over a disheartening truth. She hoped this particular lie would turn out to be true, but in the meantime it appeared to appease Winthrop.

51

"That changes things," he said. "With testimony that puts Elfie in the company of a credible witness, I may be able to overcome the damage done by the jailhouse stabbing." His tone turned skeptical. "This Miss Clary isn't a hooker, is she?"

"No, she isn't," answered Quinn, seizing on his use of the present tense. "I plan to interview her tomorrow."

"Good. Bring me her statement as soon as you can and any other information you can garner. Where they were, what they were doing, who else may have seen them. I'll expect a report by tomorrow evening." He swatted a mosquito away from his ear. "You really should tack cheesecloth over these windows."

When he was gone, Garnick swung his feet off the desk and handed her a paper fan with a picture of Jesus. "I'll see if I can rustle up a few yards of wove wire tomorrow and cover the windows. Meanwhile, it's leave 'em open and skirmish with the skeeters or dissolve into a puddle."

She sat down, tilted her head back, and fanned her neck. "Thank you for not commenting on the way Winthrop made light of the attack on Elfie and turned her into the villain. He was a real dose."

"You think so? I didn't notice much difference."

She was too wilted to smile.

"I surmise your parley with Gentle Annie didn't go so well."

"She's a cantankerous old buffalo, but helpful to a degree. I learned that Jack Stram beat up one of her girls, Jemelle. Coincidentally, Jemelle is the one Elfie stayed with for a few weeks."

"And Jemelle can vouch for Elfie?"

"I don't know. I didn't have a chance to ask. Stram spoiled her looks and she can't work so Annie gave her the heave-ho."

"You know where she went?"

"The madam over at the Mansion took her in."

52

"Sounds more like a leave of absence than retirement," quipped Garnick. "What about Stram? Does Annie know where he lurked off to?"

"Probably the hospital. She gave him quite a lashing." Quinn's headache had abated, but she couldn't seem to string her thoughts together in a coherent way.

Garnick sat down across from her in the client chair. "You want to tell me what's got you so down in the mouth?"

"A photographer from the *Tribune* ambushed me outside Annie's and took my picture. If it's published..." her voice broke. She cleared her throat and composed herself. "My sisters, my mother-in-law, my landlady, they'll think the worst. I don't know what Winthrop will do."

"The picture taker didn't know who you are, did he?"

"No. He'd aimed his camera at Annie's front door and I walked out at the wrong moment. He may be the same scandal monger who's been writing about Elfie and the Kadinger murders."

"Did he give you his name?"

"Fen Megarian. He calls himself a star newsmaker. I should have shown him my gun and threatened to shoot him if he didn't give me the plate. I was too stunned."

"Maybe we should ask this Fen fella what he'll take to part with the plate. We've got information to swap if he's minded to play fair. Maybe we can even slip him in to see her with us tonight."

"Your friend Captain Chesterton agreed to let us in?"

"For a write-off of his poker debts, he'd help break her out. But feelings over what happened run high amongst the guards, so it'll have to be late, after the day shift has gone home."

She brightened. "You make it sound easy as rolling off a log. Do you think Fen will still be at the *Tribune* office?"

***

He wasn't and none of the other reporters or typesetters knew where to find him or when he would next appear. To Quinn's relief, Fen Megarian had not submitted a story or a photograph today.

"We'll pay him a visit tomorrow," said Quinn. "Let's go to Madam Lou's now and talk to Jemelle."

"It's too late. By now, the sporting district's already a-swarm with rowdies and drunkards."

"But you can handle them, Garnick. You can clear the way."

"I'm pleased you recognize what a fearsome figure of a man I am, but I'd be no match for a mob of brawlers. Besides, this Jemelle girl would prob'ly druther keep her distance from men for a while. Lou's will be safe as church in the morning. You can go by yourself after we talk to that photographer. Madam Lou's known to be as polite and refined as Annie is rough."

Quinn didn't think a foray into the parlor of so polite and refined a call house at this early hour would be dangerous, but she hadn't yet recovered from her encounter with Annie. "All right, but I don't want to just sit around until midnight, or whenever it is that Captain Chesterton said he would let us into the jail."

"Let's visit somebody else on your witness list. You said you wanted to talk to Miss Delphine's bridesmaid. The Allbright house is on our way downtown."

CHAPTER 7

"This is it," said Garnick, curbing Leonidas in front of an elaborately decorated house with a mansard roof and molded cornices. Bonneted dormers graced the upper floor and gothic bay windows projected from the wall on either side of a wide porch.

Quinn tidied her hair and dress as best she could. "Miss Allbright will think I'm a beggar."

"I'm of a mind to beg for a glass of water," said Garnick. "If her pa's at home, he'll ask us in." He followed her down the walkway, neatened his shirt and hair, and banged the horse-head knocker.

A woman's voice sang out, "I'll get it, Mag." The door breezed open and a doe-eyed young woman with blond ringlets and a beaming smile appeared. "Oh." The smile drooped as if she'd expected company considerably more to her liking.

"How do you do," said Quinn, taking in the frilly pink dress and pink-tinged lips. She handed her a business card. "I'm Mrs. Paschal and this is Mr. Garnick. We're here to see Miss Josabeth Allbright. Is she in?"

"I'm Miss Allbright." She studied the card and caught her lower lip between her teeth. "You're detectives?"

"That's right. We're investigating the death of Mr. Rolf Kadinger and his daughter, Delphine."

"Do you work for the police?"

"No, ma'am," said Garnick. "I spoke to your pa a while ago and he thought you might have some special knowledge about your friend, Miss Delphine, how she felt about the unfortunate occurrence at her wedding reception and so forth."

"My father is out for the evening. But if you're not working for the police, is it the insurance company that hired you?"

"To be honest," said Quinn, "Miss Jackson's attorney hired us."

"Oh my goodness."

"May we come in?" asked Quinn.

"Well…" Miss Allbright bit her lip and dithered.

"We'll be as brief as possible," said Quinn encouragingly. "I'm sure you want to hear more of the story."

"Yes. Yes, of course. Do come in."

She led them into a room anchored by a large round table upon which rested a bouquet of multi-colored flowers. Heavy, plush chairs and ottomans were interspersed with smaller ladies' chairs in vibrant colors and expensive fabrics. "Do you care for a glass of cold lemonade?"

"That would be mighty kind," said Garnick.

"Mag," she called over her shoulder. "Bring that pitcher of lemonade into the drawing room. And three glasses." She turned back to Quinn and Garnick. "I've never met a detective before. It's frightfully venturesome for a woman, is it not?"

"Not today. Not in such pleasant company."

"I don't know what I can possibly tell you. I read about the Jackson girl in the newspapers. They say she did it because of unrequited love."

At their hostess' bidding, they seated themselves and a black woman in a white cap and apron arrived toting a

56

sterling tray with lemonade and slices of pound cake. She set out plates, served the drinks, and disappeared.

Garnick said, "There may have been others with a motive for murder besides unrequited love."

Josabeth's pretty brow contracted. "Whatever do you mean?"

"Did Miss Delphine ever mention anybody with a grudge against her daddy?"

"Delphine never gave a thought to business, not Mr. Kadinger's or even Burk's. She didn't think it was ladylike to ask men questions about what they did outside the drawing room."

"She sounds very demure," said Quinn.

"Oh, she could be a little forward sometimes, but never in a way that detracted from her femininity. I still can't believe she's gone. And in such a frightful way!" Josabeth shivered, making her ringlets dance.

Quinn adapted her first question to what she assumed was the customary association between Josabeth and Delphine. "You must have been much in society with Delphine and her fiancé before they were married. What kinds of things did they talk about in the drawing room?"

"Burk is truly spellbinding. He tells amazing stories about his exploits during the War, running gunboats for General Grant out of Fort Defiance and infiltrating Confederate garrisons to disable their cannons. He makes everything sound thrilling. From the moment she met him, Delphine was enraptured. She had another suitor but gave him the mitten. No one could hold a candle to Burk."

Quinn exchanged a look with Garnick. "What was her former suitor's name?"

"Oh, Delphine kept *him* a secret. I don't know how they met or when, but she didn't go out among her friends with him. I had an inkling Mr. Kadinger didn't like him or wouldn't have liked him if he'd known him. It was very strange."

57

"Was he of inferior social standing?" asked Quinn.

"His pedigree wouldn't have mattered so long as he was hardworking. Mr. Kadinger started out as a lumber shover loading and unloading logs onto boats. Whoever the man was, I know he asked Delphine to marry him. She tried to discourage him in a nice way, but he wouldn't be put off. When she told him she had accepted Burk's proposal, he became quite angry."

"In what way?" asked Garnick. "How did he demonstrate his anger?"

"Delphine didn't tell me what he said. Something rather frightful, I gathered. He demanded she return some jewelry he'd given her."

"And did she?" asked Garnick.

"I don't know."

A rejected suitor with a bone to pick shot to the top of Quinn's witness list. "Did Delphine ever say why she didn't disclose his name?"

"It was at his behest. Something about his work."

Quinn wondered if she had inadvertently stumbled into another Pinkerton plot replete with false names and nefarious purposes. She salted away this steamy tidbit to mull at a later time. "Did Delphine know about Burk's *informal* relationship with Elfie Jackson?"

"The woman attached herself to him. Like a leech, that's what Delphine called her. The leech showed up in Rock Island penniless, a runaway from some little prairie town, all rags and fleas. Burk tried to help her, protect her from the kinds of sordid things that happen to her sort, but she willfully misconstrued his kindness."

"Too big-hearted for his own good," observed Garnick drily.

"Precisely," declared Josabeth, the gibe going over her head.

Quinn brushed aside the need for tact. "Mr. Bayer's kindness continued after he relocated to Chicago. He and Elfie shared lodgings, did they not?"

"Certainly not. Mr. Weyerhaeuser maintained an office for his purchasing agent. Burk made that his quarters. Out of the goodness of his heart, he paid for a room for her. No one could possibly hold him responsible for what she did, although the poor man blames himself. He's desolated by Delphine's death."

Quinn tried to reconcile the competing versions of Bayer – the callous one who treated Elfie so cruelly, and the bighearted one who rescued her from a life of shame. Whichever version was true, he had endeared himself to Delphine and, from the way Josabeth talked, she was smitten as well. There was no chance she'd say anything less than complimentary about "Burk" and Quinn took a different line. "You mentioned insurance. Do you know which company insured the Kadinger home?"

"My father said it's the Illinois Casualty, the same as he uses. He says they'll probably investigate, but they're bound to pay because it wasn't the insured's fault."

The banging of the doorknocker brought Josabeth abruptly to her feet, cheeks flushed. "Oh!"

It didn't take a clairvoyant to see that this was the caller she'd been expecting. The considerate thing would be to thank her for her hospitality and leave, but Quinn had a premonition that she was about to meet Burk Bayer. She rushed to forestall Josabeth from bidding them a swift adieu. "We don't wish to impose upon you and your guest, Miss Allbright, but we have a few more questions of a most urgent nature."

She appeared flustered, but before she had time to respond the maid ushered a tall, lithe man into the room. "Mr. Bayer," she announced. Without waiting to be asked, she picked up the empty lemonade pitcher and whisked it back to the kitchen to be refilled.

59

There was no denying Bayer was nice to look at. His auburn hair, combed back from his forehead, luxuriated rakishly behind his ears but didn't touch his perfect white shirt collar. Smooth-faced, straight-nosed, and attired in a smartly tailored tan frock coat, he cut a debonair figure. Josabeth held out her hand. He grasped it warmly. "Miss Allbright, how kind you are to invite me."

She blushed. "I'm so pleased you could come, Mr. Bayer. May I introduce Mrs. Paschal and Mr. Garnick? They are...detectives."

Quinn and Garnick both stood and Bayer's eyes flickered over them as if taking their measure. As if calculating the value of a load of logs, thought Quinn.

"Has Miss Allbright done something that warrants investigation?" he asked with an arch smile and shook their hands.

Garnick chuckled. "That's a good one. But no, sir, as we told the lady, we're here on behalf of Miss Elfie Jackson. Her lawyer's working on a theory of reasonable doubt, which is another way of saying it could've been somebody else burned your father-in-law's house. I hope that doesn't upset you."

"No. No, it doesn't upset me. It surprises me only that she has an attorney. However could she pay?"

"A group of women who care about justice," said Quinn.

"That is welcome news indeed. I pray you discover it was someone other than Elfie, detectives, so that I may stop tormenting myself with ifs. If I'd never opened my door to her, if I'd never told her where I was going when I left Rock Island, if I'd been in the house that night. I will do whatever I can to help you with your investigation." He smiled at Josabeth and she visibly relaxed.

Mag returned with a fresh pitcher of lemonade and a glass for Bayer. "Shall I serve now, Miss Allbright?"

"Yes! Good heavens. Let's all sit. Please take the chair beside me, Mr. Bayer."

60

They made themselves comfortable. Mag poured fresh lemonade all around and repaired to the kitchen. While Josabeth plied Bayer with cakes and sympathetic chitchat, Quinn sipped her drink and mused on his seemingly open, accommodating attitude. Perhaps she had judged him unfairly. In any case, his conduct toward Elfie, whether caring or cruel, did not excuse Elfie if she'd set the fire.

Garnick drained his lemonade and waded into the conversation. "We'd be grateful for any help you can give us with our investigation, Mr. Bayer. As I understand it, you work for Mr. Fred Weyerhaeuser."

"I did until a few weeks ago. Following my marriage, I left Weyerhaeuser's employ and entered my father-in-law's business. It's not a direct competitor of Weyerhaeuser so there were no hard feelings."

"Do you know anyone who might've held a grudge against Mr. Kadinger? Any workers or customers riled up enough to want to do him dirty?"

"No one I've heard of. I'm just now beginning to go over his business records with his clerk."

Quinn said, "We were told there were two legal claims made against him. One by a saw filer named Murphy and the other by a builder, Mosley."

"Those were small claims, settled out of court with no hard feelings."

"What about yourself, sir?" Garnick sounded pained at having to ask. "Any enemies or disgruntled lady friends other than Miss Jackson?"

"No. And while I befriended Elfie Jackson, or tried to, she was never my *lady*."

Quinn marked the vicarious indignation on Josabeth's face and refrained from any suggestion of an improper relationship. "Was your wife Mr. Kadinger's sole heir?"

"Yes."

"And you are hers?"

"By law Delphine had no will, but as she was her father's only heir, so now am I."

"Your short marriage has made you a very rich man," she said, avoiding Josabeth's eyes.

"Perhaps." His voice went hoarse. "But lonely. And profoundly sad."

Josabeth bestowed upon him a moist, adoring gaze. "It's simply beyond the pale that Delphine's brother is being such a lout. He makes the situation so much more painful for you."

Quinn was perplexed. "Delphine had a brother?"

"Verner is something of a black sheep," said Bayer. "He and his father didn't get along and Mr. Kadinger sent him to Germany to learn steelmaking from his cousins. He found working in the mill beneath him. He returned to Chicago a few months ago, demanding a position in his father's office. Instead, Rolf offered to start him out as a stevedore loading and unloading ships. Verner became enraged. There was a salvo of harsh words and they parted on bad terms."

"And Verner doesn't benefit from his father's estate?" asked Garnick.

"After they fought, Rolf had his lawyer draw up a new will the next day."

"Leaving you the caboodle?"

"Leaving my wife the caboodle, although that may ultimately amount to a pittance. Rolf invested heavily in water-loan bonds and Miss Allbright's father informs me the city is on the point of default. I'll be lucky to recoup pennies on the dollar."

Those pennies added to the assets of Kadinger Lumber and the insurance on the Kadinger home would probably see him through to his next opportunity, thought Quinn.

"It's of course more money than I'd have made in three or four years working for Weyerhaeuser, even with bonuses, but at such a cost." He gave a melancholy sigh. "To think it came to me through the intentional malice of a woman I

62

helped and trusted. I had worried Rolf might start a fire by accident. After feuding with Verner, the old gentleman began adding a quaff of whiskey to his nightly routine. Actually, he was tippling pretty heavily."

"Did he leave nothing at all to his son?" asked Quinn.

"The only thing he left Verner was a spittoon."

Garnick whistled. "If I don't mistake his meaning, that's a right nasty insult."

"Rolf used snuff. Verner called him a filthy snuff eater and a lot worse. Delphine tried to persuade her brother to apologize and make peace, but he turned on her."

"And now he's turned on poor Mr. Bayer," said Josabeth.

"Miss Allbright is referring to Verner's stated intention to contest his father's will. I offered him a liberal remittance, but he turned up his nose. I guess there's no way to placate such a hoard of hard feelings."

Hard feelings seemed to be a recurring theme with Bayer, noted Quinn, and Elfie wasn't the only one who harbored them. "Have you no suspicion at all that it was Verner who set the fire?"

"It's a ghoulish thought, but...I really don't know." He stared into his lemonade and appeared to ruminate. "A prodigal son may be welcomed home, but only if he asks for forgiveness and shows a trace of humility. Rolf Kadinger wasn't willing to slaughter the fatted calf and shower Verner with money unless he bowed to his authority. Verner said he'd sooner see the old scoundrel in hell. He might still have apologized and been welcomed back into the family, but he couldn't contain his rage and resentment."

"I gather he didn't attend your wedding?" continued Quinn.

"No."

She said, "We were told a small fire disrupted your party at the Tremont. Did you ever learn how it started?"

63

"No. I'm sure you were also told that Elfie had been barred from entering the hotel."

"Do you think Verner could've set the fire to spite his father?" she asked.

"I don't know."

"Any idea where Verner might be found?" asked Garnick.

"The letter he wrote Mr. Kadinger's lawyer bore the return address of a gentleman's rooming house on Pine. Somewhere near Farwell Hall, I believe."

"There was also a housemaid," said Garnick. "We'd like to talk to her if you know where she hied off to."

In her excitement over the discovery of Delphine's angry former suitor and resentful brother, Quinn had almost forgotten about Rhetta Slayne.

A cloud scudded across Bayer's face. "Poor Rhetta. She came to me last week weeping. She blames herself for not being able to find Delphine in the smoke. Of course it was a miracle she escaped with her own life. I gave her a character reference and suggested she inquire at the Walker Ellis house. I don't know if she did."

"Oh, Mr. Bayer." Tears welled in Josabeth's eyes. "You are such a generous soul to worry about others when you are in such pain."

Quinn felt a perverse urge to stick a pin in Josabeth to bring her to her senses, but she was clearly enthralled, just as Delphine had been. "Where is Rhetta now?"

"I wish I knew. When construction is completed on my new home, I'd be happy to employ her."

Quinn set her empty glass on the occasional table next to her chair and stood. "Mr. Garnick and I have detained you long enough. You have been most helpful."

They all rose and shook hands again.

Garnick gave Bayer an extra few pumps. "One widower to another, sir, I know what you're going through. Time heals is an old saw, more hopeful maybe than seems thinkable to you right now, but memories fade. I reckon you'll outlast your grief."

"Is that how it was for you, Mr. Garnick?"

"More or less. One last question if you don't mind."

"Yes?"

"Where were you on the night of the fire?"

That fazed him. His pupils became pinpoints and his lips compressed in a thin line. "That morning I took the train to Rock Island to meet with a lumber trader. Mr. Harrell Paulson of Second Street if you care to verify. I lodged at a tavern on Third Street. I don't recall the name. No one knew where to send a wire. I didn't find out what had happened until my return two days later."

"Not being there to save her, nor even to say goodbye." Garnick's voice was warm with fellow feeling. "That's a hard thing to live with."

"It's an agony. The police said she was burned beyond recognition."

"Then I reckon it's a mercy you never saw her. Well, thank you for your hospitality, Miss Allbright, and condolences to you, sir, for your loss."

Quinn said, "Rest assured, Mr. Bayer, we'll do everything in our power to get to the truth and relieve you of your torment."

From the combustible look he flashed, he understood her innuendo perfectly.

CHAPTER 8

Lightning split the sky in long jagged shafts and thunder rolled like caissons. Quinn felt the reverberations in her bones. The carriage rocked and pitched in the gusting wind and hailstones pelted the wooden awning.

"Be careful what you wish for, Garnick," she called, but the roar of the storm drowned out her voice.

The streetlights were buoys floating in a lake of darkness. Theirs was the only carriage on the street, or the only one she could see. The big horse plodded steadily on in spite of the hail and crashing thunder. She reminded herself to ask Garnick if Leonidas had been a warhorse. Both horse and driver must be soaked. Sheltered and mostly dry in the passenger seat, Quinn couldn't help but feel guilty. They'd been bucked and buffeted for nearly an hour when they turned onto Clark Street and a fork of lightning lit up the huge marble building that housed City Hall.

"You get out here and run inside," Garnick shouted over his shoulder. "It's the side door off to your right. The jail's in the basement. Chesterton should be there waiting for us. I'll find a cover for Leonidas and join you in a few minutes."

Quinn had passed the City Hall many times, but never gone inside. Some said it was haunted. Many men had been hanged from a scaffold erected at the top of a staircase somewhere in the eastern end of the building. If Elfie were to be convicted and sentenced to death, she would be hooded, noosed, and dropped from that same scaffold with the public and an avid cadre of newspaper reporters looking on. Quinn banished the thought and darted through the squall. The pea-sized hail peppered her bonnet and a raucous clanging added to the din. She glanced up and saw the bell in the cupola whipping wildly back and forth.

The door had been left unlocked, but when she pulled it open a blast of wind blew it back on its hinges and slammed it against the outside wall. She wrestled it shut and turned around to get her bearings. Ahead of her was a long, gloomy corridor like a tunnel in a catacomb. This was her first time inside a jail. Where was the police bureau? Where was Captain Chesterton? Where were the cells?

A strong smell of disinfectant stung her nose and throat. She took a minute to shake beads of hail off her hat and cape and calm her nerves. A slur of voices from somewhere deep in the catacomb started her moving. After a short march, a door on her right opened and two uniformed men entered the hall. They wore stern expressions and long-barreled sidearms.

The sterner of the two put up his hand. "Are you Mrs. Paschal?"

"Yes."

"In there." He jerked his thumb. "The captain's fit to be tied. Where's Garnick?"

"On his way." She hadn't expected to be showered with flower petals and applause, but she thought Chesterton and Garnick had an agreement. Did the police resent them for visiting the woman who'd stabbed their colleague?

She lifted her chin and stepped inside. Captain "Chez" Chesterton filled the small room, his legs spread wide, arms folded over his chest. A muscle in his jaw rippled as if a mouse were wriggling under the skin. "Where's Garnick?"

"He's on his way," she repeated. "Has there been more trouble with Miss Jackson, Captain?"

"If that was all...thunder and tarnation!" He fixed her with a blameful stare. "Except for Garnick being a John Reb and too darn lucky at cards, I'd have put him down as a right guy. Sensible, feet on the ground. You must be some kind of Delilah to gull him into this private investigator nonsense."

"I didn't gull him into anything and it's not nonsense. You wouldn't belittle a Pinkerton investigator that way."

"That's because the Pinks stick to rousting bank robbers and guarding trains. They mostly keep their noses out of everyday murder."

"Sorry to keep you waiting, Chez," said Garnick, dribbling rain and hail on the floor. "The two guards I met outside told me you were in a bearish temper. What's eating you?"

"Paschal and Garnick, detectives, that's what's eating me." He took a card off his desk and waved it in front of their noses.

"Give me a squint." Garnick took it out of his hand. "It's ours, all right. You find a misspelled word?"

"What I found is a dead man. That card was in his pocket."

"I surmise this ain't a case of natural expiry?"

"None of your jokes, Garnick. The muggins was shot in the head. Twice for good measure."

Quinn did a quick inventory of the people she'd given the card to. The young desk clerk at the Tremont, the obnoxious hotel manager, Annie Stafford's bouncer who had passed the card on to Annie, Josabeth Allbright. Moses' horns, had Josabeth passed it on to Burk Bayer? "Who is he?" she asked. "What's the dead man's name?"

"He had no wallet," said Chesterton. "No cash, no papers. Nothing but your damn...I beg your pardon, ma'am, nothing but that calling card you're holding in your hand, Garnick."

"We've been handing them out since April," said Quinn. "They're advertising."

"I know what it is." The mouse under Chesterton's jaw wriggled. "Maybe you'll recall if the gent on a slab down the hall is one you pitched your services to. Let's go, detectives."

"There's no cause to be snide," she said with an edge of defiance. "Are you going to renege on your promise to let us see Miss Jackson?"

Garnick was quick with a softener. "I've known the Captain long enough to know he's a man of his word. Sounds like there's been a turn-up that wants our two bits worth. Let's have a look at this deceased gent, Chez. He ain't so unsightly he'll unnerve the lady, is he?"

"Not if she's got a strong stomach."

They walked a few doors farther down the corridor and Chesterton showed them into a brightly lit room with an even stronger smell of disinfectant. This was the police morgue. Three bodies had been laid out on sawhorse tables and covered with sheets.

Chesterton yanked the sheet off the one in the middle. "Look familiar?"

"Holy Mother," murmured Quinn.

"He *was* a client of ours," said Garnick. "Name's Handish. He's wanted in Cairo for killing his wife. He claims he didn't do it and hired us to find the man who did."

"Does that man have a name?" asked Chesterton.

"Stram. Jack Stram," said Garnick, turning over Handish's shirt collar.

"What're you gawking at?"

"Some kind of a wax smirch. Dried sweat, dandruff, hair, could be a spot of Macassar oil and maybe a tetch of red-eye gravy down the front."

"Trying to show off your fancy detective know-how, Garnick?"

"Just to give you a flavor, in case you ever need our professional guidance."

Chesterton harrumphed and threw the sheet back over Handish. "Did you get a lead on Stram?"

70

"No. We never did."

"Some detectives you are. Well, you can forget about him. Looks like he found Handish first. I hope your client paid in advance."

"Where," asked Quinn, "did you find Mr. Handish?"

"In an alley back of Lou's Mansion. No point asking questions around there. If any of Lou's girls saw anything, they'll play deaf and dumb. Anybody gets himself murdered in that neighborhood, it's his own fault and nothing for the police to waste time on. But I appreciate the lowdown about Handish's trouble in Cairo. I'll wire the sheriff down there. Maybe there's a reward."

CHAPTER 9

Elfie sat hunched against her cell wall, arms hugged tight around her knees. Still but alert. Coiled, thought Quinn as she sat down on the foot of the cot and faced her. She wasn't pretty, but something in the singularity of her features, the lustrous hazel eyes and heart-shaped face, made it hard to look away. Her black hair straggled around her face and she had dark crescents under her eyes. They smoldered with what Quinn imagined was a pent-up store of anger and fear.

Introductions having been made with no response from the prisoner, Quinn said, "We're here to help you, Elfie. May I call you Elfie?"

"Call me what you like. The rest of the lot in this place do."

"All right, Elfie. And you call me Quinn. I believe you're innocent and so does Mr. Winthrop. He's optimistic he can win an acquittal for you, but we need to know where you were and who you were with on the night of the fire. That was July fifth. Tell us everything you can remember."

"Have you talked to Burk?"

Quinn wasn't surprised at how quickly Burk's name cropped up. He seemed to have enchanted every woman he met. "We have talked to him. He says he wants to help us find evidence to prove you didn't set the fire."

No reply.

Garnick slouched against the iron gate. "Are you hungry, ma'am?" He pulled an apple out of his pocket. "I've been locked up, myself. The grub, if the turnkeys remembered to bring it, was so bad I near-about starved." He held out the apple and she grabbed it.

There was no "thank-you." She hid the apple behind her back and hugged her knees again.

Quinn tried a different approach. "Annie told me about a friend of yours, Jemelle Clary. Were you with Jemelle for all or part of that night?"

No reply.

It dawned on Quinn that if she were going to pry anything out of Elfie, she would have to use Burk as the lever. She left the cot and idled about the cell, hands behind her back. As if thinking out loud, she said, "Maybe it was Burk who set the fire. Maybe he did it in order to take possession of his father-in-law's money and business. Money has tempted a lot of men to murder, hasn't it, Garnick?"

"They say it's the root of evil."

Quinn waited for a response from Elfie. None came and she went on. "In addition to the value of Mr. Kadinger's business, there's sure to be an insurance settlement for the loss of the house. Burk made a great show of saying how anxious he is that you be absolved of guilt, but I don't believe him. If he hadn't told the police you were intent on punishing him for desertion, he'd be the first person they suspected. It wouldn't balk them for a minute that he was in Rock Island at the time. Isn't that right, Mr. Garnick?"

"Like I said before, he could've hired it done. Come to think of it, he could've hired a lawyer for you out of his own pocket if he'd wanted to."

Elfie sat rigid and dumb as a wooden doll. Quinn had expected her to contribute something to her defense, to rail against Burk or curse the woman he deserted her for. But

74

her feelings, whether hate or thwarted love, remained banked behind those smoldering eyes.

"Did you punish him for leaving you, Elfie? Did you set that fire?"

Nothing.

Quinn wanted to shake her. "If you don't bestir yourself and deny it, you may as well confess, save the Christian ladies who paid for your lawyer the money, save Mr. Winthrop the time and bother of preparing for trial, save Garnick and me the bother of hunting up people who'll testify to your good character. But if you believe Burk has set you up to take the blame, for pity's sake stand up and fight."

Elfie pounced off the cot with such suddenness Quinn fell back against the wall. Garnick stepped forward, a hand raised to stop her, but whatever the feeling that animated her died aborning. Her shoulders sagged. "What is there to fight for? I'm damned. Even if I'm acquitted and turned out into the world, I'm a ruined woman, a supposed slut for men like that fat guard to make sport of. Burk took everything – my money, my maidenhood, my self-respect. But I could never hate him. If he asked me to come back to him, for no other reason but to scrub his floor, I'd do it."

Quinn racked her brain for something cogent or compelling or comforting to say, but her thoughts snagged on a discrepant fact. "I thought you were penniless."

"I am now. My mother had money. I stole four thousand dollars from her so Burk could buy a parcel of land. When she discovered what I'd done, she disowned me." Elfie sank back onto the cot. "I didn't care. It made Burk happy. He sold the timber to Weyerhaeuser for a profit. Mr. Weyerhaeuser was impressed by Burk's bargaining skills. Last spring he made him his chief purchasing agent and sent him here to Chicago. If I hadn't robbed my mother to please him, he'd have stayed in Rock Island and none of this would have happened." A sob tore from her throat with such a rasp of despair that Quinn drew back in alarm.

75

"If you'll let us," said Garnick, "we can help you, Elfie. Just tell us whether or not you set the fire. Won't neither of us judge you if'n you did. I'd wager you never meant anybody to die."

"Dying is all that'll help me. If I can't have Burk I want to die."

"Stop it," said Quinn. "Suicide is a mortal sin, worse than murder, and that's what you'll be doing if you don't quit this sniveling and show some grit. You've let Burk turn you into a doormat to wipe his boots on. If you refuse to help yourself and get yourself hanged, don't think he'll lay flowers on your grave. He has a brand new sweetie."

Her head snapped up. "Who?"

"Delphine's bridesmaid. She, too, comes from a well-to-do family. Her father's a banker."

"Whatever Burk's scheming at, I know he loves me."

Garnick said, "Maybe he had second thoughts about abandoning you and hatched a plan to get rid of his new wife so he could marry you."

"We're already married. In the eyes of God."

"Did you ever go to Delphine and tell her that?" asked Quinn.

"She wouldn't listen. She called me a liar and a parasite. She was a fool. Her father told her as much. He said she was blinkered when it came to Burk and he wasn't going to give his approval until he got an explanation from Burk."

"You talked to Rolf Kadinger?" Quinn was taken aback. Winthrop said Kadinger should have done more to protect his daughter and apparently he tried. Either Bayer's explanation satisfied him, or the marriage went forward without his blessing. "When did you have this conversation?"

"I don't know. Right after Burk left me, sometime last April." Her arms fell limp onto her lap and her body seemed to uncoil. "Mr. Winthrop showed me the newspaper. I know what they're saying about me, that I'm like that witch in the play, Medea. I'm not. It's Burk who's like Jason."

"How's that?" asked Quinn.

"Wanting it all, not understanding the heartache he caused. But if Medea truly loved Jason, she was a fool. He offered to keep her as his mistress after he married the other woman, but it wasn't enough for her. If Burk kept me as his mistress, I'd be happy."

"But Burk didn't offer you that consolation," said Quinn. "Did it make you unhappy enough to kill his wife?"

"No. I swear I didn't set that fire. I could never do anything that...that horrible."

Garnick sawed a finger across his chin and looked thoughtful. "Fighting in the war, Mr. Bayer must've got used to horror. Then too, he had a financial motive for murder."

"Don't you go thinking that. Burk can't help loving money, but he wouldn't kill for it. He just waits and it comes to him. And he wouldn't want me to be blamed for what happened. You're wrong about him. All he did was answer the police's questions. It was the police put me here, not Burk."

"Why do you defend him?" demanded Quinn. "After the way he's treated you?"

She shrugged and hung her head.

"Were you at Annie's the night of the fire?" asked Garnick.

She nodded.

"Can Jemelle vouch for you?"

"The day the police came for me, she told them I'd confessed to her. She pulled a shawl out of my trunk. It was singed and smelled smoky. She said I'd worn it that night and if they looked, they could probably find scraps of it where the fire started." Elfie locked her arms around her knees and curled into a tight ball. "Somebody must've paid her to trump up that story. One of her customers maybe. It wasn't even my shawl."

77

"Do you have a specific customer in mind?" asked Quinn.

"There was one. He came five or six times, always during the day. I know they didn't go to bed. He never stayed long enough to get out of his clothes. Jemelle made me leave, but I didn't go far. I waited out of sight down the hall. I heard him say, 'It's worth fifty bucks to you if you give out a line of dirt on her.'"

"Did you hear Jemelle's answer? Or anything else from either of them?"

"No. I didn't hear my name, but the way he looked at me gave me the all-overs."

"What did this palm greaser look like?" asked Garnick.

"Tall, rangy, light-haired. He had a bushy horseshoe mustache."

Quinn's eyes met Garnick's. "Isn't that how Handish described Florrie's killer?"

"Sounds mighty like."

CHAPTER 10

The storm had passed, leaving the city chilled and strewn with garbage and downed tree branches. Streams rushed through the ditches on either side of the street and washed over the wood paving blocks in low spots. An eerie quiet had descended. The only sound was the clop and splash of Leonidas' hooves and the clacking of the carriage wheels. It was two o'clock in the morning, moonless and black. Quinn had never felt so wide-awake. More than the shock of Handish's murder, more than her astonishment at Jemelle's venality and Stram's vileness, she puzzled over Burk Bayer's unshakeable hold on Elfie.

Garnick let her off in front of her boarding house and walked her to the door. "Why," she asked, "does Elfie continue to defend him? Is she in a trance?"

"I've got no answer, Quinn. Like the Good Book says, love beareth all things."

"*All* things? That's not love. That's slavery. Why should all the misery be hers alone to bear?"

Garnick had no answer to that one either. "I'll meet you at the office in the morning and we can go see that photographer fellow. After that, if you're still squeamish to go by yourself to Madam Lou's, I'll drive you. I don't hold out much hope for Jemelle doing Elfie or our case a good turn."

They said goodnight and Quinn tiptoed into the house and up the stairs to her room. She sloughed off her dress, pulled on her nightgown, and brushed her teeth, but she had no inclination to sleep. Frustration and the prospect of defeat pecked at her and she couldn't erase the picture of Elfie cooped up in a dark cell waiting to die while Jemelle gloated over her thirty pieces of silver and Burk enjoyed his dead wife's fortune. He'd evidently convinced Rolf Kadinger that his relationship with Elfie was chaste, but he wouldn't want to go through the same awkward explanations with Josabeth's father. That gave him a dandy reason to incriminate Elfie.

Was Bayer deliberately hazy about where the Kadinger's maid had disappeared to? It seemed fishy from the beginning that the girl would flee the fire never to be seen again by anyone except Bayer. A macabre idea insinuated itself into Quinn's thoughts. The woman who died in the fire had been burned beyond recognition. What if that woman was the housemaid and the coughing escapee was Delphine? What if she faked her death to help Bayer inherit her father's estate?

Elfie's plight continued to prey on Quinn. And that wormy *Tribune* reporter would continue to make hay selling drivel about the pathetic fate of the "vengeful witch."

The Medea book sat unopened on the bedside table. She picked it up and leafed through, too distracted to delve into "the supernatural elements." There was a long colloquy with a nurse and Medea and a "chorus." It wasn't a smooth read, what with all the bitter cries of lamentation and woe. Quinn skimmed the long speeches. It seemed that Jason, Medea's husband, abandoned her to marry a princess and advance his station in life. His defection devastated Medea. Until then she had done everything he asked of her, even killed her own brother to save him. She prayed to the gods that she might die. The chorus commiserated. They cursed men who unlocked the secrets of female desire and disclaimed

80

responsibility for the pain they caused. "*Whither wilt thou turn?*" they chanted. "*What protection wilt thou find? In what a hopeless sea of misery heaven hath plunged thee.*" Medea rebuked Jason for his treachery, for having lost all shame and allowing the king to exile her, but then she appeared to come around and even sympathize. She sent conciliatory gifts to his bride-to-be – an exquisite dress and a coronet of beaten gold. But Medea had laced her gifts with poison and when the princess put them on, they burst into flames that devoured her flesh. Her anguished father knelt to embrace her body and he, too, was burned alive. "*O' Medea,*" chanted the chorus, "*How dread a scourge is love!*"

Quinn closed the book. As she struggled to fall asleep, that was the line that echoed in her memory.

***

Vulture-like, Fen Megarian hunkered atop an open roll-top desk and lectured to a flock of avid looking young men. "Those bodies that washed up against the water intake crib in the lake had to have been weighted. Two miles out and six fathoms under? Of course they were weighted! Some bloodthirsty sailor butchered them and threw them overboard. And the tenders charged with protecting the purity of Chicagoans' drinking water were too liquored up to notice. Now there's a story to be chased down, boys. Whoever catches it can make a reputation for himself in the trade."

"Gosh, thanks, Mr. Megarian. I'll sure try."

"Me, too. I'll start by talking to the crew that recovered the bodies!"

"Keep your stories bubbling, boys. Full of storm and strife. The racier the better. Readers will lap it up, especially the ladies. Underneath those decorous bonnets and fine manners, they've a taste for blood and mayhem."

Quinn and Garnick stood at the back of the group, listening. Her eyes felt sandy from lack of sleep and under *her* bonnet, impatience and aggravation sizzled. When Megarian's audience dispersed, Garnick stepped forward and handed him the agency's card. "My name's Garnick and this is Mrs. Paschal. We'd like a minute of your time if you please, sir."

"Detectives?" The little man hopped off the desk and eyed them with interest. "You're the gal whose image I caught in front of Gentle Annie's hookshop."

"I trust that card corrects any misunderstanding of my purpose for being there," said Quinn. His contemptuous tone made her want to defend Annie. "I called on Mrs. Hyman regarding an investigation Mr. Garnick and I are conducting. Whatever reason you had for taking that photograph, it's libelous, a violation of my rights and I demand that you give it to me."

"A photograph's not libelous. It's true of itself."

"Not if it invites misunderstanding," she said.

He leaned forward and cupped his ear. "I didn't hear a reason to give you a mustard seed, much less an expensive photograph."

"If it's money you're after, I'll pay for it. How much?"

"That depends. Just who or what are you investigating?"

"The Kadinger murders," said Garnick. "That bubble with enough storm and strife to suggest a reason?"

Megarian's eyes sparkled. "Take a load off, detectives. Let's talk turkey." He boosted himself into a chair that was too high for him. His legs dangled.

Garnick dragged over two chairs. He offered Quinn one, but she was too wound up to sit. She said, "You're the reporter who's been writing that tripe about Elfie Jackson, aren't you? Painting her as some kind of sorceress. Comparing her to Medea."

82

"It's called giving the public what it wants, missy, fodder for moral outrage. I covered the production of *Médée* at the Opera House, even wangled an interview with the dame who played Medea." He placed his hand over his heart and declaimed. *"Her wonderful expression of the eyes and pathos of voice imparted to Medea a womanly nobility. She evoked gasps of pity for a Medea who braved all things for her husband, faltered at no crime he required her to commit, gave all for his love, and so intertwined herself with him that to be thrust away and supplanted by a rival was an affront not to be borne."* He lolled back in the chair and latched his hands behind his head. "Tripe? Tripe, you say? That's romantic poetry."

"Medea is a myth," said Quinn. "An imaginary character with supernatural powers. Her broken heart, her vengeance, they're imaginary. Elfie is a real person. You can't meld them into one love-warped being just because it sounds romantic."

"I had a confab with Bayer and the story he told has a lot of parallels between Elfie and Medea."

"You sought him out?"

"Other way round. He'd read my critique of the play. Very flattering he was. He'd seen the performance last January and my insights lingered in his mind. After his wife and father-in-law were murdered and the police arrested Elfie, he felt a need to talk. He swears there was nothing between him and Elfie. She was his 'domestic' as he called her, but the girl became enamored. The man's beset by worry he might've done something unintentionally to lead her on to imitate Medea."

"How would she know what to imitate?" asked Quinn. "Are you telling me he took his 'domestic' to the theater with him?"

"That's right. There's no side to him. Thinks of himself as a man of the people. He worked his way up from peddling cordwood, hobnobs with lumbermen of every stripe and color. He paid Elfie's way for as long as she lived in his house, bought her whatever she needed. Maybe that's what confused her. He even paid for a room for Delphine's maid after the fire."

Quinn recalled Bayer saying that Rhetta Slaney had come to him weeping. In spite of his heartless treatment of Elfie, he sounded like a man with no class bias. She resisted the temptation to like him for it. "Do you know where the maid lives now?"

"Sure I do. I interviewed her, or tried to. Flighty as a feather. On the night of the fire she heard angels chanting. Says that's what saved her."

Like an infernal Greek chorus, thought Quinn. "What's her address?"

"Twelve Rush Street, but you won't get anything out of her but gibberish."

Garnick said, "We met with Elfie in her cell last night."

Megarian dropped his conceited pose and sat up straight. "How much did that cost you? The coppers wouldn't let me near her."

"We've got our ways. We could help you perk up your poeticizing if'n you was to work with us, give over that misleading image of Mrs. Paschal and shine a kindlier light on poor little Elfie."

"What's in the deal for Fen Megarian?"

Quinn saw a way to use the man's smugness and conceit to her purposes. "Imagine the story you'd have if you inject a hint of doubt about Elfie's guilt. There are other suspects, other motives. If our investigation uncovers anything of significance, we would share the results with you. You could create a sensation in the city."

"Hmm." Megarian pursed his lips and appeared to weigh the merits.

"I've got no gift for telling," said Garnick, "but your readers might enjoy a build-up of speculation and suspense before you gratify their taste for blood and mayhem with the

84

tragic outcome. *Was the beauteous Delphine the villain's true quarry or did her father short-weight some Wisconsin timber pirate who went loco on him? Who started the fire at the Bayers' wedding party? Did the coppers nab the real killer or is a mad-dog pyro-maniac still on the loose?* And so on like that."

"You underestimate your flair for telling, Mr. Garnick. Who are these 'other suspects' you claim to have?"

Quinn baited the hook. "Did you know Delphine Kadinger had a suitor before Burk Bayer? He wasn't very happy being supplanted by a rival. Indeed it may have been an affront not to be borne."

"Who is he? What's his name? Where's he from?"

She smiled. It occurred to her that a dose of Megarian's grandiloquent rhetoric on the front page of the *Tribune* just might draw out the mystery man and lead him to reveal himself. "Do we have a deal?" she asked.

"You're going to feed me the facts as soon as you ferret them out?"

"Promptly. Without fail."

"I won't slant things Elfie's way if I don't think your information's reliable."

"Understood."

"Then you're on, missy." Megarian reached inside the big desk for the plate with the compromising image. "But you'd better come up with something good."

"You leave it to us, sir," said Garnick. "We'll give you a gripper and that's a bottom fact."

CHAPTER 11

Quinn's spirits soared as she and Garnick walked out of the *Tribune* building. She hadn't realized how much she'd dreaded the repercussions from that photograph. Detective Paschal, self-styled heroine and daring non-conformist, afraid to lose her respectable, cozy niche at the boardinghouse breakfast table, afraid of the opinion of a bunch of prissy old hens. It was an unbecoming truth to acknowledge, but she put these contradictions out of her mind. A problem that seemed unsolvable as she tossed and turned last night had vanished in the morning sunshine. She felt almost giddy. "Did you see the way Megarian's eyes glittered when you reeled off that litany of possible story lines? You were masterful, Garnick."

"Just following your lead."

She climbed onto the driver's bench beside him and adjusted the brim of her bonnet to shield her eyes from the sun. "What do you make of the man, Garnick?"

"You mean besides being the bow-leggedest banty rooster in Cook County?"

She laughed. "Besides that. Is he an unscrupulous hack or a gullible hack? He acts as if he swallowed Burk Bayer's story hook, line, and sinker."

"Megarian's too cynical to believe anybody's story flat-out. He's like a bloodhound when it comes to nosing out skullduggery and rumors of skullduggery. We've put him onto a new scent. He won't wait to hear back from us. He'll go sniffing out folks with ties to the case same as us."

"Let him. We now know where Rhetta Slaney lives. As soon as we've talked to Jemelle, we'll go to Rush Street and interview her. She can't be as muddle-headed as everyone says. We'll get the facts out of her."

"Me waving the carrot and you the stick."

"Is that what I do? Well be that as it may, we make a grand team. We're going to solve the Kadinger case and soon. I just know it." Quinn toyed with her wedding ring. "What do you suppose possessed Bayer to feed Megarian that rigmarole about Elfie? Does he hate her so much he wants the entire city of Chicago to hate her? And she talks as if she adores him no matter what."

"I can't say. The embranglement between those two is a head-scratcher."

"Embranglement. Is that a Southernism?"

"You Yankees got a better word for two people with stories as crisscrossed as a Chinese knot?"

"I can't think of a single one." She laughed. Life would be boring without Garnick's zany turns of phrase and keen observations. Impulsively, she turned to kiss him on the cheek. At just that moment, he turned toward her. The kiss landed on his mouth.

The instant of surprise gave way to fervent affirmation, a torrent of sensations, and a laying on of hands that took her breath. Their lips remained engaged for a long time.

***

Garnick pulled up in front of Madam Lou Harper's Mansion and set the brake. "What happened back there wants airing, Quinn. You can't cut and run and act like nothing's changed."

88

She was still disoriented, unable to translate feelings into words. Every nerve in her body was throbbing. A line had been crossed, boundaries blurred. They could never again be the same way with each other. She didn't know what to say, how to be. In her imaginings, she had pushed this contingency into a clear-eyed and convenient future, but the future had sneaked up on her.

He said, "I know things went farther than you expected."

"A little." It was her fault. She'd been the instigator, played the wanton and blatantly enjoyed the experience. In the middle of a public street in broad daylight. What must he think?

"I think that lets you know how I feel about you. How I've been feeling. I need to be clear if the way you answered me back, I mean, do you feel the same way?"

She looked across Monroe toward the brothel. It had a fresh coat of blue paint, geraniums bloomed in the window boxes, and a pair of snow-white rabbits grazed on the lawn behind the wrought-iron gate. There wasn't a "Why Not" sign to be seen, but in her mind's eye they beckoned from every window. "Not here for mercy's sake."

Garnick gave a sigh of impatience, but the unseemliness of the venue appeared to register. "Before the day's out then. You go on in and talk to Jemelle. I'll wait for you out here. No sense ganging up on the poor girl and her beat up, nursing a broke tooth."

"No. It's important that we both hear everything she has to say."

"You'll pull more out of her on your own, woman-to-woman."

"I didn't get enough sleep last night. I'm flurried and out of focus and I don't want to miss anything because my mind's on, on kissing. Besides, she may be more disposed to answer a man's questions."

"I doubt that, but I reckon we'll find out." He secured Leonidas to an ornamental bronze hitching post and followed her across the street.

They entered the house through a red door into a handsomely furnished salon. A young woman wearing lip rouge, Rimmeled eyelashes, and a low-cut indigo dress met them with a gracious welcome, as if they were a married couple checking into a respectable hotel.

Garnick handed her a card. "We're here to see Miss Jemelle Clary."

"Regarding a personal matter," Quinn added.

She scrutinized the card and handed it back. "It's early. Jemelle may not be awake."

"Please tell her we're detectives and it's vital that we ask her some questions. We'll wait."

"I'll see." The woman rolled her hips and glided out of the room trailing a cloud of lavender.

"She was holding that card upside down," said Quinn.

"She's prob'ly got other talents besides reading."

Heat scalded Quinn's neck and cheeks. I've been spending too much time in sex dens, she thought, and buried her embarrassment in a copy of *Harper's Weekly* magazine. It seemed a rather lofty publication for a brothel, especially if the hostesses couldn't read, but Madam Lou had a reputation for catering to the gentry. The ambience of the place was definitely a cut above Annie's. The salon where they waited was tastefully appointed with chairs in muted colors. It could have been modeled on Miss Josabeth Allbright's drawing room.

After a few minutes, the woman in blue returned. "Jemelle says to go out in the back garden and make yourselves at home. She'll come out soon as she's dressed."

They followed the hostess into a small, private plot with a gazebo surrounded by tall, flowering hedges. A clematis vine climbed up the gazebo's pillars and gingham cushions embellished the bench encircling a table.

"Would you care for a glass of tea?"

"Yes, ma'am," answered Garnick. "That would be real nice."

Quinn scooted around to the far side of the bench, careful not to meet Garnick's eyes. Thoughts in disarray, she removed her bonnet, brushed at imaginary smudges on the brim, and rummaged for an excuse to postpone this impending declaration of feelings.

A grandmotherly woman in a conservative dress served them tea and cookies. The sun rose higher and intensified its heat on the back of Quinn's neck. She lifted her braid and touched her neck with drops of cool water that condensed on her tea glass. "How long have we been sitting here? Maybe Jemelle asked her friend to entice us out here with a pitcher of tea so she could make her getaway out the front."

"Why would I do that?" She was tall and slender, older than Elfie by at least a decade. The bruises were still visible, but her striking red lip salve had the effect of making the rest of her face seem like empty terrain.

Garnick said, "Thanks for coming down to talk to us, Miz Clary. If you could help us hunt down Mr. Jack Stram, I'd be pleased to give him a licking in payback for what he did to you."

"I ask no odds." She bared her upper lip over the broken tooth and sidled onto the bench next to Quinn. "You didn't come here to cry over my lumps. What do you want?"

"All you know about Jack Stram and Elfie Jackson," said Quinn. "Start with the money Stram offered you to lie about Elfie."

"You go to hell." Jemelle jumped to her feet.

"You first." Quinn pulled her back down. "Bearing false witness will buy you an express ticket. Have you no sense of decency?"

"Let's hear Miz Clary's side," said Garnick. "We can see for ourselves what Stram did to this lady. Did he threaten you with more of the same if you crossed him?"

Quinn could see she'd alienated Jemelle and Garnick was trying to back and fill. She added her amends. "Yes, I'm sure that's what happened. But we can protect her, can't we, Garnick? We can keep Stram from hurting you, Jemelle, if only you'll tell us where he is and why he asked you to make up that lie about Elfie."

"Who do you think you are, calling me a liar? Who says?"

"Annie Stafford," lied Garnick. "She was listening at the keyhole."

Jemelle's bruised cheek twitched.

Quinn said, "Annie didn't like the fact that one of her best earners let a friend interfere with business and she didn't like one of her girls wasting valuable time with a man she didn't bed. Is that why you didn't offer her a cut of what Stram paid you?"

Jemelle plucked a rolled cigarette from behind her ear and hung it in the corner of her mouth. She reached for the bowl of Lucifers on the table, but Garnick reached it first. He struck the match on his thumbnail. She leaned in for the light and sucked until the end of the cigarette glowed red. She held it between her thumb and forefinger with her pinkie pointed up and blew a mare's tail of smoke out the side of her mouth. "What Annie thinks is neither here nor there. The old sow don't give a toss what happens to Elfie Jackson."

"She will if she's called to give testimony at Elfie's trial," said Quinn. "She'll be forced to swear to what she heard."

"So what? It's her word against mine."

"You don't want to get athwart of Annie," said Garnick. "You saw what she did to Stram, whipped to a pulp. Why don't you air up and give us the story?"

She kinked her lip. "If you're so interested, what'll you pay for a different story?"

"Nothing," said Quinn, "but I'll do everything in my power to make your life as difficult as possible. I'll tell the police it was you who killed that man in the alley."

"Hey, now!"

"No need for things to come to such a pass," said Garnick. "We're agreeable people. What if I was to put in a word for you with a dentist fella I know? Get him to give you a reduction rate on a new chopper?"

"I ask no odds. All I want's to be left alone. I don't know nothing about a shooting."

"I believe you," said Garnick. "Stram prob'ly did it. The dead man had been looking for him. If Stram's got anything besides bone between his ears, he's on a beeline for the territories by now. He won't be back to dun you for a refund of that fifty."

She stubbed out the cigarette on the table. "A man named Handry or Handsy gave Stram the fifty he paid me to say Elfie set the fire. The burnt shawl, too. He told me to make sure the police found it in her trunk if they was to show up."

Quinn started and sloshed tea on her hat. "Ned Handish?"

"Could be. Yeah, that sounds right."

"Did Stram say why Handish wanted Elfie blamed for the fire? Was Handish the one who set it?"

"Jack never said, but why else would he pay to pin it on Elfie?"

"Did you meet Handish?"

"I never seen him. Stram said he killed a woman down in Cairo. If Stram done him, I guess he got what he deserved."

The specter of the body on the morgue table skirred through Quinn's mind. She blinked it away. "Tell me how you came to befriend Elfie. Annie said you both lived in Rock Island."

"Her family moved to town about the time the war started. Her pa worked for the railroad. Him and his wife traded at the dry goods store my folks ran. Elfie was always underfoot, cadging licorice and making a nuisance. Always watching me and asking about the boys waiting outside for me to finish my chores and go walking."

"When did she meet Burk Bayer?"

"Sometime after I got married and left Rock Island. I'd seen Burk around. He was a good-looker and you could tell he was hungry. He was gonna make it big or die trying. Little Elfie musta picked up a few of my tricks to rope in a goer like him. She shouldn't have been surprised when he chanced on a rich girl and cut her loose."

"Did you ever see Bayer at Annie's?"

"If I had, I'd have myself another fifty. Him turning up in a whorehouse would've stuck in his fiancée's craw."

Garnick edged around the circular bench to get the sun out of his eyes and took over the questioning. "How did you and Elfie stay in touch after you left Rock Island?"

"My man took off and I ran out of money. I wrote home for help but that lot of brimstone preaching gospellers would as soon stone me as spare me a nickel. I knew Elfie had a little put away on account of Burk's salary from the sawmill so I wrote and asked her for a loan. She sent me a few dollars. When she turned up at Annie's after he chucked her out, I figured I owed her."

"Is Stram a Rock Island man?"

"He wasn't there when I was."

"You didn't know him before he showed up at Annie's to buy your connivance?"

"The first time I seen him, all he wanted was to mingle limbs. It was a week or so before he mentioned Elfie. After that he came back a few times to yammer about the set-up."

"How could he have known you were Elfie's friend," Quinn asked, "or supposedly her friend?"

94

"Ask Elfie. I don't know who she woulda told about me or where I worked. All I know about Stram is he's a mean drunk and a dead weight with his heels to Jesus."

Quinn could have lived a happier life without that vision in her mind. "Why'd he hit you, Jemelle? You agreed to do what he asked."

"He thought that fifty covered as much mingle-mangle as he wanted. I thought different." She stood up to leave.

"Wait." Quinn caught her hand. "Will you sign a statement and swear what you've told us today is the truth?"

She smirked. Now she had something to sell. "What's the name of that dentist?"

Garnick scribbled something on the back of a card and handed it over. "Whatever it costs, tell him it cancels out his I.O.U. to me."

She stretched her sinuous anatomy in a provocative way, tucked the card between her breasts, and started back toward the house.

Quinn called after her. "We'll be back with that statement."

Garnick stood up, raring to leave. "We don't need to go back through the house. Let's cut through the gap in the hedge, have a look at the alley where Handish was shot."

Quinn dipped a cookie in her tea and exulted. Jemelle's admission had ousted her other worries. She and Garnick had scored a momentous success. Jemelle's testimony would vindicate Elfie and bring into the agency a trove of paying clients. "We have to report what we've learned to Winthrop right away. He can draft a statement for Jemelle to sign and we can get back here before she changes her mind."

"Hurry up then. Full chisel."

They were on the far side of the hedge when a cornsilk blonde in a vivid pink dress ran out of the house and clasped her hands to her heart. "Garnick! Sissy told me you were

here. I knew you'd come back to see your lovey-dove
Minnie."

CHAPTER 12

Winthrop's office reflected the man – neat, orderly, and meticulously clean. The afternoon sun flooded every nook and cranny, but Quinn saw not a speck of dust. Winthrop sat at his desk poring over a thick, leather-bound tome. He didn't look up as she entered, but held up his hand to preempt interruption. Her thoughts were still back at the Mansion. She see-sawed between the urge to cry and the determination not to appear foolish. Or judgmental. Or jealous, which she was not. She was embarrassed by her behavior and surprised by Garnick's, that's all. She couldn't let him see *how* surprised. How...disconcerted. This meeting with Winthrop would give her time to digest the revelation and revise her assumptions.

After what seemed a long time, he marked his place in the book, closed it, and regarded her with a sullen countenance. "Mrs. Sinclair. I had hoped to see you yesterday."

Quinn could barely recall yesterday and was in no mood to be reprimanded. "I was busy working on the case, both yesterday and today."

"Were you able to find the alibi witness you promised?"

"Yes, but there is more to the story than what we expected."

"Please sit down and brief me."

Quinn gave him a detailed account of her interviews with Elfie and Jemelle, the intrusion of Ned Handish and Jack Stram into the case, and the chilling news of Handish's murder. "Handish gave Stram money to bribe Jemelle to supply the police with a made-up story and a scorched shawl, which she claimed Elfie had worn on the night of the fire."

"I can't believe the police withheld information from me about the Clary woman. This is the first I've heard about any shawl. And you say this Handish person hired you to track down Stram?"

"Yes, it's very strange. He said he'd been wrongly accused of killing his wife, but insisted it was Stram, not him."

"Sounds the kind of brute who'd naturally end up dead in an alley. What can we expect now from Jemelle Clary?"

"I convinced her, I mean Garnick and I convinced her to retract her accusation against Elfie and admit the shawl was a ruse. If you prepare a statement with the right legal terms, I'll see to it she signs today and in front of witnesses. Even if she changes her story at Elfie's trial, her waffling will give the jury reason to doubt."

"Excellent work, *Detective* Paschal. You elicited a lot more from Elfie than I did. And a woman like Jemelle, I wouldn't have known how to interrogate her. You and Garnick are to be congratulated. Where is he, by the way?"

"He stayed behind at the brothel. To make sure Jemelle doesn't bolt and run. I took the horse-car."

"Good thinking. The two of you make an efficient team. I was out of sorts when I last spoke with Garnick. I want to apologize. No question I misjudged the man."

"He can be hard to read sometimes." She forced a smile and pressed ahead with her report. "Jemelle characterized Burk Bayer as a man bent on making money, come what may. He's the one who benefits most from the Kadingers' deaths."

"Bayer's an unprincipled reprobate. I wouldn't be surprised if he killed his wife for her fortune and will eventually go back to his mistress. Water seeks its level."

If Quinn weren't preoccupied with other concerns, she would have chided him for his snobbery. But she couldn't let herself be sidetracked. "Bayer fixed himself up with a pat alibi, but he could have paid Handish and Stram to set the fire, then sent Stram to buy Jemelle's false witness against Elfie, or beat it out of her."

"Yes. And with Elfie in prison, she could cause him no more embarrassment."

"After doing his level best to incriminate her, Bayer has the gall to express his hope that you prove her not guilty."

"I didn't know you had interviewed Bayer. When and where was this?"

"In Edmond Allbright's drawing room the day before yesterday. He was visiting Miss Josabeth Allbright at her invitation."

Winthrop crimped his mouth in marked distaste. "I heard he was ingratiating himself into the Kadingers' social set."

"He said Rolf Kadinger had a son, Verner. Mr. Kadinger wrote the boy out of his will, which made Verner extremely angry."

"Verner Kadinger has asked me to represent him."

Quinn was dumbfounded. "Why you?"

"I assume he saw my name somewhere in connection with the criminal case against Elfie. He's been out of the country. He may not know any other attorneys."

"But you can't represent him *and* Elfie! What if the jury doesn't believe Jemelle's retraction and you have to argue that Verner had a motive to murder his father? He was in Chicago a whole month prior to the fire and had a nasty row with him."

"I haven't accepted him as a client yet. We've communicated only by telegram. But if you believe Bayer is

99

guilty of the murders, I should think you'd be pleased if I could uphold Verner's claim to the estate and prevent Bayer from profiting from his crime." He pulled his watch out of his pocket. "I've scheduled a meeting with Verner for four o'clock tomorrow afternoon. I'd like you to attend and take notes. Now, give me a few minutes and I'll prepare that statement for Jemelle Clary."

Quinn wanted very much to meet Verner Kadinger, although she didn't relish the idea that Winthrop would take Verner on as a client. She wouldn't like it if he represented Geneva Sinclair at the same time he was representing her, regardless how finely he split the hairs.

The wait while he crafted his lawyerly statement was excruciating. She needed to keep moving, to keep thinking about the next thing. To keep *not* thinking about the cornsilk blonde Garnick had been mingling limbs with. Minnie. She permeated Quinn's thoughts like cheap perfume. Minnie was the reason he didn't want to accompany her to Lou Harper's hookshop. Minnie was the reason he'd been dousing himself with Florida Water and getting his hair barbered.

"How does she spell her name?" asked Winthrop.

"Who?"

"Jemelle Clary?"

Quinn spelled it like it sounded. She didn't think Jemelle would object.

Winthrop's gold-nib fountain pen scratched slowly across the page, pausing every other word. At the end of her endurance, she got up and browsed a shelf of thick law books and statutes, some as heavy as andirons. She opened *Bouvier's Law Dictionary* to **Doubt**, defined as "The uncertainty which exists in relation to a fact, a proposition, or other thing; an equipoise of the mind arising from an equality of contrary reasons." Quinn's mind stretched in equipoise like a clothesline hung with contrary reasons and contrary feelings, not to mention a load of dirty linen. How could she have so misread Garnick? What was it Josabeth said? Elfie misconstrued Burk's kindness. Apparently naïve prairie girls weren't the only ones liable to misconstruction. The one thing about which Quinn had zero doubt, she had to conquer this ridiculous urge to cry before she saw Garnick again.

She wrested her thoughts off personal matters and considered *Bouvier's* definition of **Reasonable Doubt** – "proof to a moral certainty as distinguished from an absolute certainty." By her lights, Winthrop had already compiled more than enough reasonable doubt to win Elfie's acquittal. As soon as she had obtained Jemelle's signature, she would go back to the jail and give Elfie the good news. Maybe she could suggest a way for Elfie to earn a living and live independently. If Winthrop could cajole a settlement out of her in-laws, maybe she could afford to hire Elfie as a receptionist and buy a second horse and buggy so that she and Garnick didn't have to spend so much time together.

She shelved the book and wandered around. A collection of ambrotypes and cabinet card photographs caught her eye. Displayed on top of a pine pie safe, they added a homey, sentimental touch to the office. Quinn wouldn't have thought Winthrop had a sentimental side. One of the older ambrotypes showed an elderly gentleman posed with two children at his knee, a boy and girl. The boy in short pants had a robust, chesty look. She guessed it was the young Winthrop. The facing picture of a middle-aged woman with a haughty, down-the-nose mien was probably his mother. The cabinet photo featured a flamboyant young woman sporting a spiky tiara and intricately carved eardrops in the same design. Her hands were crossed theatrically over her bosom to exhibit cameo bracelets with dancing cupids. Could she be Adelaide Ristori, the Italian actress who portrayed Medea?

On the wall facing his desk, he had tacked a playbill advertising last January's production of the play at Uranus

Crosby's Opera House. The poster depicted a red-robed, gimlet-eyed Medea facing down her domineering husband while a cauldron of poison brewed behind her back. Quinn opened her mouth to tell Winthrop that she had now read the play, but the door swung open and a black-haired lunatic barged in. He had a scoop nose and small, blazing eyes that broadcast fury.

"Are you Winthrop?"

"I am." The lawyer stood. "Who might you be, sir?"

"Verner Kadinger."

"You are early, sir. Our meeting isn't scheduled until tomorrow."

"Forget that. I need advice now."

"If you must." Winthrop held out his hand.

Kadinger was either too rude to take it or too blinded by fury to see it. "I won't
let that greedy swine steal what's mine. Papa was a vindictive old scoundrel, but he wasn't mad. He was a Kadinger. He wouldn't give what he worked for all his life to a bloody fortune hunter."

"This is Mrs. Sinclair," said Winthrop, calling his attention to Quinn. "I've asked her to take notes of our meeting."

Verner half-turned but offered no greeting. He drew a telegram out of his sack coat. "What's this *improper influence* you say here? Can you get the will revoked if Bayer flimflammed the old man?"

"If it can be proven," said Winthrop. He handed Quinn a notebook and pen and pulled out a chair for her next to his desk. "Let's sit, shall we, and start from the beginning. Why do you believe your father was flimflammed?"

"I'm my father's only son. I'm the only legitimate heir."

"Tell me the name of the attorney who read the will. I need to see it for myself."

"Caleb Cranston."

"Did you attend the reading?"

"I stood up, I told him it's a fake. My father didn't want that bloody bastard to get his hands on one cent of his money. Cranston, he insisted it was Papa's true testament, authenticated by witnesses, leaving everything to Delphine contingent on her marital status at the time of his death. But that can't be right. He knew better than to trust Delphine or any husband she might have chosen. That bastard Bayer is the author of this fake will."

"You are unduly exercised," said Winthrop. "Please calm yourself. There's a lady present."

Verner slung a blistering look at Quinn. There was something feral about him, something wild and unpredictable. "Don't try to put me in my place. I've had enough of that. Are you going to help me or not?"

"I can try. Are you prepared to retain me as your counsel?"

"I guess. How much?"

"Fifty dollars."

"I'll mail you a check."

Winthrop's face said, "I'll take you seriously if and when it clears the bank." His voice said, "Tell me why you think the will is a fake?"

"The original left everything to me, what's left after his crack-brain investments."

"Could your father have misplaced the first will or left it in the keeping of a different attorney?" asked Winthrop.

"He was a pigeonholer. Everything in its place, every number in its right column, every decimal point exact."

"Is it possible the original will was burned in the fire?"

"I don't know. Maybe Bayer stole it."

Quinn hesitated to further incite Verner, but his rant had tapered off and he seemed to have his temper under control. She said, "Mr. Bayer told me your father bequeathed you a spittoon. Was that in the will Mr. Cranston read?"

103

He jumped out of his chair with such force that it toppled and crashed behind him.

"You've talked to him? What kind of humbug is this?"

Quinn bounced out of her chair and moved to safety behind Winthrop's desk as Verner stomped around the office, muttering and flailing his arms. "What kind of a damned lawyer's trick are you pulling?"

"You are overwrought, sir." Winthrop's equanimity raveled. He looked genuinely alarmed. "I beg you to restrain yourself. Come and sit. There is no trick. As part of her investigation into the arson, Mrs. Sinclair had occasion to speak with Bayer. And what did he tell you about this, um, cuspidor, Mrs. Sinclair?"

"He indicated that the elder Mr. Kadinger and Mr. Verner Kadinger didn't get along. The younger Mr. Kadinger ridiculed his father for dipping snuff and the spit...the cuspidor was his father's posthumous rejoinder."

Verner made a gnarling sound in the back of his throat.

"We can explain away such family tiffs to the court," said Winthrop. "I'll consult with your father's clerk. He may be able to validate your claim. Clerks often know their employers' intents and purposes."

"Jones," muttered Verner and circled back toward the desk. "He worked for Papa for twenty years. He'll tell you how Bayer twisted him around his finger."

Winthrop recovered his poise and settled into the chair behind his desk. "Did you remain close to Delphine while you were away in Germany? Did she write to you?"

"Nothing but twaddle. 'Met charming European actor at McVickers Theater' and 'Pearl eardrops for my birthday.' She was too vain to live."

"Do you still have her letters?" asked Winthrop.

"My sister was an imbecile!" A mist of spittle sprayed from Verner's mouth. "A sap for any sweet-talking masher who whispered in her ear."

"Do you remember the names of any of the mashers?" asked Quinn. "One of them became angry when she rejected him. He may have set the fire."

"Why harp on that? All I want's my money. If you can't get it for me, take your *improper influence* and be damned!" He ripped the telegram in half and barged out as furiously as he'd barged in.

"The man's unhinged," said Winthrop. "He clearly hated his sister."

"True, but if there was a will in his favor somewhere in the house, he wouldn't burn it and wreck his chances to inherit." Quinn deliberated the truthfulness of Verner vis-à-vis Bayer. Had Bayer persuaded Kadinger to disinherit his son or had he destroyed the old will and forged a new one? She still chafed over the fact her husband's mother had falsified a deed to cheat her out of her inheritance. She said, "I wonder if Mr. Kadinger's bad investments relate in some way to his death."

"Verner is a madman. He wouldn't know a sound investment from a sack of salt. His father probably made business expenditures for necessary equipment that Verner believes should have gone instead for his personal upkeep."

"I guess that's so." Both of Rolf Kadinger's children seemed remarkably self-indulgent. Quinn thought about Delphine's pearl eardrops and recalled Josabeth saying her secret suitor had demanded his gifts back. "If you need to mention another suspect at Elfie's trial, Delphine had a secret lover before she married."

"Who told you that?"

"Her bridesmaid, Miss Allbright."

"Did Miss Allbright give you the name of this man?"

"No, but I'm going to interview Rhetta Slayne. She probably knows more of what went on in the Kadinger household than anybody and I've found out where she lives."

"The fire fighters questioned her and she knows nothing. Another interview would be a waste of your time." Winthrop gathered up the pieces of the torn telegram and dropped them in the rubbish pail. "I'd prefer you spend an afternoon with Elfie and see if you can liven her up a bit. If she presents herself in a sympathetic way in court and Jemelle Clary sticks to her statement, we can declare victory."

"Don't you want to find the murderer?"

"Finding the Kadingers' murderer is unrelated to winning an acquittal for Elfie, but it would strengthen the defense if Stram could be induced to confess that Bayer paid him to kill his wife. If you discover any clue at all as to where he's gone to ground, report to me immediately."

"Rhetta Slayne may have seen him on the night of the fire. Maybe she noticed something that would lead us to him."

"She was blithering that night and if she saw anything, she'll already have forgotten. Put that witless housemaid out of your mind and rest on your laurels. You've saved a woman from the gallows, detective. I want to take you for a celebratory dinner at John Wright's restaurant. I shall pick you up tomorrow evening at seven." He gave her an assessing look. "It's in the Opera House, you know. There's always a dressy, upper-crust crowd in attendance. But I'm sure you have a suitable frock stowed away in the back of your wardrobe, something you wore prior to your widowhood. It doesn't have to be the latest mode. Simplicity has its own style."

CHAPTER 13

By four o'clock a gaggle of boisterous customers had congregated on the front lawn at the Mansion. Quinn looked on from a block away and debated how to enter without being accosted. She assumed Garnick had stationed himself in the salon or possibly outside Jemelle's door. Regardless of his whereabouts, she would probably have to announce herself to the woman in the indigo dress.

An approach through the hedge in the back seemed the least risky. Eyes lowered, resolutely deaf to any come-on, she skulked down an unpaved, overgrown lane that dead-ended in the alley behind the brothel. She hurried along beside the hedge, careful to step around the blood-drenched spot where Handish's body had lain and stole into the back garden. Garnick sat under the gazebo with Jemelle and two other people, Fen Megarian and the woman in indigo.

Garnick said, "I reckoned you'd be getting back about now, Miz Paschal. Seems the *Tribune's* star reporter searched out Miss Clary same as us."

Megarian saluted her with his notebook. "Afternoon, detective. I wasn't sure you and Garnick would pay me another visit after you got the photograph. Big Annie told me I might find you here and I'm glad I came. Like Garnick promised, it's a gripper of a story, if what Jemelle says is half true."

"She's about to swear that it's all true," said Quinn. "Micah Winthrop, Elfie's lawyer, drew up a statement for her to sign. Under penalty of perjury."

"Wide is the gate and broad is the way," intoned Megarian, burying a pencil in his stork's nest of hair.

"What's that supposed to mean?" asked Jemelle.

"People generally reach the conclusion they want. Sometimes it's true and accurate, sometimes not. A reporter sifts through a range of opinions and conclusions. It's my job to turn the hodgepodge into a tale that'll titillate the public, one that beguiles them to shell out and buy a copy."

"Weaving a fantastical myth into a real-life tragedy is shameful," said Quinn. "It's malpractice."

"Oh, just let me sign the blasted thing and be done," said Jemelle. "I can't get quit of you gassers soon enough."

Quinn took the statement out of its folder and smoothed it out on the table for her review.

Garnick held out a pen.

Jemelle took it and scrawled her name in a slashing script. "There. Now will you all please go away and leave me be?"

"Hold on," said Megarian. "She can't swear to something she didn't read. Let's hear it read. I want to compare what you told these detectives with what you told me, missy."

Quinn picked it up, but Jemelle snatched it out of her hands. "I'll do it." She read, haltingly but with seeming comprehension. When she finished she dropped it on the table and fumed off into the house.

Garnick slid the document across to Megarian. "Add your John Henry at the bottom. You're a witness that it's her own signature."

Megarian signed and Garnick handed it to the woman in indigo. "Now you, Sissy. Your name in full if you please." He looked at Quinn. "I beg your pardon, ladies. Miz Paschal, this is Miss Sissy Dinkins."

"How do you do," said Quinn.

"Pleased to meet you." She signed and stood. "Can I go now?"

"Sure. And thanks for your time." Garnick handed the document back to Quinn. "Exhibit One for Elfie's defense."

Megarian slithered off the bench and grinned. "Don't miss the poetic threads I weave into tomorrow's paper, detectives." He tapped his notebook against his forehead and followed Sissy into the brothel.

Suddenly Quinn found herself alone under the gazebo with Garnick.

He said, "Leonidas is hitched a ways down the lane. I'll drive you back to Winthrop's office to drop off the statement, or home if that's your druthers. We can talk on the way. I need to explain myself."

She panicked. Of all the talks she didn't want to have at this particular time, a heart-to-heart with Garnick ranked foremost. And of all the reactions she didn't want to convey, disappointment and disapproval took priority. Not that she felt disappointment or disapproval. There was a twinge of punctured vanity, a sense of diminished closeness, a belief that someone of Garnick's caliber could do better than Minnie. But these feelings were mean-spirited and hypocritical given the way she, herself, had behaved. She'd thrown herself at him like a love-addled hoyden, then misunderstood the ardor of his response. Any man invited to take such liberties would have responded the same way. It was humiliating. Least said, soonest mended.

"Heavens sakes, Garnick, you don't owe me an explanation. Please." She put on a hectic smile. "Absolutely we have to talk. I've a hundred things to tell you. Verner Kadinger showed up at Winthrop's office while I was there. He's an absolute wild man, knocked over the furniture, looked as if he wanted to knock me down and you wouldn't believe the spiteful things he said about his father and sister. You remember what Bayer and Josabeth said about him.

They weren't exaggerating. We definitely need to question him. I was thinking you could deliver Jemelle's statement to Winthrop and see if you can locate that rooming house on Pine where Bayer said Verner was living. While you're doing that, I'll take the horse-car over to Rush Street and interview Rhetta Slayne and by tomorrow, we'll have even more to talk about."

She handed him back the statement and tried to ignore the reproach in his eyes, a look that said he was being unjustly done by.

"The horse-car doesn't go anywheres near Rush, Quinn."

"I'll transfer."

He held her eyes for a long moment. She could feel the bond between them stretch.

He said, "Nothing I can say if you've made up your mind. We'll cross paths sometime tomorrow. Don't forget your bonnet." He went out through the gap in the hedge and she saw she'd left her tea-stained bonnet behind when she tore out in a rush to Winthrop's office. With a catch at her heart, she retrieved it and stuck it on her head, probably lopsided. She removed the hatpin and stabbed it through the crown to secure the confounded thing. Her aim was off, the pin nicked her scalp and she winced. The tears she'd been holding back for the last few hours began to spill.

She ripped off the bonnet and sat down to feel sorry for herself. She was exhausted. This day had already lasted a thousand years and still the relentless sun beat down on her neck. Inside the brothel, somebody played *Goodnight, Ladies* on the piano. It was a sign. She retraced her steps through the hedge and down the alley and trudged to the nearest horse-car stop. But by the time the omnibus arrived, she had shelved the idea of visiting Rhetta Slayne. She needed a cool bath. She needed time to absorb the shifts and turnabouts in this awful day and to think. More than anything, she needed sleep.

***

The voice shrilled and resounded again and again. "Get out", cried Elfie. "Get out, get out, get out of here." A man cursed and something smashed.

"Where is she?"

"No one here – stop! Where are you going?"

Elfie screamed.

"Light! Light a lamp!"

Quinn burrowed deep under a blanket, making herself small, hiding from the invader. In the dark of her cell she fondled the hilt of a knife. If she had to fight –

"Mrs. Sinclair! Wake up!"

"Elfie?" The jail was black as the inside of a cave.

"Mrs. Sinclair!"

Somebody was pummeling on the door, jiggling the knob. Quinn sat bolt upright. Her hand flew out and fastened around something round and solid. She broke out of the dream. She was holding the finial of her four-poster bed. The voice wasn't Elfie's, but Mrs. Mills' and she sounded frantic. The house must have caught fire. Quinn threw on a wrapper and flung open the door.

"There's a drunkard in the parlor." The lamp wobbled in her landlady's hand. "He forced his way inside. Miss Nearest has gone next door for help. Miss Franks is down there with him. She's in a state. I think she's fainted."

"What man? What does he want?"

"He wants to speak to a Detective Paschal. I told him no such person lives here. This is a home for ladies, but he refuses to leave. You're so confident and strong-minded. Maybe you can ward him off while I tend to Miss Franks."

An assortment of possibilities scrolled through Quinn's mind, none of them good. Megarian? Annie's bouncer? She was still unsettled by her dream. What if Elfie had been raped or murdered and Captain Chesterton had come to tell

111

her? Mother of God, what if Garnick had gotten drunk and decided to gloss things over in the middle of the night? Nothing could surprise her now. She said, "I'll go down." She took the derringer off the dresser and slipped it into her wrapper pocket.

"That's a gun," blurted Mrs. Mills.

Quinn nudged her landlady aside and padded stealthily down the steps. Two lamps had been lit, but they were both in the entry hall and most of the parlor was in shadow. She drew in a calming breath and stepped into the light.

"You look more the ticket than the rest of these peahens." The man had a thicket of whitish-blond hair, a drooping mustache of the same color, and deep-set, stone-cold eyes. He wore a red kerchief around his neck, baggy trousers, and a billed kepi cap. "Why are you looking for me?"

"It's the police who are looking for you, Mr. Stram. They think you murdered a man in the alley behind Lou Harper's Mansion."

"What kind of cock and bull is that? What man?"

"Ned Handish."

"Never heard of him."

"He *was* looking for you before you put two bullets in his head. He said you strangled his wife to death in Cairo."

"What was her name?"

Quinn stiffened. How many women had he strangled? "Her name was Florrie. Florrie Handish."

"Never heard of her neither. You're barking up the wrong tree."

Quinn had been thinking that same thing ever since Handish's case collided with Elfie's. There were too many wrong trees. She couldn't see the forest.

"Git, you old boiler!" Stram shouted over Quinn's shoulder.

She looked around. Mrs. Mills was goggling like an owl. Quinn said, "Please go back upstairs, Mrs. Mills. I'll attend to this matter."

"What about Miss Franks?"

Quinn surveyed the shadows. A whimper arose from the darkest corner of the couch. "Miss Franks, there's no need to be afraid. Please go with Mrs. Mills."

She jumped up and scurried across the room into the landlady's outstretched arms.

Mrs. Mills clucked and patted. "We can't leave you alone with this ruffian, Mrs. Sinclair."

"Sure you can," said Stram. "Mrs. Sinclair, if that's what she calls herself, is tickled to see me. She's been asking for me in every whorehouse in town."

The women gasped.

"Miss Nearest will be back any minute with the police," said Mrs. Mills. "You'd better get out of here, mister."

"We'll both get out." He clamped a steely hand around Quinn's arm and dragged her out the door.

Her heart stuttered. The man was a killer. His vise-like fingers dug into her flesh, but she didn't cry out or try to resist. With her free hand she caressed the derringer in her pocket. Behind them the door spanked shut and she heard the deadbolt click. Stram towed her around the side of the house, past the small garden toward a vacant, overgrown field. A humpback moon cast just enough light to make out the ground in front of her. The darkness felt suffocating. Stram could strangle her out here and she wouldn't be found for days, but curiosity eclipsed fear.

"How did you find out where I live?"

He stopped under a tree and leaned in close. "I got friends looking out for me."

The liquor on his breath nearly gagged her. She wrenched her arm free and backed away. "Who told you I was asking about you?"

113

"Jemelle and me had a reunion earlier this evening. She said she told you I paid her to lie about the Jackson chippy. That's bogus, like everything that comes out of that whore's mouth. I should've busted her head."

Quinn's stomach knotted. She should have given Jemelle money to hide out in a hotel for a few days. "Did you beat her up again?"

"Jemelle's too smart to need another lesson." He leered. "An edgy bundle like you on the other hand—"

She whipped out the derringer and pointed it at his face. "Make a move toward me and I'll shoot off your ears."

He let go of her arm and took a step back.

Quinn felt a boost of reassurance. "How'd you find Jemelle? What 'friend' told you she was at the Mansion?"

"A girl at Annie Stafford's. Sue. I was seeing her regular before Jemelle."

From what Quinn could see of his face in this light, he didn't look as scared of the gun as she would have liked. He twirled a fob attached to his watch chain. It looked like a spent cartridge, the one Handish had mentioned. She tightened her grip on the derringer and put another foot of distance between them. "You followed me here from the Mansion?"

"Ain't you the clever minx. Yeah, I snoozed till the lights went out, but now I'm bright-eyed and bushy-tailed."

Like a skunk, thought Quinn. "Jemelle said Handish was the one who gave you the money to buy her off. Did he set the Kadinger fire? Did you help him?"

"I told you I never heard of Handish."

"You're lying."

"You listen now, Paschal or Sinclair or whoever you are. The somebody who hired me ain't somebody you want to tangle with. What I did for him's my business and he'd be one crazed zu-zu if he knew I was still knocking around this town."

"Crazed what?"

114

He leered. Either the alcohol was tripping his tongue or it was an obscenity. "I don't know who lit up that house and I don't want to know. What I want's to stay living. You and your chum Garnick noising my name around, you're making it hard."

"You say you don't know anything about Handish or the fire, but you know who hired you to bribe Jemelle."

"You gonna believe that lying slag?"

Quinn widened her stance and leveled the gun at his chest. "Tell me. Who was it?"

"You don't look much of a terror, puss. I'm gonna gamble you ain't the type to shoot a man point blank, not 'less he's fixing to take your toy away from you and whack you in the head with it."

Quinn tried to swallow, but her throat constricted. Did he mean to lunge at her? She heard a whirring in her ears, like the whir she'd heard after her father walloped her. Her confidence drained away, but she'd never lacked for bravado. "You don't know me, Mr. Stram. You would not be the first man I've shot. I'm asking you again, who hired you?"

"Jemelle said your aim was to get Elfie Jackson off. You did that, or her lawyer will. If I was you, I'd forget about the man who hired me. Somebody higher up probably hired him. Swimming upstream's a dangerous bet. Fish do it and they end up dead." He twirled the cartridge at the end of the chain. "I'm gonna turn around and walk away now. Quit dogging me and you won't see me again. There's places in this town where a man can disappear and that's what I mean to do."

"Are you afraid of him? The man upstream?"

His lip lifted and she caught a flash of white teeth. "He's a pit viper. He can change his skin, but not his fangs. Or his cold blood." Then he turned and loped off toward the street. She called after him, but he didn't look back. Questions tumbled and tossed through her mind like kernels in a

115

threshing machine. Was it possible he'd told the truth about not knowing Handish? Had Jemelle lied, spinning a story her interrogators wanted to hear? She was devious enough to betray Stram just as she'd betrayed Elfie, but there could be no doubt that she knew Handish. If she didn't, she couldn't have come up with those sound-alike names.

Somewhere in the dark, a coyote howled. It reminded Quinn of all the secret watchers she couldn't see. An answering chorus of yips reminded her how lonely she was at this moment. She listened, goosebumps rising, and watched the moon slide across the sky until the coyotes went quiet. Until her heartbeat slowed and her slippers became clammy from the dew. The world seemed murkier and more baffling than ever. One thing was sure, it wouldn't get any less baffling standing in a snaky field in her nightgown and wrapper. She pocketed the derringer and picked her way along the stubbly path back to the house.

Mrs. Mills was waiting on the front porch. She held up a lantern by which Quinn could see her ordinarily friendly face engorged with righteous indignation. "Intolerable," she said. "I run a house for respectable ladies. Tenants who use summer names, who associate with drunkards and visit bawdy houses, saints preserve us! I won't abide it. You are no longer welcome in my home. Please remove your belongings and be gone by the end of the day tomorrow. In the circumstances, you needn't ask for a letter of recommendation."

Chapter 14

Quinn folded the last of her garments into the trunk, closed the lid, and looked around at the comforts she had enjoyed for the last time. The big four poster with the feather tick mattress, the screened window with a view of the garden, the upholstered chair where she liked to sit and read her books, the writing desk – bare now except for the empty plate she'd brought up from the kitchen yesterday afternoon with a slice of Mrs. Mills' fresh baked spice cake. How quickly life could turn topsy-turvy.

The aroma of Mrs. Mills' coffee tantalized, but breakfast was an amenity reserved for the respectable residents. Last night's confrontation with Stram had robbed her of that designation. She scraped a few remaining crumbs off the plate and licked her fingers. For Mrs. Mills to evict her on the basis of a single event she didn't understand, without giving Quinn the opportunity to defend or explain, was small-minded and insulting. But there was nothing to be gained from self-pity. What was done was done. She straightened her back and finished packing her books. She could tote the box downstairs herself, but she'd need help moving the trunk. For the time being she had no place other than the office to move things to. In normal times, she'd ask Garnick to collect her effects and drive her around to look for another boarding house. But their bond of mutual understanding and reliance was frayed. She wasn't sure how frayed, but in the wake of the kiss, in the wake of Minnie, it didn't feel right announcing she had no place to sleep. She would take the horse-car downtown to the Tremont and hire a hackney.

The office afforded no privacy in which to dress for her fancy night out with Micah Winthrop, so she would have to start the day in her best finery. She cinched her stays and pulled on a blue-green walking dress with a basque bodice and a somewhat narrow skirt. The color and style looked rather fetching on her although she had no illusions she would live up to Winthrop's grand expectations. Somehow she'd have to get word to him to pick her up at her office and have ready an explanation as to why she no longer resided at Mrs. Mills' Home for Lady Lodgers. She foresaw an uncomfortable night ahead, in more ways than one. Recalling for him her brush with Stram, she didn't think she'd sound as daring as she'd led him to believe.

Careful not to stab herself again, she pinned a diminutive "Cocodette" bonnet into her hair, dropped the derringer in her purse, and gave the room a final once-over. She eyed the satin-cased goose down pillow with a pang, half-tempted to steal it. What with her other supposed transgressions, thievery wouldn't surprise anyone. It would only confirm their evil opinion. She wouldn't give the old prudes the pleasure. She left a note on top of Miss Nearest's copy of *Medea* promising that someone would arrive to transport her belongings by no later than six o'clock and quit the premises with her head held high. Assuming the ladies were watching her down the walkway, she rolled her hips like the woman at Lou's Mansion.

She breakfasted at the Tremont and was pleased to notice the eyes of several ladies linger admiringly on her dress. After eggs, coffee, and an excellent pastry, she engaged a hack and directed the driver to take her to 12 Rush Street and wait. The house had a rundown, ramshackle appearance. A hand-lettered sign poked up out of a laurel bush and advertised "Rooms for Rent, Single Women (No Colored or Irish). From the name, Quinn had assumed Rhetta was Irish. Maybe like Quinn, she'd quashed her accent. More likely, Bayer had rented the room in his name and the landlord never met the tenant.

The woman who answered Quinn's knock was pale and distinctly peaky. Her eyes were puffy and red-rimmed as if she'd been crying, her hair disheveled, and her gray sack wrapper draped about her like a wet flag.

"Are you Rhetta Slayne?"

"My misfortune."

"I need to talk with you, Rhetta."

"'Bout what?"

"About your former employers, the Kadingers. May I come in?"

She didn't say yes but stood aside and Quinn pressed forward into a drab, sour-smelling hallway. "Is there someplace we can sit down?"

The girl turned and shuffled into a large, dark room with a trio of tatty armchairs. They looked a perfect habitat for fleas. "Where will you be most comfortable, Rhetta?"

She flumped into a squishy brown lounger. Quinn spotted a straight-backed wooden chair with no padding and dragged it across the room to sit facing Rhetta.

"Who're you? Did Burk send you?"

Quinn noted the familiarity. "My name is Quinn Paschal. I'm a detective. Mr. Bayer didn't send me. In fact, he told me he didn't know where you were."

"I made him promise not to tell anybody."

"He told a journalist named Megarian."

"Yes, but Burk was here with that funny little man and made sure he didn't bully me."

"I see. Well, I won't bully you and I'm sure Burk would want you to answer my questions."

"'Bout Delphine?"

Again, she displayed an unwonted familiarity with her former employer. "Yes. How long did you work for the Kadinger family?"

"'Bout a year. She was a fast one."

"How do you mean fast?"

"Flirty. Free with her favors. She let a man into her bedroom through the window on days when her da was at work. I heard them cavorting, but she said she'd skin me alive if I snitched."

Quinn was flabbergasted. She had imagined the secret suitor at least came in by the front door and paid court in the parlor. "How many of these assignations do you know of?"

Rhetta's shoulders climbed halfway to her ears, which Quinn took to signify more than a few. "Did she invite Mr. Bayer into her bedroom before they were married?"

"Not Burk. He's got too much consideration."

Another one with a crush, thought Quinn. "And he didn't know his fiancée had a lover before him?"

"The way he worshipped her? He couldn't have had a glimmering. I wish I'd have told him, but he probably wouldn't have believed me. Delphine had her ways, that one. Mr. Kadinger never knew either."

Quinn finally understood why Delphine hadn't resented Burk's unsanctified union with Elfie. She'd had one of her own. "Tell me about the other man. Did you ever hear his name?"

"No. She laughed and called him a shammer and a make-believe gallant, whatever that means. Pot calling the kettle black is what *she* was, telling her daddy one thing and Burk another. Telling me I oughtn't to be doing the same as her or I'd get myself knocked up. It made me mad, only now I wish I'd of listened."

"You're pregnant?"

She nodded "I'm sick to the gills and I wish I'd have been burnt up in the fire like her."

120

"Will the father not take responsibility?"

Rhetta slumped face forward and started to bawl. If Garnick were here, he would've offered an apple or a dollop of cheer or the name of a doctor on call at a reduced rate. Quinn could offer nothing. A refrain from the Medea play flitted through her mind. *Whither wilt thou turn? In what a hopeless sea of misery heaven hath plunged thee.* Delphine had a rich father and a bridegroom on the hook if she had fallen pregnant. A girl like Rhetta suffered the perils of lovemaking on her own with no one to turn to for help but Burk Bayer. Quinn wondered if there was a guilty conscience behind his charity. "Is Burk the father of your baby?"

"Lawd, no! Burk would do the right thing."

"He didn't do right by Elfie," said Quinn.

"She wasn't knocked up. Anyhow, everybody says she's a witch." Rhetta started to sniffle and the sniffles turned to sobs.

Quinn waited until the waterworks tailed off to a hiccupping mewl and handed her a handkerchief. "Were you at the Kadinger home when Elfie visited Delphine?"

"No."

"She told Delphine that she and Burk were husband and wife under the common law. Delphine professed not to believe her, but her father wasn't so sure. Did you ever overhear a conversation between Mr. Kadinger and Burk about Elfie?"

"No, but the old gentleman thought the world of Burk. One time I heard him tell Burk he was the son he wished he would've had."

That wasn't what Elfie heard him say when she saw him in April. Kadinger had obviously warmed to Burk by the time of the wedding. "Tell me about Delphine's brother Verner. I understand he and his father clashed."

"Loud enough so I heard them from the kitchen. Verner said the old gentleman was squandering his inheritance on a bunch a worthless bonds. Mr. Kadinger said if he didn't

121

mend his ways and get a job, there'd be no inheritance, but if he was willing to work, he could move up the ladder at Kadinger's like Burk did at Weyerhaeuser. Verner was bellowing mad, called Burk a bootlicking schemer and Mr. Kadinger a harebrained old so-and-so, words I can't say. There was some low talk with Delphine I didn't catch, but on the way out Verner said when the old buzzard died, which he hoped was soon, he'd come to his funeral and spit in the casket."

The legacy of the spittoon became clear. Whether or not Verner carried out that threat, his father spat last when he cut him out of his will. Or Burk heard about Verner's taunt and added the spittoon to a will he forged. How difficult would it be to create an authentic looking legal document? Or perhaps Kadinger had written a new will in anger, not yet decided whether to finalize it, and Burk had made sure it got signed and witnessed without his father-in-law's knowledge. "Did Verner come back later and try to patch things up or beg his father to reconsider?"

"I never saw him after that or heard tell of them making matters up. 'Course he could've gone to see Mr. Kadinger at his office."

"Is that where Mr. Kadinger kept his private papers?"

"I wouldn't know about that. He kept a little bankers safe lock box in his study on top of the mantelpiece."

"Was it in its usual place on the day of the fire?"

"I don't know. Delphine had me ironing dresses and polishing jewelry all day and I didn't get in to dust the study. Oh, Lawd." She began to blubber again.

"What is it, Rhetta?"

"I was gonna put it back. I just wanted to wear it for a little while and look fine, but then..."

"The fire," finished Quinn. "What did you take?"

"This. Her *other* man gave it to her." She pushed her shabby wrapper sleeve off her right hand to show a large, yellow-gold filigree ring. The center stone was gold-bezeled ivory with an angel carved in relief. "In all the confusion I forgot and then later I was too ashamed to tell Burk. And...and...and he's been so good to me." More tears. "It's like the Bible says, coals of fire on my head and it's too late to give it back now."

"I'll give it back to him," said Quinn. "I'll tell him I found it where the arsonist dropped it."

"Would you?" She slipped it off her finger and handed it to Quinn.

It was at least a quarter pound of unmitigated ostentation. And of course there'd be an angel. "I'll be sure Mr. Bayer gets it. I imagine he'll have need of a ring in the near future." She put it in her reticule and led Rhetta back to the subject of Delphine's clandestine lover. "You must have seen him sneaking in and out of the house. What did he look like?"

"During the winter he wore a heavy coat with a cape and a Boss of the Plains hat pulled over his ears. I never got a look at his face. By spring when the weather broke, he wasn't coming around anymore. Delphine took up with Burk around the end of March or first of April and that's the same time I met my...oh." She started to weep again.

"There, there." Quinn got up and roamed around the room, scouting for a bottle of sherry or brandy. Failing that, she found her way to the kitchen and brewed a pot of tea. When she returned to the parlor, Rhetta was at least sitting up straight. Quinn placed a cup in her hands and gave her a minute to revive. "Maybe your beau will develop feelings of remorse and come back to take care of you, Rhetta. But you can't sit around crying in hopes that he or Burk or a choir of angels will save you. Burk thought there might be a place for you in the Walker Ellis house. Even now it's worth a try. Did you inquire?"

"The Ellises wouldn't hire the likes of me."

"Even on Burk's recommendation?"

"He may think he's one of 'em 'cause of who he married, but he ain't been out of Rock Island long enough to cut the ice with those swells."

"What about your mother? You told the firemen you were going home to her. Does she live in the city? She'll take you in until the baby's born."

"I don't know. She lives in St. Charles."

"Well, write her a letter and ask. If she says yes, I'll make sure you get there. Will you do that?"

"Uh-huh."

"I have only a few more questions. Josabeth Allbright told me Delphine's secret lover didn't like it when she rejected him for Burk. Did you overhear their falling-out?"

"The last time he was with her, they yelled a lot. She said, 'He's twice the man you are.' And then he said, 'You'll be sorry.' And she was sorry, wasn't she? Maybe if she'd married him instead of Burk, Elfie Jackson wouldn't have set the fire and she'd be alive today."

"And you'd still have your job and a nice place to live."

"Not when she found out I was in a fix. I could see she was looking for a way to get rid of me anyhow. I'd seen too much. But she might've given me some money."

If she didn't, you'd probably have blackmailed her, thought Quinn. And as for seeing too much, I wouldn't award you a ribbon. "Can you remember anything at all about the man that would help me identify him? His voice? His walk? Did you notice the color of his hair above the collar?"

"Uh-uh."

Quinn scoured her brain, but she couldn't think of any more questions Rhetta could answer. She poured the wretched girl another cup of tea and rose to leave. "You be sure to write that letter to your mother. I'll stop by again in a few days and you can let me know if you want a ride to St. Charles."

124

"She'll say she taught me better than to let myself be seduced by a bounder. The easiest thing is for me to die. Wouldn't break anybody's heart."

"I'm sure you're wrong about that, Rhetta. Your mother loves you, and you must have friends and family you're not thinking about right now."

"They'd be better off with me in the ground. Maybe this baby will kill me."

Rhetta was as fatalistic as Elfie. Quinn's heart went out to her, but she had worries of her own. She marshaled a parting platitude. "It's darkest before the dawn. Perhaps your man was waylaid by some emergency and as soon as he's out of the briers, he'll come back and marry you. When did you last see him?"

"The night of the fire."

"He was *there*? At the Kadinger's house?"

"We were in bed in my room and he heard a noise. He left me to go look around. I was feeling all comfy and contented and I must've dozed off. If it hadn't been for the angels singing..."

"Did he go outside?"

"I thought so. I thought he wanted a smoke."

"And he didn't come back?"

"Uh-uh. The firemen were all shouting and yawping, 'Who's in the house? Who else? Where?' I looked but didn't see him in all the uproar. I got afraid maybe he'd been careless and dropped a match and Delphine would blame me for the fire. I didn't know she was going to die. And then it hit me maybe *he* was dead. I ran to the church and prayed for him all night long. But in the morning, there was no sign of him in the ashes. Jack just absquatulated, plain and simple, and took my poor heart with him."

Quinn froze. The name was common as coal. "What's Jack's full name?"

"Jacques Stram. But everybody calls him Jack."

CHAPTER 15

Quinn wouldn't have believed anyone could find Jack Stram seductive, but there was no disputing with desire. She marveled at the sheer stamina of the man. Jemelle, Sue, Rhetta. Jemelle may have faulted his prowess, but Rhetta seemed besotted. The qualities that drew men and women together mystified Quinn. What did Elfie see in Burk? What did Delphine see in him? And what did Stram see in Rhetta?

Perhaps it was the time she'd spent in brothels of late, but Quinn had started to suspect a transactional aspect to too many pairings. Not all were motivated by love, nor even by lust. Stram may have enjoyed a few amorous couplings with Rhetta, but what else did he gain from his courtship of the Kadinger's live-in housemaid? Quinn didn't believe for one instant they'd met by chance. Stram, or the person controlling him, had engineered that meeting. Who?

Was Delphine's lover the man upstream? Had he paid Stram to distract Rhetta from his bedroom frolics with Delphine? Or was Burk Bayer the one who pulled Stram's strings? He may have doubted the fidelity of his reckless bride-to-be and hired Stram to keep an eye on her. Verner couldn't be ruled out as Stram's master. By placing a spy in his father's house, he may have hoped to learn where the will was kept and steal it, himself. Or perhaps he asked Stram to eavesdrop on Bayer, to listen for something he could use to discredit him and persuade the old man not to change his will in Delphine's favor. Regardless of who hired him, Stram had lied when he said he didn't know who set the fire. If he didn't do it himself, he saw who did, perhaps spoke to him, very likely aided and abetted him. Winthrop might not be interested in pursuing the murderer now that he had his reasonable doubt about Elfie, but Quinn was more curious than ever.

All of this creative imagining energized her. She loved being a detective. The more secrets she uncovered, the more she wanted to uncover. How many of those secrets Winthrop could be billed for, or would pay for if billed, dampened her outlook, but only a little. The murderer wouldn't remain hidden much longer and when she found him, she could sell the story to the *Tribune* or the *Evening Journal*. She couldn't wait to tell Garnick what she'd learned from Stram and Rhetta and to find out what he'd gleaned from his meeting with Verner. She climbed into the waiting hack and directed the driver to take her to the office. This round-trip ride with the wait time would cost even more than her breakfast, but at this moment she didn't care.

Her qualms about talking with Garnick had melted away. Nothing changed the fact that he was her partner and best friend. She should have guessed he had a woman. He wasn't a hermit. Released from prison in a city five hundred miles from home, widowed and friendless and alone, he'd naturally sought female society. If she disapproved what sort of female society, she wouldn't permit prejudice or wounded pride to blight their partnership. That impetuous kiss had unbalanced her, unbalanced them both. She hoped Garnick had lost the desire to explain himself, but if he did say something, she would be rational and understanding and things would return to normal. They would put their heads together, evaluate the suspects and motives, and come up with a plan of action.

Her belongings had to be transported from Mrs. Mills' boarding house by the end of the day, but that would be a waste of Garnick's time. In a fit of extravagance, she struck a deal with the hack driver. When he let her out at the office, she gave him the address and cautioned him not to answer nosy questions. He drove off and she practically ran into the office. Garnick wasn't there.

The tide of excitement ebbed. Where was he? He wouldn't have left the door unlocked if he intended to be gone long. Maybe he'd just stepped out for lunch. She went to the rear window to see if Leonidas was hitched in his usual spot under the shade of an arching white oak. He wasn't, but the window had been screened with a sheet of woven wire since yesterday.

Restless and impatient, she sat down to wait. As soon as the hack driver returned with her trunk, she'd be free until Winthrop...drat! She'd forgotten about their dinner engagement. He had to be told to call for her here. His office was more than a mile away and the day was growing hotter by the hour. Even if she could find an available hack to take her partway, her dress would be noticeably the worse for wear by the time she got back. She returned to the window, hoping to spot some loafer willing to deliver a message for the price of a beer. Even if she found a willing runner, there was no guarantee that Winthrop would be in his office and no chance the runner would get the message right unless she wrote it down.

Dear Mr. Winthrop

She crossed that out and began again.

Mr. Winthrop,
Please call upon me at my office this evening. Much has happened and I am preparing a report based on my interview with Rhetta. She doesn't know where Jack Stram is,

129

but she gave me a ring that Delphine's lover bought for her. It's quite distinctive and I believe we can trace the purchaser by inquiring among local jewelers. I will safeguard it in our office – Did that sound insufficiently prudent? *– in our office's undetectable secret safe tonight and will visit the likeliest shops tomorrow.*

Respectfully yours,
Mrs. Sinclair.

She crossed that out.

Respectfully,
Detective Paschal
P.S. I will visit Elfie tomorrow as you suggested.

She copied the note over as corrected, sealed and addressed it, and went outside to look for a runner. A well-scrubbed boy of about twelve with ginger-colored hair and freckles came by dragging a collie puppy on a rope. She showed him a half-dollar and a grin broke from ear to ear. "Yes, ma'am!" He took the envelope and set off at a fast clip. The laggardly collie looked back at her with foreboding eyes. Or maybe that's the way she looked at him.

Where *was* Garnick? She needed him to volley ideas back and forth, to help put things in perspective.

Having promised Winthrop a report, she went back to her desk and took out the Jackson file. As she filled in the newly discovered facts, she strove to line up the connections. The one character who didn't connect to the Kadingers in any way she could discern was Ned Handish. Was the big man who paid them twenty dollars to find Stram the same man who choked his wife in Cairo? What if he was paid to impersonate Handish by someone who wanted to locate Jack Stram but didn't want his identity known? It made no sense. The murderer had used Stram to suborn Jemelle to lie to the police. He must have known where to find him. And what became of all that money Handish had on him?

Moses horns! What if Handish was Delphine's secret lover? He was big and ugly and his rough manners wouldn't fit in with a well-to-do family, but the Kadingers had become well-to-do in a rough business. Rolf was a snuff-dipping ex-lumber shover who'd worked his way up from the docks. Delphine may have seen something of him in Handish, or she may have been attracted to Handish's raw physicality and air of danger. Sexual predilections were inexplicable.

A sound startled her. She looked up to see Burk Bayer smiling at her through the door pane. His auburn hair gleamed with flecks of sunlight and his come-hither gaze was unmistakable. In her current state of mind, Quinn was immune to sexual allure, especially Bayer's. Notwithstanding his kindness to Rhetta, he remained a cad in her estimation. She affected a pleasant expression and waved him in.

He entered with the lithe, cat-like grace she recalled, more like a dancer than a lumberman. "Pardon the presumption, but you look especially charming this afternoon, Detective Paschal. You must have no criminal apprehensions on your calendar for today."

"Only if the criminal drops in and surrenders. Is that why you've come, Mr. Bayer?"

"I sensed a certain antagonism at our first meeting, detective. May I ask why you seem to hold me in such low esteem?"

"Other than your cruelty to Elfie, I believe you are what the sensation novels refer to as a lady-killer and an adventurer."

"Ah." His mouth curved in a half-smile. "May I sit?"

"Of course."

"You're an attractive woman. Have you never been the object of a passion you couldn't return?"

"That is an impertinent question, sir."

131

"You claim the sole right to impertinence? Don't be so coy. I sense a conflict."

"I am not amused by your repartee, Mr. Bayer. I am, however, curious about your relationship with Elfie. You say she was nothing more than your housekeeper and yet you lived together as husband and wife, you provided for her and appeared with her in public as if she were your wife."

"She wasn't coerced. It was her choice."

"And that choice has ruined her. She stole money from her mother for you. Have you no sense of gratitude? Of loyalty?"

"She's not ruined. She has no children to raise and she understood from the beginning I would never be bound to her. Elfie's a knowing girl. She'll outgrow this obsession and find another man to take care of her."

"And you will find another wealthy woman and acquire her fortune. You have captivated Miss Allbright already. Is she your next victim?"

"Victim? Come now, Detective Paschal. You've had the opportunity to observe Miss Allbright. She has worked hard to make herself eligible for a certain kind of marriage. She is beautiful, empty-headed, and utterly compliant. If I marry her, she will deem it the crowning achievement of her life. As for my affair with Elfie, thousands of men and women cohabit with no intention to marry and thousands who do marry take their pleasure with prostitutes like Jemelle Clary."

Bantering about prostitution with this preening peacock gave Quinn the fantods. Her thoughts skidded to Garnick and Minnie and she couldn't disguise her discomfort. "How did you come to know of Jemelle, Mr. Bayer? Did you take your pleasure with her while you were married to Delphine?"

"I know about her because her name is reported in today's paper." He took a folded page out of his side pocket and set it on the desk.

Quinn brushed it aside. "Why did you encourage Fen Megarian to paint Elfie as a modern-day Medea. Was it your intention to make her the scapegoat in your wife's murder? Did you pay Jemelle to fabricate evidence against her?"

"Forgive me for remarking, detective, but in spite of Mr. Garnick's homespun manner, he is an altogether more courteous and sensitive inquisitor."

"Well he's not here. Will you not answer my question?"

"I didn't pay Jemelle or anyone else to fabricate evidence. I went to Megarian because I needed to talk to someone. Elfie raved and raged when I told her I was leaving. She wished she was dead, that I was dead, that Delphine was dead. And then Delphine *was* dead, murdered in a way reminiscent of that play I'd taken Elfie to see. I thought Megarian would be a sympathetic listener. I didn't expect him to make it into an extravaganza."

"Land sakes, he's a reporter. How could you not have expected it?" Quinn's stays felt too tight, her dress too hot, and an extravaganza of anger seethed under her Cocodette bonnet. Bayer was putting on a performance, trying to be winsome. "Were you aware Delphine had a secret lover?"

His face darkened. "I'd have thought such coarse slander beneath you."

"If you don't believe me, ask Miss Allbright. Delphine confided in her, although it was Rhetta who heard what went on in Delphine's bedroom."

"If it is your purpose to blacken my wife's memory and humiliate me," there was a poignant little catch in his voice, "you have succeeded."

Quinn couldn't tell if the emotion was real or played for show, but if his purpose was to make her feel less cocksure of her preconceptions, *he* had succeeded. "I'm sorry if you didn't know."

"I suppose it's the detective's prerogative to lay bare the secrets of the dead. No hard feelings."

133

She didn't know how to respond. "I spoke with Rhetta this morning. She said the affair went on until April. She wanted to tell you but didn't think you'd believe her. If it's any solace, she didn't see the man again after Delphine met you."

"I didn't know Rhetta was such a busybody. But she was right. Nothing she could have told me about my wife's character would have made any difference."

Because it was only Delphine's money you wanted, thought Quinn, but she bit back a retort. The desire for money didn't necessarily preclude finer feelings. She said, "Verner insists that he's his father's legitimate heir and the will Mr. Cranston read was a fake. He claims the original will was stolen or destroyed and that you substituted a new one naming Delphine, the brand-new Mrs. Burk Bayer, the only beneficiary."

"He would say that, wouldn't he?"

"Do you deny altering Rolf Kadinger's will?"

"I do, but I won't deny altering his opinion of his son." Bayer pushed to his feet, patently offended. "Verner is incapable of getting along in this world unless a living is given to him, but Rolf knew that before. What he didn't yet know was the reason Verner had to leave Germany."

"And what reason was that?" she asked.

"You're the detective. Ask him yourself."

"And where did you dredge up this dirt about Verner, Mr. Bayer?"

"Rolf made no secret of his son's escapades. The business in Germany was the last straw." He dropped a business card for Chicago Bank onto her desk. "I came to tell you I've opened an account for Elfie in the hope she'll be acquitted. If she is, give her that."

Quinn turned it over. There was a hand-written account number on the back.

"It should be enough to see her through until she's pulled herself together. Tell her it's a gift from the Christian women who are paying her lawyer."

"You should give it to her. It would mean a lot coming from you."

"The only thing she wants from me is the one thing I can't give." He expelled a rueful little sneeze of a laugh and started for the door.

"Wait!"

He stopped and turned back.

"I'll give you a receipt." She took her time writing, double-checking the numbers of the account, while she organized her thoughts. His good deeds nonplussed her. She blotted the ink dry and handed him the paper. "Do you know Jack Stram and Ned Handish?"

"I saw Stram once or twice. A malicious looking ne'er-do-well. I didn't like the cut of his jib. Rhetta found him charming, to her lasting regret as I'm sure you discovered. Another example of a one-way passion. The name Handish doesn't ring a bell. Who is he?"

"That's what I want to find out. He may have had something to do with your wife's murder."

"You sincerely don't believe Elfie's guilty, do you?"

"I do not. There are more believable motives for murder than being forsaken by a man. I'm determined to get to the truth."

"Take care you don't let that determination lead you into jeopardy." His eyes twinkled. "Only those with nothing to lose can afford to pull the Devil by the tail."

CHAPTER 16

It was that twinkle that galled. Quinn didn't know if she'd
been threatened or mocked. She stared at the closed door,
her hand itching to hurl something. Her fingers were
clenched around the base of a cut glass inkwell when
Garnick walked in. Her heart did a little somersault. She
relaxed her grip and tried to sound nonchalant. "You must
have rubbed shoulders with Burk Bayer on his way out."

"We swapped howdy-dos," said Garnick, equally
nonchalant.

"Did he say anything besides howdy?"

"Said he was sorry he missed me. I reckon that was a
mite steep."

"He didn't say anything else?"

"Nothing of note."

"It may be. Tell me."

Garnick gave her a quizzical look. "He asked how my
wife died."

That jolted Quinn. She'd never asked. Had she really
been so self-involved? She'd wondered about Lucy, of
course, but only in superficial ways. What she looked like,
whether she read books, what she and Garnick laughed
about, how they related to each other. The questions a
caring friend should have asked – how Lucy got by during
the war while Garnick was away fighting, the manner of her

death, how it affected him – these Quinn had neglected. She felt a ripple of shame. "How *did* she die?"

"The typhoid. It took her and the baby."

Another jolt. Quinn had no idea there was a baby. She was preparing herself to ask the child's name and age but couldn't find her voice.

Whether it was the look on her face or the pain of remembering, Garnick turned his back and poured himself a glass of water. "It's another roaster out there. You want one?"

"Yes, please."

He poured another glass and set it on her desk. He spun the client chair around backwards, straddled it, and leaned his chin on the top rail. "We'd been married just over a year when I was conscripted into the Confederate army in sixty-two. In February they sent me to defend Fort Henry and then Fort Donelson. I musta brought the side bad luck 'cause we lost both battles. After Donelson, the Yanks took a few thousand of us Southrons captive and I ended up here at Camp Douglas. Lucy and Gabe died that June. Her sister tracked me down and got a letter through."

Quinn sipped the water and tested her voice. "Gabe. Was he your namesake?"

Garnick laughed, instantly dispelling the pall of sad memories. "You finally pried it out of me, detective."

She had to laugh, too. "You're a hard case. Gabriel. Like the Archangel."

"Let's keep it down-to-earth with just plain Garnick. But now you got me talking, you want to ask me about anything else? Or anybody?"

She knew he meant Minnie, knew he wanted to make things right between them. The feeling in his eyes was palpable as a touch. What would happen if she simply held out her arms to him? But something paralyzed her. She'd rushed into Thom's arms and after the first transport, after the anticipation ended and consummation was achieved, all she'd felt was disappointment and lukewarm duty. Bayer had planted an idea. Maybe she was afraid she couldn't return Garnick's feelings the way she couldn't return Thom's. Or was she afraid he couldn't return hers?

"Quinn?"

She felt as if she were standing on the edge of a cliff. They both were. Whatever they said to each other now would either push them over the edge or pull them back. They could remain friends or they could leap into a sea of complicated and unfathomable emotions. She took a sip of water. "Were you able to interview Verner Kadinger?"

He swung off the chair and walked over to the drinks table. He kept his back turned while he poured another glass of water. When he about-faced, his expression was neutral, his tone casual. "Yeah, I whiled away a few hours jawing with Verner last night. I was just about to sum it up for you."

Quinn felt abruptly let down. Had she wanted him to push harder? Had she outsmarted herself? Too late for regrets. The moment had passed. "Burk Bayer hinted at some kind of serious trouble that forced Verner to leave Germany. Did he say anything about that?"

"No. He mainly maundered on about injustices done to him on this side of the pond. The man's got no head for whiskey and no fondness for the recently departed."

"What did he say about his sister?"

"Vain. Headstrong. Heedless of every rule her folks laid down. When she was fifteen, her pa sent her abroad to a finishing school for young ladies in Switzerland. After a few months, the teachers discharged her for being a disruptive influence and she came home, more unruly than ever."

"She took lovers," said Quinn in a matter-of-fact voice and embarked on a full report of her conversation with Rhetta. She had just dropped the bombshell about Jack Stram when the hack driver walked in bent-necked with her trunk hoisted across his shoulders.

"Where you want me to set it, ma'am?"

"Here. Behind my desk please."

He unburdened himself and rolled his shoulders. "Hang on. I'll fetch t'other box."

He went out and Garnick gave her a questioning look.

"I've been evicted," she said. "Stram found out where I live and came calling in the middle of the night. He raised a hubbub. Mrs. Mills drew the wrong conclusion and wouldn't give me a chance to explain."

Garnick cocked an eyebrow. "I know how that can go."

"Anyhow, Stram worked for someone else, Bayer or Verner or maybe Delphine's lover. I think he's afraid of the man. He says he wants to disappear."

The hack driver returned with her box of books, set it down with a grunt, and rubbed his neck. She thanked him and paid him a dollar over the agreed amount. He was on his way out the door when she remembered her date with Winthrop and wondered if the boy and his laggard collie had delivered her letter. Best to be sure. "Sir! Will you deliver a message for me? The address is only a few blocks from here."

"What and where?"

"I'll write it down." She dashed off a note and in yet another rush of extravagance, gave him two more dollars.

Garnick busied himself riffling through one of her books. The door closed behind the messenger and still he didn't meet her eyes. He acted as if he'd lost interest in Stram or anything else she had to say. When she couldn't stand the silence any longer, she said, "Rhetta gave me a ring we may be able to trace to Delphine's mysterious gallant, but unless Stram decides to confess his crimes and name the man who hired him, we'll never know what happened. It's maddening."

Without looking up, he said, "It's like this Elfie Jackson case was cooked up by the devil just to vex you."

"We're detectives. It's our job to be vexed about our cases."

140

"Up to a point. Winthrop's got enough arrows in his quiver to shoot down the charges against her. Maybe we should leave well enough alone and move on to other cases."

"And never know who committed the murders?" Garnick closed the book and studied her as if she were a weathervane and he was trying to gauge the direction of the wind. "This is no run-of-the-mill killer, Quinn. He's smart and he's apt to know who's after him. Don't forget the bullet that came within a gnat's whisker of killing you as we were leaving the Tremont after your talk with Enoch Bean. If Stram found out where you live, so can the killer. You're playing a dangerous game."

"We've always known there'd be danger. If you don't want to continue—"

"I'm not obligated. You already made that clear."

She averted her eyes and stared out the window. It stung to have her impertinence thrown back at her. "I don't want to..." what was the word Chesterton had used, "to *gull* you into something you don't want to do, Garnick."

"And I don't want you to wind up in a gunny sack at the bottom of the Chicago River. But seeing as how quit ain't in your vocabulary, you may as well hear the rest. Verner knows the bub who wooed his sister this past winter before Bayer waltzed in."

"That's tremendous! Who?"

"Alderman Henry Tench. He's one of Mayor Rice's inner circle and the city council's main go-between to Cap Hyman and his lovely bride Annie. For a cut of the profits, the council makes sure the coppers don't clutter up the neighborhood and harass the pimps or customers. The money seeps down through the system. Chesterton's a good egg, but he's a go-alonger. He takes his sweeteners and passes a taste on to the men under him."

"Everybody feeds at the trough," said Quinn, channeling Annie.

"That's the system, but access to the trough isn't free and the folks who oversee the graft are ruthless as weasels."

"Annie told me the Kadinger murders had the council running scared. Small wonder if an alderman was keeping company with Delphine."

"If Stram's on the run from Tench, he'll have a hard time slipping the net. He could end up like Handish."

"The thing I don't understand," said Quinn, "is how Verner knew about Tench. Delphine kept their meetings secret."

"Maybe Verner happened upon a mash note."

"That sounds logical. I'm going to dinner with Winthrop tonight. He wasn't keen to press on with the investigation, but if he sees a chance to expose high-level corruption and make a name for himself, he may decide it's worth proceeding with the investigation. He could become the next mayor. Governor, even. He can cook up a pretext for us to interview the council members and we will know soon enough if Tench is the killer."

Garnick's mouth twisted into a crowbar, one side up, one down. "Sounds like you and the silver-tongued esquire got the problem solved already."

"Give him his due, Garnick. He's a bit pompous and overbearing, but Micah has a brilliant legal education and a quick mind. He'll see ways of doing things we can't."

"A regular sage, I reckon."

"Garnick..."

"Aw, let it go. Enjoy your evening with the gov." He slammed out the door.

Gadzooks, did he think she meant to spend the night in Winthrop's bed? The rift between them seemed to grow wider by the minute. In a stormy frame of mind, she jerked open the folded paper Bayer had left on her desk. It was the front page of the *Tribune*. Bayer had marked the lead article in column four.

Questing through the vilest haunts of the most depraved and degraded creatures in our city, detectives hired by Micah Winthrop, the attorney representing the accused murderess Elfie Jackson, have found a witness they believe will exonerate the defendant. These are not the hardened detectives of the Pinkerton Force, but an amateur pair, one of them a woman who, although she risks being taken for one of these disreputable cyprians, moves among them undaunted, showing neither shock nor repulsion. She has styled herself with the alias Mrs. Paschal, but this reporter has ascertained that she is the widow of the late Thomas Sinclair, whose father John Paul Sinclair is Envoy Extraordinaire to France. Her partner, a former secessionist named Garnick, calls the prostitutes by name and treats them as equals.

The witness deposed by the detectives is Jemelle Clary, whose marred face and broken teeth give testimony to the vile and vicious persons she is paid to service. Her affidavit disavows the statements she first made to the police and asserts that a man named Jack Stram paid her $50 to incriminate Elfie Jackson. Mr. Winthrop's challenge at the trial will be to persuade twelve jurors that a woman who sells her body for one dollar and her eternal soul for $50 can be believed on any subject.

"Devil to pay," said Quinn. "There'll be the very devil to pay for this."

CHAPTER 17

Torches of radiant yellow light lined Washington Street and illuminated the sumptuous marble façade of the Crosby's Opera House. The massive five-story building, home to a 3,000-seat auditorium, lecture and concert halls, and numerous galleries, was renowned as the finest public building in the West. The four allegorical statues on the parapet above its arched entrance represented painting, sculpture, music, and commerce and proclaimed in shimmering stone the cultural advancement of the city.

Winthrop shepherded Quinn through the horde of elegantly accoutered upper-crusters milling about in front. They passed through the imposing portal and strolled along a spacious corridor bordered by frescoes, mirrors, and statues. Commerce dominated the first floor, but in a high-class way. There was a piano store, a sheet music store, a confectioner's shop, and at the end, John Wright's opulent dining establishment.

A waiter attended them to their reserved table. Quinn took her place like a condemned prisoner sitting down to her last meal. Winthrop had spent the afternoon reviewing documents at the courthouse and had not yet seen Fen Megarian's toxic front-page commentary. She wondered how many courses she would enjoy before one of Winthrop's acquaintances approached the table and exclaimed, "Is this that detective who consorts with cyprians?"

"It's rather sudden," said Winthrop, "your moving from Mrs. Mills' house, isn't it?"

"Yes." She wished she'd thought to drag her trunk behind Garnick's desk where it wouldn't have been noticed. "A room became available in a more commodious place. I was afraid someone else would take it if I didn't move immediately."

"Where is it? I assume I'll be escorting you to your new home tonight?"

Another waiter appeared, presented them with menus embossed with gold lettering and withdrew. "What do you recommend, Mr. Winthrop?"

"I like to think that over these last few months we've become friends. Please call me Micah and, with your permission, I'll call you Quinn." He smiled in a way that gave her fresh cause for unease.

"What do you recommend, Micah?"

"The quail is excellent, also the boned turkey. The prairie chicken patties are the specialty of the restaurant. In honor of your success, I think we should order a bottle of claret. What do you say, Quinn?"

She didn't know if her father's penchant for whiskey predisposed her to intoxication, but it made her leery of spiritous beverages. Her mother-in-law seldom missed a chance to deplore the "Irish sots" that plagued her beautiful city, but unless she had revealed Quinn's ethnic roots to Winthrop, he wouldn't know. Perhaps that explained his rashness. Frazzled nerves explained Quinn's. "Claret sounds delightfully festive," she said, and settled on the chicken patties.

A different waiter came and Winthrop ordered for her. While he questioned the waiter about the wine, she made a visual tour of the restaurant – swagged draperies, damask tablecloths, tall vases with varicolored flowers in every

146

corner, and carpet as soft and thick as clotted cream. Huge circular gasoliers adorned with clusters of pendulous glass beads hung from the ceiling and the dulcet strains of an orchestra floated through the air. "It's like a palace," she said.

"I thought you'd be impressed."

The other diners were decked out in the latest fashions and colors – mauve and periwinkle and drake's neck. The two matrons at the next table wore swanky gowns and expensive jewelry. Their waterfall hairstyles must have taken their hairdressers all day to plait and rope and pin. They laughed and chattered with each other as if the men sitting across from them weren't there. It crossed Quinn's mind that the disregarded men might drive their wives home after dinner and seek more appreciative companionship with one of Lou Harper's hostesses. If sympathy for visitors to Lou's implied a collapse of her morals, she wasn't minded to analyze the reason.

Yet another waiter materialized and held out a wine bottle as if he were presenting a newborn baby. Winthrop examined the label minutely. "You may pour," he said at last. When the wine was pronounced acceptable and the waiter had gone, Winthrop touched his glass to hers. "To you, Detective Paschal. And to our growing friendship. Quinn."

She took a rather large sip and eked out a tentative smile.

"I must compliment you on your dress. Most charming."

"You are very kind, Mr. Win–"

"Micah."

"Micah. And that's a handsome suit you are wearing."

"Thank you. It's bespoke, tailored and hand-stitched by a British firm on Michigan Boulevard." He swirled the wine, sipped, and grew thoughtful. "Tell me about your conversation with Rhetta Slayne. You constantly surprise

147

me with your ability to insinuate yourself into the confidence of unstable women."

He'd be a lot more surprised after he saw Megarian's article, but one surprise at a time. "A lot more has come to light since my meeting with Rhetta. Garnick spoke with Verner Kadinger last night."

"And what did that lunatic have to say? Anything more about the missing will?"

"No, but something that may lead to the murderer."

"I'm on tenterhooks."

She didn't like his tongue-in-cheek tone. "You should be. Verner says that Henry Tench was Delphine's lover before she married Bayer. Everybody knows the city council takes bribes from the brothels and heaven knows what else. If Tench is as ruthless as Garnick thinks–"

"*Alderman* Tench?" Winthrop's face broke out in blotches almost the color of the claret.

"Yes. Alderman Henry Tench."

"Who else have you told about this? Who has that idiot Kadinger told?"

"Garnick and I have told no one. I can't answer for Verner."

The dinner arrived. While the waiters lifted the cloches and sauced the meat, Winthrop's red blotches faded and he appeared to simmer down. Quinn fortified herself with more wine. The name Tench had an intimidating effect. Garnick had shown real concern and he was more accustomed to dealing with dangerous men than Winthrop. When their servers bowed and moved off to tend to other patrons, she said, "There's a possibility Tench killed the Kadingers."

"Do please keep your voice down. That is preposterous and defamatory and, really Quinn, beyond the pale."

"No it's not. What if Delphine knew too much about his graft and dealings with brothels and gambling dens and threatened to tell her father and anyone else who'd listen?"

148

"Are you suggesting you want to investigate Tench? I forbid it. You are not to question him or any other alderman. You have no idea the Pandora's box you'd be opening."

The introduction of another mythological troublemaker grated on Quinn's already raw nerves, and the idea that Micah Winthrop would claim the authority to forbid her from doing anything rankled to the bone. She imbibed a large sip of claret and took her irritation out on the prairie chicken patty. There was a lull in the conversation during which she questioned his grasp of the situation, his competence, and his professional integrity. If he was this flummoxed over a perfectly reasonable supposition, there was no hope of mollifying him after he read Megarian's exposé. When she looked up again, he was staring at her in a peculiar way.

"I can see you don't like being told what to do."

"Not much."

"I'm sorry, Quinn. I shouldn't have been so overbearing, but I have to think of my standing in the community. I want someday to have a thriving law practice, more client files than my mother's old pie safe will hold. You may think me shallow, but that's one reason I attend cultural events and plays at the Opera House. It's important to meet the right people, like the Episcopal Women's Charitable Society that engaged me on Elfie's behalf. Their husbands elected the Common Council members, including Tench. I've heard the rumors about his arrangement with Annie Stafford, but I can't be associated with any effort to tie him to the Kadinger murders. It's too explosive."

"Don't you want to find out who killed them and bring him to justice?"

"Not as much as I want to build a solid, respectable legal practice." He meditated upon his claret and swirled again. "Naturally, one wants to believe that Elfie Jackson is innocent, and of course I will exert my best efforts on her behalf, but she may have done exactly what the prosecution claims. She's emotionally unstable and Jemelle Clary is not the most credible witness."

"I believe there are more plausible suspects, Tench included."

"You've shown commendable ingenuity in this investigation. It comes down to respecting the limits. Does that make sense?"

"I suppose."

"Someday I hope to marry a woman with your kind of intelligence to assist me in my work." He smiled an unctuous smile. "There's not any kind of understanding between you and Garnick, is there?"

The turn was too sharp. She nearly fell out of her seat. "You are very opaque, Mr. ...Micah."

"I mean, an intention to become engaged?"

"There is not."

"I didn't think there would be. You're too clear-sighted to make such an ill-considered match. Garnick's an able enough fellow, witty in a broad sort of way, but obviously less educated than a woman of your quality deserves."

Her glass of claret was almost empty, not enough left to make tossing it in his face worthwhile. She wasn't sure if the red haze swirling in her head was caused by wine or anger, but she needed to get away. "Is there a ladies' retiring room in the building?"

"On the second floor." He stood and pulled out her chair. "Shall I order dessert for you? Wright's serves a beautiful array of decorated cakes."

"I like strawberry," she said, and steamed off to find the toilet.

She should have showed him Megarian's article as soon as he stepped foot inside the office tonight. Better to have terminated the relationship on her turf than waiting for the axe to fall in this pretentious temple of prettified aristocrats. Respect the limits, ha! He couldn't divert her from her

150

investigation with overcooked chicken patties and blarney. The man was detestable! Insufferable!

The ladies' room was fit for a queen. A row of silk-skirted dressing tables stood against one wall, each topped by its own gilded mirror and overhung by a crystal gasolier. On the facing wall were private closets painted with colorful murals evocative of the fashion plates in Godey's Lady's Book. Two attendants stood by to help ladies out of and back into their garments. A few ladies primped in front of the mirrors, powdering their noses, and spiffing their hair. Others rested on chic ottomans and velvet *chaises lounges* straightening their stockings and chatting.

An attendant held open a compartment door for Quinn and she slunk in like a hunted fox to its den. What if Winthrop withdrew from her lawsuit? She'd been counting on that widow's dower. She'd paid him to get it for her, invested in his skills and his reputation and his promises. He'd so far failed, but without him, she'd have to pay another lawyer and start all over again. Winthrop would say it was her just desserts. Megarian's story undermined both Elfie's case and her own. The Devil had made a day's work of messing with her. She could scarcely breathe, gripped as she was between mortification and fury – like the jaws of a pincer.

After a few minutes and a silent vent of Irish curses, she made use of the facilities and regained her composure. Time to face the music. She opened the door as a tall woman with a silver duchess chignon and a majestic nose swept out of the adjacent compartment.

"Geneva!"

"You!" Her mother-in-law's eyes dilated with rage. "How dare you speak to me!"

The lady on the ottoman sat forward, all ears.

"You have splashed the Sinclair name across the front page. *In amongst the cyprians!*" She turned up her

151

imperious nose and sneered. "Thom must be turning in his grave."

"That article was wildly exaggerated. An ambush. I have never used the name Sinclair in the course of my business, Geneva." The very name tasted like vinegar. Why was she apologizing to a forger?

The woman on the ottoman leaned across to whisper to the woman on the chaise.

"Let's find a private alcove somewhere down the hall and talk," said Quinn. "We need to clear up some things."

Geneva scoffed. "This much is clear. You are a never-ending source of disgrace. But know this, you impudent Irish baggage, you *detective*, you'll never see a cent of Sinclair money. After the humiliation you've heaped on us, I'd rather burn it. If that lawyer of yours hasn't realized the vulgar little grubber he's representing, you can be sure I'll set him straight. Henceforth, you are dead to me." She threw up her head like a bee-stung horse and stamped out of the room.

Quinn lifted her chin, smartened her hair, and winked at the open-mouthed onlookers. "Don't be fooled by her highfalutin talk, ladies. In the sporting houses on Hair Trigger block, Geneva Sinclair is known as Jigging Ginny."

There was an audible gasp. Pleased with herself, Quinn returned to the restaurant. A piece of strawberry cake with white frosting awaited her and her wine glass had been replenished.

Winthrop stood to reseat her. "I was getting worried you wouldn't come back."

"That would have been rude after you've treated me to this excellent dinner."

As Winthrop rambled on about the complexities of preparing for a jury trial, she savored the wine and let her thoughts drift. She would not be cowed by a starchy lawyer who thought he was smarter than everybody else, or a snake-in-the-grass reporter who thought he could muck about with people's lives, or the high-and-mighty Geneva Sinclair who thought she could get away with forgery and fraud. If the Devil meant to swallow her whole, he'd have to do it sideways with her kicking and clawing all the way. She'd find another place to live, another lawyer, and the right words to soothe Garnick's feelings. Together, they would figure out who killed the Kadingers if they had to take on Henry Tench and the whole city of Chicago.

A queer peace settled over her. She chased the last mouthful of cake with a big sip of wine and smiled. "Geneva Sinclair is attending a lecture at the Opera House this evening. I ran into her upstairs and she's extremely eager to speak with you."

"That's good news. I'll call on her tomorrow."

"No, tonight. I'd like you to seek her out and hear what she has to say, Micah. Please? I've a hunch tonight will be the turning point in the matter of Sinclair versus Sinclair."

"All right, if you insist, but I can't leave you sitting here all by yourself."

"But that will be heavenly. That is to say, I shall be watching the comings and goings of all these fashionable people and daydreaming about what I'm going to do with all that Sinclair money."

CHAPTER 18

The street in front of the Opera House was a hive of activity. A dozen carriages disgorged fresh arrivals, but a steady stream of people was leaving as Quinn was and she had to vie for a free hack. The day's twists and turns had sapped the last drop of energy. She looked forward to spreading a quilt across her desk and giving in to sleep. With all the wine she'd drunk, she wouldn't miss Mrs. Mills' feather bed and goose-down pillow.

When eventually she caught a ride, she closed her eyes and drowsed against the back seat. Micah would be fit to be tied when he returned to the dining room after his chat with Geneva and discovered that his disgraceful client had done a bunk. She envisioned his shock, his red blotches, his plaints of offended respectability. The picture made her giggle.

A jangle of bells and clamorous shouts brought her back to attention. The hack pulled to the curb and she stuck her head out the window as a steamer fire wagon thundered past, horses galloping headlong. They were on Pine headed east. She watched the steamer swerve right onto State. A hose cart raced close behind. When they had passed, Quinn's driver pulled into the street and followed the hose cart. The fire was in the same general direction as the office.

It was after nine o'clock but still light enough to see a plume of brownish smoke boiling into the sky.

The hack gained speed and jounced Quinn all over the seat. She braced herself with both hands. Thoughts of Rolf and Delphine Kadinger sprang to mind and she crossed her fingers no one was trapped. She peered out the window again. In the distance flames shot skyward. The acrid smell of burning wood filled the air. Some poor soul was having a worse day than her. The fire wagon had veered out of sight, but the hose cart was just careening onto Adams.

The fire was on the same street as her office. She tensed. What were the chances of a coincidence? By the time the hack made the turn, there was no doubt. The fire wagons had stopped directly in front of Garnick & Paschal.

"I don't want to get no closer," said her driver. "My horse ain't trustable around fire."

"Then let me out." The carriage was still moving as she jumped out.

Heat gusted against her face and she brushed in vain at ashes and cinders that rained all around. The little one-room building was enveloped in flames. Where was Garnick? She began to run. She drew up at the hose cart, panting, and a man reached out and grabbed her arm.

"Stay back. You'll get yourself burnt up."

"Is there anyone inside?"

"Can't say. It's too hot to send a man in."

"But you have to. That's my office. My partner may be inside."

"If you don't let us work, somebody's for sure gonna die. Now move back and keep out of the way."

The hose men unrolled their leather hoses and lugged them to the steam pump. Men shouted and exhorted each other to hurry. A sprinkle of cinders fell onto her sleeve and she batted them away.

Garnick sometimes worked at night, nailing screens in the windows or installing shelves. But this afternoon he had left in a temper. He had no reason to return. No unfinished project, no partner to argue with. He was probably off somewhere playing cards with Chesterton. Even if he'd been inside when the fire started, he'd have left when he saw he couldn't put it out by himself, wouldn't he? Dread swamped her. What if Stram had showed up and something God-awful happened?

At last they got the hoses attached to the pump and high, arcing fountains of water gushed into the inferno, but the water seemed only to fuel the flames, whipping them higher and hotter. They leapt into the white oak behind and its upper branches flared like a hundred fiery candles. If Garnick were here, he'd have tethered Leonidas under that tree. She moved around to get a view of the rear but couldn't get close enough. The blaze was too hot.

Sick with fear, she crossed to the opposite side of the street and watched the fire devour the little office upon which she had founded her new life as an independent woman, listened to the whoosh and crackle of a burning dream, breathed in the smoke of her disappearing history. Everything she owned in this world, everything that wasn't on her back or in her purse was feeding those flames – clothes, books, letters, keepsakes. All gone. All up in smoke. Someone had done this to her deliberately. A reflux of wine and prairie chicken and fury rose in her throat. Her knees buckled and she sat down hard on the curb.

After an hour, there was no more water, no more building, and no more history to save. Nothing was left of Garnick & Paschal but a skeleton of charred wood and the singed shingle that had blown off into the street. In the gathering darkness, shadowy figures with lamps trawled through the rubble. The moon rose ghost-like over the ruins.

"We didn't find a sign of anybody inside," called a sooty-faced fireman crossing the street toward her.

She sent up a silent Hail Mary. Garnick was alive.

The fireman picked up the shingle and handed it to her. "Sorry we didn't get here in time to put it out for you. Looks like she started on the east side in a trash barrel. Somebody could've emptied pipe dottle or a live ember from a cigar in it. From what we can tell, it burned slow a good long while before it caught and got to climbing the wall."

She nodded. No one could convince her this was mere happenstance.

"You need a ride home, miss?"

"I am at home. That was it."

"Where you want us to take you then?"

"I don't know." She felt numb, bereft of all power. The fire brigade might as well leave her to wait for the hearse. A hotel was out of the question. She'd spent all her cash on breakfast and hack fares. She'd been to Garnick's cabin just once. It was at the edge of a wood somewhere to the south. Even if she knew how to find it she couldn't be sure he'd be there to let her in or want to after the way she'd deflected his attempt to put things right and disprized his opinion while making much of Winthrop's brilliant legal mind.

"You got family somewhere?"

"No." Going back to her family wasn't an option. After her father's murder, she and her mother had become estranged. Her sisters lived in Springfield and her only woman friend, Norah, had moved to Omaha with her husband a year ago. The only other person who cared about her was her brother Rune, whose last letter had been posted somewhere in Canada.

"You can't sit here in the street all night, miss. It ain't safe."

She looked at him, but he seemed oblivious to the irony.

"Ain't you got no place?"

The smoke burned her eyes and throat and lungs. It felt like she was breathing the ashes of her life. "Take me to West Monroe Street. Number two-nineteen."

"Land O Goshen, I wouldn't have guessed you was *that* kind."

"I'm not, and if anyone thinks otherwise, be advised I have a loaded pistol in my purse."

***

Madam Lou's Mansion was lit bright enough for the man in the moon to ogle the girls. The hose cart driver could scarcely take his eyes off the coquettes who dallied about the lawn in the glow of red lights. Quinn hopped down and hurried into the foyer. The first person she saw was the grandmotherly woman who'd served her tea under the gazebo. Tonight her lips and cheeks were rouged and her pink dress clung to her body in a way that flouted the laws of both age and gravity. Her blue eyes danced with merriment as she laughed and flirted with a gentleman half her age.

"Excuse me," said Quinn. "Can you please tell me where to find Jemelle?"

The woman drew in her chin and gave her a dubious look. "What happened to you? You're bedraggled as a guttersnipe."

Quinn rubbed her face and her hand came away black. "Somebody burned down my office." Still carrying the shingle, she held it out to show, then feeling too much like a beggar, tucked it under her arm again. "I thought that if Jemelle isn't working, she'd let me wash up here and spend the night in her room."

"You must be hard up, diddums."

"I'm temporarily without lodging."

"Temporarily, eh? With a clean face, you'd be taking enough. You sure you don't want me to set you up in a new career?"

Quinn didn't know what to say.

159

The woman laughed. "I'm joshing you, diddums. Never let it be said Lou Harper turned away a damsel in distress."

"Are you Madam Lou?"

"The one and only. And you're the gal detective trying to get Elfie Jackson out of jail." She shooed the young man into a parlor where somebody was playing the piano and people were dancing. "You come with me, Detective Paschal."

She led Quinn up a winding, carpeted staircase, down a wide corridor with numbered rooms like in a hotel. Quinn pictured a lather of lust and mingling limbs behind the closed doors. She tried hard not to picture anyone she knew. On the last door a heart-shaped plaque read "Lou's Boudoir" in gold letters. Lou waved her inside.

It was a pretty room. The brass bed was covered in a pastel patchwork quilt and the air had a clean, citrusy smell. Quinn didn't think Lou entertained in her boudoir.

"There's water in the pitcher next to the washstand. Freshen up and make yourself comfortable. There's a wrapper in the armoire. I'll have a tub bath poured for you and send Sissy to fetch you when it's ready. Maybe one of the girls has a street dress that'll fit you. That one you're wearing is a goner."

"Thank you. Thank you very much."

"Glad to oblige."

"Is there a key to lock the door?"

Lou's eyebrows swooped low over her nose, paused in apparent disbelief, and swooped up again nearly halfway to her hairline. "I wouldn't have thought a female game enough to call herself a detective and bold enough to spend the night in a bawdy house would be all niminy-piminy and shy. But if you're skittish, don't be. You won't be bothered. All of my guests are domesticated." She left in a gale of laughter.

Quinn yanked off her silly bonnet and smoky smelling dress, riddled now with burn holes, and pitched them into the wastebasket. She poured water into the washbowl and

160

scrubbed her face. First Annie Stafford and now Lou Harper. What was it about her that provoked such uproarious laughter from whorehouse madams? It was irksome in the extreme.

Was Madam Lou *really* joshing when she offered her a job? A hundred hard-up girls with no place to sleep and no family to take them in must have walked through her door, girls like Elfie and Jemelle, girls in trouble like Rhetta. Lou, herself, may have been a damsel in distress once, alone and impoverished with no choice but to prostitute herself. Quinn wasn't that desperate yet, but if this day had taught her anything, it was the suddenness with which circumstances could change. She had lost her home, her business, her personal belongings, her pride, and the belief that she was somehow exceptional. The grim face in the mirror above the washstand stared back at her. "There's nothing for it now. Nothing left to lose. Go on and pull the Devil by the tail. Pull it and hang on till you're licked or he is."

CHAPTER 19

Madam Lou ordered a camp cot set up behind a Japanese screen for Quinn. It was hard and narrow and Quinn's thoughts were not conducive to slumber. The plinking of the piano downstairs and the bumps and moans coming from the next room didn't help. Sometime after midnight the piano went quiet and Lou came to bed. After a while, her rhythmic snores had a tranquilizing effect and Quinn fell into a mercifully dreamless sleep.

***

The insistent trill of a red-winged blackbird encroached into the edges of her consciousness. The scent of honeysuckle filled the room and the sun teased at the edges of her pillow, enticing her to open her eyes. She stretched her arms. Mrs. Mills was frying bacon this morning. It was a normal summer day.

A man's loud, hooting laugh ruptured her reverie and she snapped awake. Alert. In the present. In the boudoir of the head hooker. She jumped up and peeped over the top of the screen. Lou was gone, her bed already made. The French porcelain clock on her bedside table said eight o'clock. Quinn went to the window. A happy customer was waving good-bye to a woman she couldn't see.

She turned back to the room. The question "what now?" thrummed in her brain. The burnt shingle of Garnick & Paschal with its broken chain lay on the floor beside the cot. Had Garnick arrived at the office already this morning and found it gone? What would he think? Where would he go? Where would she go from here? She had a little money in the bank where she regularly deposited her thirteen-dollar-a-month widow's pension and the agency had a separate account with Handish's twenty dollars. She knew nothing about Garnick's finances, but she could hardly ask him to subsidize a detective agency that had been mostly her idea. If their last conversation was any indication, he'd likely say good riddance to a bad business.

She didn't have nearly enough money to replace her clothes and shoes and linens and pay for a room in a nice boarding house, too. Still, she wasn't destitute. She thought about the other women in Lou's brothel. Most had probably showed up with far less than her, their only saleable asset being their bodies.

A note had been propped against the rouge pot on Lou's dressing table. *There's a buff-colored dress on the clotheshorse that should fit you. If you're hungry, there's eggs and bacon in the kitchen. One of the girls will show you.* Quinn resolved never to disparage hookers again, except maybe Jemelle who lied as easily as she breathed. Lou hadn't mentioned her last night and, in retrospect, Quinn wouldn't have slept a wink in the same room with Jemelle. She had the look of a cornered animal, one who'd sink her fangs into anyone who got too close.

The thin muslin dress on the clotheshorse had been laundered and ironed so many times it was shiny. Quinn slipped it on and wondered which one of Lou's girls had donated it. Without the corset, it hung almost as if it were custom-made for her. She felt grateful and glad to be alive. She brushed her hair out loose and natural, no bonnets or nets or tight-wound braids. No more mealy-mouthed evasions, either. A woman who wasn't self-assured enough to say what she meant shouldn't aspire to be a detective.

Armed with fresh clothes and a sense of mission, Quinn wended her way downstairs and followed the smell of frying bacon. The cramped kitchen appeared to double as the dining room. A long communal table had been wedged between the stove and a baking cupboard with flour and sugar canisters and a kneading board. The blonde doing the frying didn't turn around.

"Whatever you're cooking smells delicious," said Quinn.

"Streak o' lean and apples. There's enough for two if you want some."

"Sure. Lou said I could also find eggs."

"I've got a basket right here. Scrambled do you?"

"Scrambled would be great."

"You're the detective who came to talk to Jemelle."

"I am. My name is Quinn. What's yours?"

"Minnie Franklin." She swiveled her head around and smiled. Without the make-up and revealing décolletage she looked twelve years old.

Quinn's brain transmitted a direct order to her mouth to smile. What her muscles did felt like a spasm. It would *have* to be Minnie. God certainly wasted no time testing her resolution to be open and frank and say what she meant. "You look awfully young, Minnie."

"Not really. Nineteen last month. The bread and butter's in the cupboard. Slice yourself off a hunk. The eggs'll be ready in a jiff."

Quinn brought the bread and a small crock of butter to the table and sat down. "Shall I cut a slice for you?"

"Yes, please."

Minnie scooped the bacon and apples and eggs out of the pan onto plates and set one down in front of Quinn. "Most of the other girls don't come to the kitchen this early and I don't drink coffee, but you can brew a pot for yourself if you like."

"Maybe later."

They ate for a while in silence. Quinn couldn't stop herself from staring, but Minnie didn't seem to take the stares amiss.

"Sissy told me Jemelle made up a story about Elfie Jackson and you and Mr. Garnick made her fess up. I could never be a detective. You must put a lot of people's backs up. Lou said you were in trouble when you came in last night, everything all burned up and no place to go. Are you scared?"

"I am, a little. Last night I was petrified. Don't you get scared doing what you...I mean, meeting so many strangers?"

"You mean like what happened to Jemelle? That wouldn't have happened here at Lou's. All of her customers are real nice."

Quinn couldn't bring herself to ask how nice Garnick was. So much for that line of inquiry, but she had other questions. Stram had been to Lou's the night after she and Garnick took Jemelle's statement. Maybe Minnie or one of the other girls had overheard a snippet of their conversation, the name of a friend or a clue where Stram may have gone to hide out. "Did you see the man who beat Jemelle? He visited her night before last."

"No. Sissy's been the parlor hostess for the last few days. You'd have to ask her or Lou. Lou doesn't miss much around here. She keeps out the bad eggs and lushingtons. That's why everybody likes working here. I'm learning a lot from Lou. Not next year, but maybe by the year after, I'll have enough money saved to open my own house."

"That's remarkable. You must have a very generous clientele."

"Most of them."

"Do any city aldermen visit Lou's place? Alderman Tench, perhaps?"

"Oh, yes. He comes in at least once a week to see Mary Gladys. If you come back for tea around four, she'll probably be here."

"I'll do that. Thanks for the breakfast and the information, Minnie." Quinn took her plate to the basin and washed it.

"Will you be with us for another night?"

"No." Had that come out sounding too emphatic? "I mean, I don't know. My life is pretty unsettled at the moment."

"Well, when you see Garnick be sure to say hallo from Minnie. It was wonderful seeing him the other afternoon. He hadn't been around since way back the end of last year. I thought maybe he'd moved back to Tennessee, but I guess he's found himself another woman. I hope she's sweet and brave."

"Why brave?" asked Quinn.

"Lou says a lot of men who soldiered in the war get crazy in their sleep and not to stay with anybody all night even if he pays. Garnick was so nice I did it anyway, but I hope never to hear such horrible nightmares again if I live to be a hundred."

CHAPTER 20

Madam Lou may have catered to the hoity-toity, but she wasn't above promoting her business to the hoi polloi. Her white-and-gold barouche carriage with "Lou's Mansion" painted on the doors in lurid purple seemed designed to attract customers and smack her critics in the eye at the same time. She made the conveyance and its liveried driver available to her girls to take them wherever they wished to go, at whatever hour, at no cost. Quinn needed to get to the Chicago Bank where $33 was on deposit, $20 in the joint account of Mr. Garnick and Mrs. Thomas Sinclair, the unmatched names a scandal in and of itself. She jettisoned whatever squeamishness remained and climbed aboard behind a buxom girl in a bright red dress who introduced herself as Hannah Mae. It was a bright, clear morning. Quinn didn't bother to hide her face as the carriage paraded through the streets eliciting a mix of foul-mouthed shouts from corner puppies and derisive stares from the respectable citizenry.

The barouche stopped in front of the bank and Quinn informed the driver she would have no further need of his services today. She strode into the bank, produced her Widow's Certificate as proof of her identity, withdrew ten dollars, and departed with as much dignity as she could muster. She hailed a hack to the Tremont where Garnick often went to catch up with his old pals, but Leonidas wasn't among the horses out front. Again she wished she knew how to direct the driver to Garnick's cabin, not that he'd be there at this hour of the day unless Leonidas had gone lame or the cabin roof had collapsed.

She thought about paying a call on Captain Chesterton. Even if he didn't know where to find Garnick, he needed to know that last night's fire was no accident. But "Chez" didn't respect her detective skills. He'd give little credence to her opinion unless it was supported by a man, preferably one of the fire fighters. She needed to get started hunting for a new place to live, but how could she sweet talk a potential landlady with her thoughts in a whirl over Garnick? It was his habit to show up at the office every morning by ten, even when there was nothing to do. She decided to go to the scene of the disaster and hope he'd be there.

The blackened stone chimney towered over the devastation like a tombstone. Quinn asked her driver to wait while she walked the perimeter of the rubble. In daylight, the loss appeared more stark. More utter and complete. Garnick wasn't here. Unless he was so out of patience with her he'd packed up and gone South, he'd know about the fire by now. He'd be here. She began to worry.

The trash barrel, what remained of it, had been pushed jam up against the building. The staves had burned and the metal ribs encompassed empty space and at the bottom, a pile of ashes and debris. She stirred it about with a stick. Was that tiny brown lump an unburned plug of tobacco or the stub of a cigar, and could it have ignited such a hot, hellish blaze? Perhaps, if fed by a few oily rags.

The fire started between the time she and Winthrop left for the Opera House and the time she returned, less than three hours, all in daylight. People traveled past the office at all hours. Even now several passersby had gathered to look at the destruction, one of them the elderly Italian woman who lived across the street. She had come into the office once to hire the *investigatori* to find her cat, Tenero. Her English was sketchy, but she was almost always peeping out from behind the curtains of her upstairs window. Quinn approached her in a calm voice so as not to upset her.

"Hello, Mrs. Baroni. Did you walk past here last night?"

Her face, wrapped in a woolen headscarf, looked like a dried apple. She eyed Quinn askance, as if she'd never seen her before. "You're not the same *ragazza* worked in there."

"Yes, ma'am. I'm Mrs. Paschal. I helped you find Tenero, don't you remember?"

"You changed your hair."

"Somewhat. Did you see what happened last night?"

"*È bruciato*. Burned up."

"Was anyone lurking around the building before the fire?"

"Lotta people watching. *Fiamme, fumare*." She gesticulated to illustrate the motion and height of the flames.

"What about before the fire, Mrs. Baroni. Did you notice anyone acting suspicious before the fire broke out?"

"Garnick."

"Garnick was here?"

"On that big *cavallo* of his. He waved at me."

"He wasn't driving the buggy?"

"No. *A cavallo*."

Quinn's worry ratcheted up a notch. What would Garnick have been doing at the office at that time of day? Was he leaving on a trip? Had he left her a message? She glanced back at the charred wood and ashes. "Did you see anybody else, Mrs. Baroni? Anyone smoking a pipe or a cigar?"

"Smoke very bad." She covered her nose with the end of her scarf and made a snuffling sound.

"Yes, but did you see anybody smoking a cigar?" Quinn mimed to get the meaning across.

"No. I gotta wash my curtains today. *Puzzare di fumo*."

Quinn thanked her and walked around the devastation again. The cast iron stove lay on its side under the chimney. A bronze hasp from her Saratoga trunk glistened in the sunshine and a blob of melted glass, the remains of her inkwell, marked the spot where her desk had stood. The only person she could recall smoking tobacco was Jemelle. Had she seen Fen Megarian's article in the *Tribune*? If she had, she would've been livid.

"Hey, you!" A tuber-nosed man in a felt bowler and loud plaid coat bore down on Quinn, shaking a walking stick above his head. "What have you done to my property?"

"I didn't do anything."

"You're one of the tenants, aren't you? Where's Garnick?"

"I don't know."

"Well, he signed a paper guaranteeing he'd maintain the place and leave it in the same condition it was in when he moved in. I should've known better than to rent to a pair of quacks. Detectives! My eye and Betty Martin! What the dickens did you do here?"

Quinn caught hold of the cane he brandished over her head. "Mr. Garnick and I are not responsible for this fire. We lost our personal property and place of business and it was almost certainly arson."

"I shouldn't be surprised. You think I don't read the newspaper? You conduct yourselves in such a way as to invite criminal trespass. You can be sure I'll prosecute to get back my money or see the both of you in jail."

"Do what you must, sir, but a man who doesn't have sense to purchase insurance oughtn't to be in the rental business."

She left him spluttering and returned to her waiting hack.

"Where to?" asked the driver.

She had to find another place to live before the end of the day, but she was angry and worried and in no fit state to

172

present herself to a choosy landlady. Moreover, a nascent plan had begun to form. "Take me to the *Chicago Tribune* building."

As if spurred by the anger in her voice, the driver took out at a precarious speed that only added to Quinn's aggravation. When she alit in front of the newspaper offices, the temptation to shoot Megarian afflicted her so powerfully she almost asked the doorman to hold the derringer for safekeeping. Instead, she balled her hands in her pockets and concentrated her energy on flushing out the little toad who had so disrupted her life. She joined a group of men on the elevating machine and rode to the second floor.

The newsboys parted as Quinn stormed across the floor. "Fen Megarian!"

He looked up, pen paused in mid-air, and grinned like a gargoyle.

"How'd you like my article, detective? Theme, plot, setting, characters. The stuff of drama, eh?"

"I call it the stuff of a smutty mind, the handicraft of a Judas. You are a despicable, unscrupulous snake, but I'm not here to enlarge upon your character. I have business to discuss."

"What's that?"

"You're about to become an adjunct member of Garnick and Paschal."

"Oh, I am, am I? What's the salary?"

"You will waive the salary and do exactly what I tell you to do or as God is my witness, I'll go to your boss with a plot, a setting, and a cast of voluptuous characters that will curl his hair."

Megarian hopped off the desk and squared up to Quinn. "What are you rattling about?"

"Your visits to the prostitutes you so blithely disparage in your articles, Mr. Megarian."

"That's a calumny. I write what the bosses want. The *Tribune* has a policy of speaking out against the brothels and crusading to shut them down."

"I'm sure it does. And anyone as committed to telling the world how vile and iniquitous they are has probably done a good deal of research. You say you went to Annie Stafford's house to find out what she'd told me and where I might be found. I bet if I asked her, she'd say you stayed to mingle limbs with one of her girls. And don't think I didn't see the lecherous look on your face when you followed Sissy into the parlor at Lou Harper's."

"You ought to be ashamed. I've never heard such raw talk from a lady."

"Like you wrote in your article, I'm undaunted. No shock or repulsion."

"See here, it's no crime for a man to visit a sporting house. Plenty of gents patronize Lou's Mansion."

"Is that the excuse you'll give your employer?"

His brow puckered. He lowered himself into a chair and appeared to consider the risk. "What is it you want?"

"I want the *Chicago Tribune* – you – to set up an interview with a certain member of the city council. It should happen very soon, first thing tomorrow morning will suit me."

"Who?"

"Henry Tench."

He opened his mouth in a round O and snapped it shut like a fish. "What makes you think he'll agree to an interview?"

"If he doesn't, you'll publish a story about his illicit doings with the brothels and skinning houses."

"That's not news. Everybody knows some on the council take a taste."

"Not Tench's voters. Not the businessmen who are trying to civilize this city and turn it into a hub of industry

174

and respectable commerce. Not churchgoers. Not the moral crusaders at the *Tribune*."

"It's one thing to denounce vice and corruption, altogether another to lay it at the feet of a powerful councilman. Anyhow, voters and landowners care more about exterminating Irish squatters and their droves of geese and goose dung than they care about prostitution."

Quinn positively ached to clobber the man. "The Irish can't be exterminated, Mr. Megarian. The English have given it their best effort. As for Mr. Tench's cozy arrangement with what your article calls 'the most depraved and degraded creatures of the city', the voters and landowners have wives and although wives can't vote, they can make life unpleasant for husbands who condone prostitution. Does that persuade you?"

Megarian dropped his chin on his chest, leaving the question to hang fire.

"Are you listening to me?"

"I'm listening." His head came up. He was wearing that triumphant grin she'd seen when he took her photograph. "I don't believe you could say anything to my editor that would cause him to sack me. My stories stoke interest and sell papers and his morals, if he has any, ebb and flow with the profits."

Megarian didn't know the Sinclairs had ostracized her. For all he knew, they doted on Quinn and applauded her decision to become a detective. All she had left was the bluff. "A telegram from my father-in-law, the Envoy Extraordinaire to France, would overcome your editor's reluctance to sack you soon enough."

The grin disappeared. "I'll set up a meeting."

"Good. Tell Tench to be in the garden at Lou's Mansion at ten o'clock in the morning and just so you know, I'll ask the questions."

CHAPTER 21

Quinn was growing increasingly worried. Garnick wouldn't have left town without leaving her a message. Maybe that was why he'd been at the office early last night, but anything he may have left for her was ashes now. It seemed a long time ago, but her thoughts harked back to the sniper who'd taken a shot at them that first day Handish walked into the office. Garnick had been sitting on the driver's bench, a perfect target. Did he have enemies she didn't know about?

Again she reproached herself for not knowing more about his life outside of their shared interests. He'd mentioned a Confederate corporal he served with and was captured with – Bradley. They had talked about starting a carpentry business after the war, but Bradley didn't survive Camp Douglas. Apart from the vet who'd treated Leonidas for colic and the shucker at the oyster depot Garnick liked, she couldn't name a single person he spent time with. Like her, he seemed disconnected, whether because of personal temperament or long habit or providential intervention.

Chesterton! He and Garnick kidded and made jest, but they appeared to like each other. They played cards together, probably swapped yarns together over a mug of beer. It was possible Garnick had told Chesterton where he was going. Anyway, she wanted to give the policeman the facts about the fire. About the *arson*. And she'd make sure he knew of her plan to meet with Tench. Even if the captain took bribes from the council, he couldn't turn a blind eye if something...untoward happened to her. Since the fire, Garnick's caution about her ending up in a gunny sack at the bottom of the Chicago River had become more concerning. But since the fire, she'd become more willing to take risks if it meant bringing the guilty devil to justice. If Fen Megarian were willing to take on the council and use his position with the *Tribune* to back her up, she'd feel a lot safer.

On the off chance Chesterton would be amenable to letting her in to see Elfie, she bought a couple of cheese sandwiches and some fruit and walked to City Hall. As luck would have it, Chesterton lounged on a bench outside the door to the jail, eating his lunch.

"Good afternoon, Captain Chesterton."

"Well, well, well. If it isn't Detective Paschal. You lose another client to misadventure? There's a fresh batch of corpses in the morgue if you'd care to look 'em over."

"Thank you, Captain, not today. My main reason for coming is to find out if you've talked to Garnick in the last twenty-four hours."

"I haven't seen him since the three of us communed over the remains of Mr. Handish. Maybe the spell broke and your partner resigned from the detective business."

"You're not the only one who wants him out of the business. Somebody burned our office to the ground last night."

Chesterton crumpled his lunch sack and got up slowly with a defiant look. The muscles in his neck and jaw bulged and squirmed. "Who did it?"

"I don't know."

"Then there's no point bellyaching to me. How do you know the fire was started on purpose?"

"The trash barrel had been pushed flush against the building and I saw what looks like the stub of a half-burned cigar at the bottom."

"Rooting in the trash, were you, detective? Why didn't the barrel burn if it was that close to the building?"

"It did burn. Whoever pushed it against the building meant for it to burn with all the evidence inside."

"But not the cigar you say started it?"

"Maybe there was water in the bottom of the barrel from that big rain we had. Oh, never mind. If you don't want to investigate, I will. But I thought you'd at least want to help me find out if Garnick's safe."

"Why wouldn't he be?"

"Because the man who murdered the Kadingers, and maybe Handish, too, knows we're looking for him."

"Elfie Jackson murdered the Kadingers and we've got her under lock and key. That piece in the *Trib* about the hooker who cooked up a story won't wash."

Quinn was sorry she'd wasted words on this lummox, but if she could wheedle her way past him to see Elfie, she wouldn't count the visit a total loss. "You're probably right, Captain. About Garnick and Elfie, too. And now with our office up in smoke, I'll have to give up the crazy notion of being a detective." She adopted a miserable tone.

"You're finally making sense."

"I know that now. I haven't helped Elfie very much, have I? But if you'll allow it, I'd like to speak with her once more before she goes to trial. I brought her a sandwich and some grapes and plums. Perhaps we can console one another."

"I can't see the harm in it. Better give me a peek inside your bag in case you're trying to smuggle a weapon."

She showed him the contents of the lunch sack. He didn't ask to see the contents of her purse and she didn't volunteer. She wondered if two women could pull off a jailbreak with nothing but a derringer.

Chesterton led her into the jail and walked her down the tunnel-like corridor, through the sharp disinfectant smell to Elfie's cell. Elfie lay huddled on her cot, black hair draggling

179

on the floor like a tattered fishing net. Chesterton opened the door and Quinn went inside.

Elfie lay so still Quinn couldn't tell if she was breathing. "Elfie, it's Quinn. I brought food. I hope you're hungry."

"You'd better eat," said Chesterton. "The cook's tired of sliding a tray of his choice vittles in front of you and coming back to find it untouched. Hurts his pride."

Quinn gave him an imploring look.

"All right, then. You've got half an hour." He locked the door and left them alone.

"A lot has happened since we last talked, Elfie. A lot of reasonable doubt as to your guilt has turned up and there's a good chance you'll be acquitted. Jemelle recanted the story she gave the police and we know Verner Kadinger had a fight with his father which makes him a suspect."

She didn't move.

Quinn sighed. As before, Burk's name was all that could bring a response. She pulled the card he had given her out of her purse. Lucky she'd thought to take it away with her or it would be ashes. "Look. Burk set up a bank account for you. I don't know how much is there, but he says it should be enough to carry you through for a while."

She rolled over and sat up. Her cheeks were sunken, her eyes glassy with tears. "Is he going to marry the banker's daughter? The one you said he was sweet on?"

"I don't know. He calls her 'compliant,' which I suppose means she'll marry him if he asks her to."

"If she's like me, she'd do anything in the world he asked her to do."

Such abject submissiveness made Quinn's teeth itch. But it was senseless to be annoyed. Acceptance of male superiority was the foundation of most marriages. Medea killed her brother for Jason. Elfie robbed her mother for Burk. Had Delphine stolen her father's will for him? "Move over, Elfie. I'll set out our picnic on the end of the cot."

"Picnic." A thin squiggle of a smile tugged at the corners of her mouth. "Are you always so chirpy?"

"No, but then I haven't been locked in jail for over a month."

Elfie tore into the first sandwich with gusto. She was gaunt as a scarecrow and slatternly from so many weeks without washing. Quinn would have to see about borrowing a clean dress for her to wear at trial and getting her a shampoo. Maybe Chesterton would parole her for a few hours. Now that she had a bank account, she could buy a dress and pay one of the women in the millinery department at the Field, Palmer emporium to style her hair. The irony wasn't lost on Quinn that since her last visit, it was *she* who'd become the pauper and Elfie the woman of means – however limited those means might be.

"You're married," said Elfie.

"My husband was killed in the war."

"But you still wear his ring."

Quinn twisted the gold band on her left hand. She had long since shed her widow's weeds, but not the ring. She didn't know why. Habit, she supposed. Or maybe guilt. "It's a kind of amulet, to protect a woman alone from unwanted attention."

"Is that what you want? To be alone?"

The answer had never been so decidedly, categorically "no," but wanting didn't work like magic. "Have some grapes, Elfie. They're really juicy. I should have asked Captain Chesterton for a pitcher of water. I'll have him bring you one on my way out. And I'll be back before the day of the trial to make sure you have clean clothes to wear. Do please eat your supper and try to stay optimistic. You have a little nest egg now and once the trial is over, you'll be fine."

"Mr. Winthrop came by this morning. He said he wouldn't call Jemelle to the stand to testify."

"What?"

181

"He said she'd been tainted by the newspaper and he'd have to rely on a sympathetic jury and Burk's good will."

"His good will? It's decent of him to contribute a few dollars for your welfare, but he's the one who told that reporter you were deranged by jealousy and driven by a desire for revenge. It's because of Burk that you became the number one suspect."

"Mr. Winthrop doesn't think Burk will say anything too damaging about me if the prosecution calls him to testify." That squiggle of a smile played across her mouth again. "I wished her dead, but wishing's not the same as lighting the match, is it?"

Chesterton returned and unlocked the door before Quinn had time to question the oddness of that smile. "Stay hopeful," she said from the bright side of the bars. "A lot can happen in a short amount of time."

Elfie nodded and took a bite of the second sandwich.

Quinn followed Chesterton back through the jail.

"When Garnick shows up, tell him I'm ready for some high-stakes poker. Seems there was a reward for your client Handish. The sheriff down in Cairo sent me a draft for fifty bucks for clearing him off their wanted list."

"Did he say anything more about Florrie, the woman Handish killed, or give any more information about the man?"

"No, but he passed on a laugh. The crazy galoot wrote him a letter saying he was innocent but didn't think they'd give him a fair trial in Alexander County. Said he'd hired himself a Chicago lawyer."

Quinn had a premonition. "Did the sheriff happen to mention the name of Handish's lawyer?"

"Winthrop, same mouth-piece that's been here quizzing Elfie Jackson. Said he'd tracked his wife's killer to Chicago and soon as he got ahold of him, the lawyer would be in touch."

CHAPTER 22

Lost in thought, only vaguely aware of her surroundings, Quinn began to walk. She'd told Winthrop about Handish. Told him Handish had hired Garnick & Paschal to find Jack Stram. Told him Jemelle said it was Handish who paid Stram to bribe her. Told him Handish had been shot dead in back of Lou Harper's Mansion and, with all of that eye-opening revelation, he hadn't so much as raised an eyebrow. That failure to remark upon the seemingly astounding coincidence that one client had blundered into the case of another, demolished the last vestige of trust in the man.

At a grocer's shop, she stopped to buy a bottle of fizzy water and continued walking. Did Handish bring his case to Garnick & Paschal on his own initiative without informing his lawyer? A supercilious snob like Winthrop probably wouldn't credit a "brute" like Handish with the ability to write, much less write a letter to the sheriff of Alexander County naming his attorney and declaring he would soon be in touch. Ned Handish had no ostensible link to the Kadingers except Stram. Did her oh-so-respectable attorney also have an undisclosed link to Stram?

The odor of burnt wood assailed her nostrils and she looked up. Without realizing it, she'd been walking toward the office, a homing instinct for a home that no longer existed. Head down, hands behind her back, she approached the ashes of her big idea, anger vying with grief. Garnick should be here. Even if all her problems were suddenly to evaporate and she could start again, without Garnick there'd be no one to share the stories with, no one to share the aggravations and the successes. Her thoughts returned to that lost moment when she'd stood on the brink and backed away. He'd opened the door, but she hesitated, afraid to take the chance. And later she'd put him off to go to dinner with Winthrop. Why were the Rubicons in her life visible only in hindsight? She seemed always to be looking back, bemused by how she'd arrived at this or that place, either too impulsive or not impulsive enough. Strange to think she hadn't cried yet. Maybe the fire had cauterized all feeling. Maybe...

"Hey!"

She lifted her gaze. Garnick was stepping around from behind the blackened stone chimney. This time there was no hesitation. She ran flat out, threw her arms around him, buried her face in his shoulder. He held her close and buried his face in her hair. Neither spoke. She listened to the steady, reassuring beat of his heart. She didn't know if she'd crossed another Rubicon. They were on the same side, together, and everything felt right again.

She was the first to find her voice. "Where the Sam Hill have you been?"

"Not where I should've been from the looks of this shambles. When did it happen?"

"Last night while I was at the Opera House with Winthrop."

"Did the fire brigade save your trunk?"

"Nothing." Anger, loss, relief, desire — they all converged and she gave in to tears.

"Jesus, Quinn. How did you—?"

"Don't talk." She was having a lot of trouble with the desire part. "Kiss me."

184

He touched his mouth to hers and blood rushed through her veins like water through a broken dike. She had joined the ranks of Elfie and Medea. She imagined the Greek chorus commiserating over her shoulder. *Ah, poor lady, woe to thee!*

Garnick broke away. "How did you make it through last night? What did you do?"

"I walked out on Winthrop at the restaurant and came back here. The fire was raging. At first I was afraid you might be trapped inside."

"Where'd you spend the night?"

"Lou Harper's boudoir."

Surprise played across his face and then suddenly, simultaneously they burst into a fit of incongruous hilarity.

"If everything falls apart and I can't find another way to support myself, Lou says she'll set me up in a new career."

"That won't happen."

"I know. But I've become a lot more understanding of those who can't find a port in the storm."

"Come on. The rig's parked a ways down the block. Let's find ourselves a quiet saloon and have a bracer and a powwow."

They stopped at a German tavern oriented to beer and family fare where women were allowed to enter by the front door. The place was crowded with stonemasons and construction workers engaged in building the new water tower and pumping station on Pine Street. The smell of frying sausages and the exuberant hum of conversation filled the big room. The detectives seated themselves at a table near the kitchen, away from the noise. Under the table Quinn's legs jittered. She was still keyed up. She needed to cool her emotions and let this heightened intimacy sink in.

Garnick said, "You look like you've got a lot on your mind."

"Megarian's write-up, Winthrop, the fire, my night at the brothel. I know you want to talk about the other...I mean, the change in our relations. I do, too, but I have to think. I have to have words for it all. Could we hold off on any more kissing for a while? It's too much all at once."

His eyes crinkled at the corners. "It's been a right eventful week." He called over the barkeep and ordered a beer. Quinn asked for fizzy water, but it wasn't on the menu. The barkeep suggested a glass of *johannisbeere*. "Red current juice. Nice drink for nice ladies." She eyed him doubtfully, but his bland face betrayed no hint of irony. He went back to the bar and she and Garnick sat in silence until the drinks were served.

"You want to talk about the case?" prompted Garnick. "Because I'm mad enough to start cracking heads."

Her confidence rebounded. They were back to business. Together. Collaborating. Her legs stopped jittering and she started to talk. All the facts and suspicions and anxieties and inferences she'd been holding in surged out in a narrative rush. She didn't slow down until the name Winthrop curdled on her tongue. "You were right about him all along."

"I was jealous. I envied his way with words. He talks like a book. Like you."

"He's a barefaced liar, Garnick. I can't believe I let him bamboozle me."

"You had no cause to doubt him. Lawyers generally try to bamboozle the party their client hires them to bamboozle, not their own client. But why didn't he come straight out and say Handish was a client? It would've been easy enough to pass off as a coincidence."

"Unless," she said, "the admission would implicate him in Handish's murder."

"Even if Winthrop's crooked as a dog's hind leg, it doesn't mean he killed anybody. Could be he's got some other kind of a swindle percolating."

"Like what?"

"There's a couple of possibilities. You asked me where I went last evening. I paid Mr. Silas Jones a visit."

"Rolf Kadinger's clerk?"

"Since Bayer took over the company, Jones has moved west, nearabout halfway to Naperville. He's a gossipy old cuss. Had a lot to say about Miss Delphine. Since her mama died, her daddy didn't have much control over her. Once or twice he tried to marry her off, but she shunned his advice. Kadinger didn't divulge the names of any of her paramours, but Silas got the impression she kept company with 'rogues and pleasurists.' The only one of her suitors Kadinger took to was Bayer. He made no bones that Bayer was marrying the girl for his money, but opined that Bayer wasn't a wastrel like Verner. He thought Bayer would help him build the family fortune."

"That sounds like he intended Bayer to inherit," said Quinn. "I guess Verner lied about the will being faked, not that lying sets him apart from anybody else in this quagmire. I still believe Bayer is lying about something. Did Jones have any idea where Kadinger kept the will?"

"In a lockbox at his home, he reckoned."

"That would have made it easy for Bayer to steal it with Delphine's help and alter it to suit himself. Blood is thicker than water, possibly thicker than tobacco juice. Did Jones know anything about Verner's shenanigans in Germany?"

"You want a jigger of whiskey first?"

"It was that bad? What did he do?"

"Two weeks before Kadinger died, he wired two thousand dollars to his brother in Arnsberg, Germany to cover damages to his steel plant caused by Verner. Seems junior flew into a rage and upended a vat full of molten metal ready for casting. It set off a fire and two workers got burned pretty bad."

"Dear God."

Garnick throttled his beer mug. "If it transpires he's the one who torched our office, I don't know if I can hold myself back from killing him."

Verner seemed prone to tantrums. It was easy to imagine him flying into a rage lobbing a kerosene lantern into the draperies. But Rhetta hadn't seen or heard him on the night of the fire and he didn't seem dispassionate enough to kill quietly, escape unseen, and avoid being caught. "Did Silas say anything about Handish or Stram?"

"Never heard of 'em."

"What about Winthrop?"

"I didn't ask. Didn't want to think about him squiring you about pitching woo."

"You needn't have worried. But you said he might be up to some kind of swindle. What are you thinking, Garnick?"

"You say he didn't want you pestering Tench or any of the other councilmen. Suppose he's their lawyer? He could be helping them fudge the way they account for their shady income. Shining up to the city leaders is one way to get that law practice he wants off to a booming start."

"That fits Micah like one of his bespoke suits."

"Here's another thing to chew on," said Garnick. "The last few months old man Kadinger's company had run up against a dearth of prime logs. To compensate, he was lending out some of his workers to the city. Jones didn't know what for. Kadinger recorded the work slips himself. There was no contract and Kadinger told him not to ask questions. It graveled Silas. In the past he'd always been trusted to oversee routine business dealings. He still kept the books and from the first of the year till Kadinger's death, the city sent the company a check for a thousand bucks a month."

"Who signed the check?"

"Tench."

"Did Bayer know about the deal with the city, or with Tench?"

"Silas couldn't say yay or nay."

"What sort of project would be so difficult the city couldn't use its own employees?"

"Whatever the job, I'd guess it's a backbreaker. Kadinger's men are laborers, used to lifting and loading logs."

"What about the city workers who dug the tunnel under Lake Michigan? They're no weaklings." Quinn's curiosity redoubled. A thousand dollars a week for six months for work so secret Kadinger didn't trust his long-time clerk with the reason and, apparently, neither did the workers who performed the work. Had they all been sworn to secrecy? "Maybe the money had nothing to do with Kadinger's workers or his company. Maybe it had something to do with those water-loan bonds Kadinger had invested so heavily in."

"If Kadinger was buying, the checks would've been going to the city and Silas would've seen the bonds or evidence of purchase."

"You're right, unless Kadinger purchased them off the company books with personal funds." She didn't know that Winthrop was involved, but if he'd been offered the opportunity to advance his prospects, he wouldn't have refused. "I'm not sure where to go from here, Garnick, but I'd dearly love to burgle Winthrop's office and ransack his mother's pie safe."

"That's a job best left till midnight when there's no coppers around to snap the cuffs on us. And after that?"

"After?"

"You'll want someplace to sleep at the end of your ransacking."

The implicit invitation started her pulse racing again. "I need to spend one more night at the Mansion if Lou will let me. I want to talk to Jemelle again and I've asked Megarian to bring Tench to the Mansion for a meeting in the morning."

She expected Garnick to demur, to look a little disappointment at least. But he seemed happy to honor her request and put off kissing to another day. He tossed off the

189

last of his beer and rose to leave. "You want to drop in on Gentle Annie this afternoon? She can tell us how Tench fleeces the brothels and maybe we can get a line on Stram's hiding place from his ex-regular, Sue."

Chapter 23

"What can I do for you, honey?" Romeo fluffed his green feathers and screeched with apparent glee. Half of a gnawed banana lay on the cage floor and a string dangled from his beak like a skinny white worm. "Romeo want some fun!" He mimicked a lascivious laugh that made Quinn's skin crawl.

A dark-skinned woman in violet bombazine rested her elbows and overflowing breasts on the pedestal table. "What's your pleasure?" she asked Garnick. "You want a threesome?"

Romeo cackled.

"We're not shoppers," said Garnick. "We've come for a word with Miss Annie."

"She expecting you?"

The bouncer, shaggy-browed and surly as Quinn remembered, erupted into the parlor, shoving a womblylegged drunkard ahead of him. "Annie ain't receiving any detectives," he growled as he walked by and catapulted the drunkard headfirst down the narrow stairwell. "Clear out, you two, or I'll kick you out next." The sound of the drunkard's body bouncing off the walls punctuated the threat.

"I hope you'll reconsider," said Garnick. "Your boss lady won't want to miss hearing what we've got to say about Alderman Henry Tench."

"I'll tell her," said the woman in violet and swished off down the hall.

The bouncer glowered. "Stand over by the bird, out of the customers' way."

There were no customers just now, for which mercy Quinn felt greatly relieved. There was a prurient suggestion in Romeo's evil little eyes and she worried that her thin dress and unbound hair conveyed an unintentional conviviality. The woman in violet swished back to the pedestal where she and the bouncer conferred in low voices. He gave the detectives a scathing look and left. The woman leaned her elbows and breasts on the pedestal again. "Annie says to hold your hosses."

Garnick nodded. "Thank you, ma'am."

Quinn fidgeted. The smells of banana and parrot droppings and the unwholesome musk of the place closed in on her, adding to her feeling of awkwardness. She wished they'd asked to meet the fat madam outdoors. The effluvium of the stockyards would have been more bearable.

A pot-bellied man with lank brown hair and a pitted face passed through and jogged down the stairs, whistling. A satisfied customer, no doubt. A few minutes later, a scrawny girl in a baby-blue dress minced into the room and assumed a pose on one of the red velvet settees. She couldn't have been more than sixteen. Quinn wondered if she was the one the whistling man had his fun with.

"Didn't I tell you to keep away from here?" Annie swanned into the room fanning her big arms and adding the bouquet of otto of roses to the smothering atmosphere. Today she wore a crimson gown almost the color of her hair. She looked as wide and spectacular as a closed theater curtain.

Romeo dipped his head and cowered against the bars of his cage.

Quinn stepped forward. "I have additional questions for you."

192

"What makes you think I'll answer 'em?"

"The right answers could save you and your husband a lot of money, Mrs. Hyman."

"Still mealy-mouthed." Her angry eyes shifted to Garnick. "Not much heft to your bodyguard here."

"But I'm nimble," said Garnick, "and I fight dirty."

She snorted. "You want to talk, follow me." She pulled a key out of her cleavage and opened a panel covered with red-and-gold wallpaper. Inside it appeared to be an ordinary office with a mahogany kneehole desk. Instead of a chair, there was a high-backed settee of sufficient dimensions to accommodate Annie's girth. She shut the panel, moved behind the desk, and enthroned herself.

There were no other chairs. All who entered here were clearly supplicants. Quinn leaned her back against the wall. Garnick stood off to the side of the desk and sawed his finger across his chin, as if mentally mapping detours around the blockades Annie might throw up.

"What's this horse manure about Tench?" she demanded.

"We know why the councilmen are quaking in their boots since the Kadinger fire," said Quinn.

"Why's that?"

"Actually," said Garnick, "it's their money collector, Tench, who's quaking. The rest are probably just trying to keep clear of any shot that ricochets off him."

"What'd he do?"

"He was Delphine Kadinger's paramour before she married Burk Bayer," said Quinn.

"Sounds like a girl with a big heart." Annie threw back her head and detonated that cannonball laugh of hers. "Who's your favorite poet?"

"What?"

"Your favorite poet. Mine's Lord Byron. Now there's a man who understood love."

Garnick laughed along with her. "Seems like I've heard something about his lordship's way with the ladies. But back to Tench. His love, if that's what it was, makes him a suspect in Delphine's murder."

"Yeah, and Elfie Jackson's love, if that's what it was, makes her the one waiting trial in the calaboose," countered Annie.

"Thanks to Jemelle's false witness," said Quinn.

"I read in the paper she's changed her tune. You must've buttered her up good."

"We pointed out the risks of not telling the truth," said Quinn.

"Jemelle's a stupid heifer, but she knows how many beans make five."

Garnick edged closer to the queen bee's throne. "Did a big, ugly cuss named Ned Handish ever come around here asking for Jemelle?"

"Didn't your partner here tell you? I don't keep tabs on my girls, nor every Ned, Dick and Harry who walks in the door."

"You sell yourself short, Annie. You don't get to be the richest brothel keeper in the Patch without being the savviest. I reckon you've got eyes in the back of your head."

"Don't try to soft-soap me, Garnick."

"Likewise, Annie, don't pretend you don't keep a sharp lookout."

"All right, for what it's worth to you, Handish was here. I wouldn't have heard of him, but my bouncer caught Jemelle squirreling a roll of bills under a loose board in her room and figured she'd been holding out on me. He took it away from her and the three of us had a consultation. Jemelle claimed somebody named Handish gave her the money but wouldn't say who he was or what it was for."

"Was Handish a courier for Tench or the council?" asked Garnick.

"Cap's never mentioned the name."

194

Quinn hadn't known about Handish's connection to the case when she first visited Annie. She still wasn't clear how he fit into the picture. "Was this consultation with Jemelle before or after Stram beat her up?"

"After. Wasn't much doubt she was lying through her teeth, but being as how she'd never rooked me before, I only took twenty. Between Cap and Lord Byron, love's turned me soft-hearted."

It was increasingly apparent to Quinn that Stram told the truth when he said he didn't know Handish. Was it possible both he and Handish worked for Tench and didn't know each other? "All we want, Annie, Mrs. Hyman, is to prove Elfie innocent of the murders and find out who set that fire. Jack Stram was at the Kadinger house that night. He knows who else was there and he's scared. He wouldn't be hiding out in fear for his life from Elfie. But if Tench did the murders—"

"Bull!" Annie rose like a breaching whale. "You sleuth-hounds have been beating your gums ninety to the dozen, but I ain't heard one thing I give a damn about, nothing that saves me a Dixie dollar."

"If Tench can be taken down a peg, the council might slack off on their extortion game," said Garnick. "That would save you some legal green."

"Pshaw! The good citizens of Chicago don't care that the council takes a bite out of my profits, or Cap's or Roger Plant's."

"They'd care if Tench killed one of their own kind and his young daughter and burned their house to cover his tracks," argued Garnick.

She appeared to turn the idea over in her mind. "The bastard's got a face like a mule. Why would he kill the daughter of a codfish aristocrat or any other woman willing to do the hogmagundy?"

"Keep it clean and mannerly, Annie. You'll make us blush."

"Then you're in the wrong place. Get to the nub. What do you have on Tench?"

"I think Delphine Kadinger was doing to Tench what he's been doing to you," said Quinn.

"Bleeding him for money? Pah! She'd be telling on herself if she went to his wife."

"Maybe she had something else to tell," said Quinn. "Something more serious than a charge of marital infidelity. In fact, maybe it was her father who was bleeding him. Kadinger's employees were doing some kind of heavy work for the city on the sly. Have you or your husband picked up any hearsay about what that might be?"

"The two-mile tunnel and the water works are finished. That's all aboveboard and a boon to the public, if you believe all the hurrahs the city pols have been giving each other. Nothing else going on except for 'em digging up coffins in the cemetery and they sure as shooting can't keep the stink off that mound of rotting Confederate meat a secret."

"Are you trying to raise my hackles, Annie?"

"I should've guessed you were a grayback, Garnick."

Quinn said, "We're going to interview a few of Kadinger's employees in the next day or two. We'll find out if Tench or his fellow aldermen were fleecing the city and paying blackmail to Kadinger, or if Kadinger was doing something illegal for the benefit of the council. But we really need to find Stram. If we can persuade him to spill the beans about the council's schemes, you may get a reprieve from their extortion."

"When the sun rises in the west."

"Another of your girls used to mingle limbs with him," said Quinn. "Sue. He visited her here after his fight with Jemelle and you. She may know where he's hiding."

"Not likely. That ninny don't know a whore-pipe from a bell pull."

Heat seared Quinn's face. The old bawd was taunting her with obscenities. "I daresay you derive your eloquence

196

from a source other than Lord Byron. But whether you help us or not, here or someplace else, we're going to talk to Sue."

"Here, then, damn it. This reprieve sounds like a lot of tomfoolery to me, but whatever you dig up against Tench, keep my name out of it. Ten years ago another moralizing mayor and his holier-than-thou vigilantes brought in a team of dray horses and leveled my lakefront brothel and every other doggery and squatter's shanty in the neighborhood. Cost me plenty to re-settle. I don't need another posse of Sunday school jayhawkers."

Annie pranced out past the bird's cage, hips rolling. "Farley! Round up Sue if she ain't *in flagrante* and bring her here. These detectives want to ask her some questions. And take Romeo out and clean his cage. How many times do I have to tell you? Birdshit ain't an aphrodisiac."

The bouncer pouted but complied without comment. Romeo rocked from side to side and ruffled his feathers, but he seemed diminished and kept mute. Annie locked her office door and sailed off into the bowels of the place, leaving Quinn and Garnick to wait.

He stared at the wall, looking glum.

"What's eating you, Garnick?"

"I can't stop thinking about those unearthed corpses in the cemetery. Must be more than a dozen I knew from the prison camp, one or two I liked."

She touched his arm. "It's a desecration, but you mustn't dwell on it. I'm sure there'll be more reverence for the dead when they're laid to rest at Oak Woods."

"I'm not worried about how reverently or irreverently their bones are treated, but think about it, Quinn. There's six thousand or more bodies buried in cheap, termite-eaten pine boxes, some just wrapped in winding sheets. Moving 'em is a whopping big operation. What if some genius dreamed up a shortcut?"

"What kind of shortcut?"

197

"Less digging, less hauling, less cost. I don't know. I'm still cogitating."

"But if all Kadinger did was provide the city with more diggers and haulers, and the city paid him, how is that illegal? Why would he not let his clerk know about the deal?"

Before the question could be addressed, a spindly girl with a wan complexion and frightened eyes scuffed into the room and gripped the edge of the pedestal table as if it were the only fixed and solid thing on a tossing ship. "I'm Sue," she said, "and I don't know nothing about nobody."

"It's a pleasure to meet you, Sue. This lady is Miz Paschal and I'm Garnick. We're trying to get a girl out of some bad trouble and we think you can help." He spoke as if gentling a fractious colt. "Would you let us buy you a bowl of iced cream? It's a hot day and I know an eatery a mile or so from here that serves chocolate and coffee flavored cream, fizzy water, too, if you're thirsty."

"I told you I don't know nothing."

"You know whether you like iced cream, don't you?"

"You think you can buy me off, but you can't 'cause I don't know where Jack's gone to and if I did I wouldn't blow on him." She kept a white-knuckled grip on the table.

"Is that because you love him or because you're afraid of him?" asked Quinn.

"If you're afraid," said Garnick, "we can see to it he won't bother you again. And if Annie didn't come straight out and say so, she wants you to own up and tell us what you know. You wouldn't want to disappoint *her*, now would you?"

"Lawd, would I rather be beaten or whipped?" She looked too frightened for sarcasm.

Quinn said, "Annie won't whip you, Sue. And if you think Stram will come back and beat you, we can move you someplace safe." She might have added, *if I can think of one*, but her objective was persuasion. "The sooner we find him, the safer we'll all be."

Annie crashed into the room like a landslide. "Sue!"

The girl spun around with a tremulous cry.

"Quit your whining and tell these nags what they want to know so I can get 'em out of here."

"But I don't know where Jack is."

"What's your best guess?" asked Garnick.

"All's I know, he once said he had an old laker boat docked near the McCormick Reaper Works and if anybody was ever to come after him for his IOUs, he could hole up on the river till they gave up."

CHAPTER 24

The McCormick Reaper Works was a busy, sprawling factory situated on the north bank of the Chicago River. An adjacent rail spur and wharf made loading the heavy reaper machines less arduous. At least twenty barges and steamers were berthed along the wharf. A forest of masts rose in front of the McCormick smokestack and a hundred men or more moiled about in a welter of noise and hurly-burly.

Garnick handed Quinn the field glasses. "Notice the last three boats at the far end. Looks like they're out of commission. Leastways no cargo being loaded. Probably waiting to be shellacked or something. I'd guess Stram's holed up in one of them."

"Here we go then."

"You best wait here. I'll reconnoiter. If I find him, I'll prod him back this way."

"No, we'll go together."

"That wharf ain't a resort promenade, Quinn. You'll hear saltier language down there than what you heard from Annie."

"I won't faint. Anyway, those men aren't ruffians or yahoos. They're just laborers going about their work."

"Men without much practice in the social graces," said Garnick. "The sight of a woman traipsing along the dock will for sure gin up interest."

"I'll shut my ears and keep my eyes on my shoe tops."

"Have it your way but hold tight to my arm."

The afternoon sun sparkled on the greasy river water. A yellow sheen, runoff from the tannery, slapped gently against a blue sheen discharged from the soap factory. Quinn had to step lively to match her gait to Garnick's. As they weaved through the crowd, she cleaved to his arm and fastened her gaze on the weathered boards of the dock. A few oglers began to close around them, hooting and calling out crude comments. As Garnick pushed and shoved through a gauntlet, her dress began to feel flimsy as gauze. She imagined a host of hot stares stripping her naked.

A pair of rummy-smelling seamen jostled them and an errant hand groped at the front of her dress. Garnick elbowed the roughneck hard in the ribs and he went down cursing. The second rowdy took a swing at Garnick, but Garnick parried the blow and the man tripped over his felled cohort. Garnick held fast to her arm and they plowed ahead as the air behind them blued with curses and insults. She shouldn't have been so stubborn about putting herself on view and at risk, but how unfair it was! Men could walk unmolested wherever they chose while women had to skitter about like prey. Garnick broke into a trot. As she pushed herself to keep up, her thoughts turned to how they could get back to the street without retracing their steps.

After what seemed like half a mile, Garnick slackened the pace and let go of her arm. "You make it through in one piece?"

"Yes." Out of breath, she bent over with a stitch in her side. "I shouldn't have put us in that situation. I'm sorry."

"Some things are learned best in the pinch of the moment, I reckon."

"By those too mulish to listen to advice." The pain in her side subsided and she looked around. To her surprise and relief, they were alone. The hurly-burly at the other end of the wharf sounded far away and the boats here had an almost derelict appearance. "There's no one to stop us. I guess we should just go aboard and search."

"This time, why don't you let me go in first?"

"But what if Stram's not alone? What if he's with a gang and they attack you?"

"Unless he saw me when I went looking for him at Cap Hyman's place, he won't know me from a tin bucket. Anyways, I don't plan to say anything to set him off till we're on safe ground. Keep on your guard and out of sight till I call out for you. You got your pistol?"

"Yes."

"Take it out now and don't scruple to use it." He vaulted onto a rope ladder and shinnied up onto the deck of a dilapidated, two-masted schooner named Hiawatha. Quinn took the derringer out of her bag and stood near the stern in a shaded spot invisible to the McCormick factory workers. The Hiawatha and the boat moored next to it, the Charming Betsy, looked seaworthy in spite of their neglected appearance. Even in a condition of disrepair, they would have been worth a lot of money. Did Stram have the money to buy such a vessel or had he seen it was disused and moved in? Maybe he had a pal at the factory who let him know there was an empty boat where he could hide out.

After a while, the sun invaded her shady spot. She moved toward the front of the boat and a sliver of shade under the curve of the prow. How long would it take to search a boat this size? Not very long, she thought. Not as long as it seemed to be taking Garnick. She moved out into the open and looked up to see if she could catch a glimpse of him on the deck. If a fight broke out, she assumed she would hear. If Garnick and Stram were talking, it had turned into a lengthy conversation. A spooky sensation, like the mercury in a barometer, rose inside her. What if Stram had sneaked up behind Garnick and stuck a blade in his back?

Something plopped into the river. She ran to the edge of the dock and craned her neck. "Garnick? What was that?"

No answer.

"Are you all right? Say something."

He didn't.

She pondered the ladder. The first step was above her head and out of reach. She laid the gun on the ground, bent her knees, and jumped for it. Her fingers grazed the rope but she couldn't get a grip. It had looked so easy when Garnick did it. She glanced around for something to stand on. A broken metal wheel lay at the edge of the dock under a scrap pile of loose planks imprinted with the name "McCORMICK." She dragged the heavy wheel under the ladder and laid a couple of planks on top. It added just enough height to bring the ladder within reach.

From somewhere on the far side of the boat came the sound of violent retching.

"Garnick?"

She lifted her skirt and pulled a strip of her petticoat through the derringer's trigger guard behind the trigger. With great care, she knotted the pistol into the fabric. The thought that it might go off if bumped crossed her mind, but a fall from the ladder onto the dock would probably kill her first. She grabbed onto the rope with both hands like a trapeze artist. It had been a long time since she climbed trees with her brother, but how much harder could this be? It wasn't a huge boat, only five steps to the rail. She began to pull herself up hand over hand, her legs swinging like clappers in a bell. The muscles in her shoulders ached and she felt the seams under the arms of her dress ripping.

The retching continued, broken by what might have been death throes or sobs. Her palms burned from the rope and her feet tangled in her skirt, but she kept pulling until her feet gained purchase on the bottom rung. She steadied herself and climbed the remaining four steps until she reached the rail and clambered over the side onto the deck. The derringer clunked against the wood and she caught her breath. It didn't fire. She untied it and holding it outstretched in both hands, edged starboard toward the sounds of the retching.

Garnick hung over the rail, dry-heaving into the river. There was nobody else in sight. She set down the gun and took hold of his arm. His breathing sounded raspy, ragged. "What's wrong?" She brushed a shock of hair off his face and felt his forehead. "Is it the ague?"

"No. Just let me be for a while, Quinn."

"If you've taken ill, we need to get away from here and find a doctor."

"I don't need a doctor." He faltered slightly but seemed to will himself upright.

"Lean on me. If you can't make it down the ladder, I'll go back to McCormick for help."

He managed a wry smile. "You *would*, wouldn't you?"

"If I have to."

"You don't. I can march under my own steam."

"So you say. It looks to me as if your steam has fizzled."

"Not the heroic impression a man wants to make on a woman."

"You've done that already often enough. Now tell me what's wrong."

He held out a piece of grimy cloth, brownish-gray with a band of faded yellow.

"It smells foul. What is it?"

"Part of a Confederate uniform. From the yellow, I'd say it belonged to a cavalryman. I threw the arm that wore it overboard."

"Only the arm?"

"I reckon it dropped off when they dumped the rest of the poor devil."

"Oh, Garnick." No wonder he was sick. "Are you sure there weren't more bodies?"

"Ninety percent."

She scanned the deck. "Where's the cargo hatch?"

"You don't want to open it, Quinn. It's dark as night down there and stinks like hell's portal. I gave it a pretty good going-over. There was just the arm, a heap of garbage and a colony of fat rats."

"You think Stram murdered the man?"

"If he did, it happened a while ago judging from the decay."

Quinn remembered Miss Nearest talking about decayed bodies fished out of the lake near the water intake crib. Megarian had also mentioned them. "Is it possible that Tench and the aldermen are disposing of those exhumed Confederates in the lake?"

"I wouldn't put any kind of deviltry past Tench, but it would cost more to haul the bodies out here to the wharf, load 'em into boats, and consign 'em to Davy Jones Locker than it does to hire gravediggers to dig fresh holes at the new cemetery."

She said, "There has to be some angle we're not seeing."

"Maybe we can prevail on the alderman to enlighten us tomorrow morning. For right now let's cogitate someplace else. I've had enough of the Hiawatha."

They climbed down. This time she centered her weight on the ropes and had less trouble. Garnick was his usual nimble self, the nausea apparently passed.

Quinn said, "This must be the boat Stram has been hiding on, but we don't know if he's gone for an hour or gone for good. There's no sense waiting. We should go someplace and get you a stiff pick-me-up."

"Naw. While we're here, let's check out these last two boats."

"Are you sure? What if there's another body or piece of a body?"

"You mean, am I apt to faint?"

"You might." She was thinking about those nightmares that had shaken Minnie.

He rumpled his hair and gave a sheepish grin. "That severed arm gave me a turn, I can't pretend it didn't. But now I know what to expect. I won't keel over."

"But what if Stram's lying in wait for you? I'd better come along."

"No offense, Quinn, but rope ladders ain't your top talent."

"Then here. Take the gun."

"No, you best hold onto it and keep a lookout. If Stram's hiding somewheres around here, it's not on one of these floating rat hutches." He leapt onto the ladder.

"Garnick?"

He looked back over his shoulder.

"Better not throw anything else in the river. It may be needed for evidence."

CHAPTER 25

While Garnick reconnoitered the boats, Quinn looked for a footpath up the riverbank to the street from this end of the wharf. In almost any other circumstances, the muddy, near vertical rut she lit upon would have been out of the question. It must have been used at one time to skid logs down to the river. Eroded and slick, it would demoralize a goat. But the thought of returning through that wolf pack of gropers made it look inviting as a cakewalk. There were shoe tracks, so someone had used it in the not too distant past. She picked through a pile of planks and rubbish and came up with a sturdy walking stick to give her an extra push.

Garnick was back before she had time to worry. He found no bodies or body parts and if Stram had been aboard, he left no sign. She pointed out her chosen route to the street. Garnick grimaced but motioned her to lead on. Using the stick to push off against and grabbing the occasional low-hanging branch to pull herself up, she reached the brick sidewalk with the Rush Street Bridge in sight. Garnick scrambled up behind and they made for the bridge.

"It's early yet," he said. "We need a place to wash up and get some rest before the raid on Winthrop's pie safe. There's a hole-in-the-wall hotel up ahead on Rush."

She didn't answer. They continued walking. Her palms, abraded first by the rope and then the stick, argued for a bath in cool water and an application of salve. Her dress, ripped and dirty, argued for a mending kit and a thorough sponging. The change in her relations with Garnick argued both sides of the hotel proposition. She had always been good with words. Why couldn't she call up words to express her feelings for him? Why did she keep stopping him from expressing his for her? She'd promised herself there'd be no more evasions, but even after her joy and relief at finding him this morning, even with desire gnawing at her, she clung to the edge of the cliff.

He stopped at a nondescript door. A letterbox nailed to the side of the building read *Hotel*. He rapped a few times. No one answered and they went inside. There was no one at the desk. He rang the bell. The harsh *brrring* jarred Quinn.

A white-haired, wraith-like woman clad in a white lace mantle toddled down the hall.

"Afternoon, ma'am," said Garnick. "We need a room for the night if you've got a vacancy."

She scrutinized them from behind the thick lenses of her gilded pince-nez. "I run a respectable house. No streetwalkers or moochers. You'll have to go elsewhere." Her face was solemn but not without compassion. Like Saint Peter at the pearly gates, thought Quinn, duty-bound to keep out the sinners.

Quinn held out her left hand, giving the woman a good look at Thom's wedding ring before turning over her skinned palm. "We're from out of town. Cedarburg. Our wagon tipped and broke an axle when the bridge swung open. We were hoping to find a room where we could clean up while it's being repaired."

"Murderation! I do apologize." She scrunched her eyes and peered at Quinn's nicks and scrapes. "Poor little thing. You must've got a handful of splinters and grit when you fell out. That swinging bridge is a hazard. Wasn't long ago it broke in half and drowned a herd of cows. Every time a tug blows its horn I jump. So then, one room, two baths. That'll be three dollars."

"Would you by chance have a jar of Cloverine salve or some other ointment for my hands?"

"I'll see what I can find."

"And a needle and thread, if you can spare it," added Quinn.

"Wait here." She disappeared into a room behind the desk.

"Cedarburg," said Garnick under his breath. "You've a rare gift for invention, detective."

Quinn slued her eyes at him. Her invention had situated them in a room with a single bed. The cliff was crumbling under her feet and he knew it.

The woman returned with a spool of white cotton thread and a card of needles. "Ten cents for the notions. The calendula oil's on the house."

"That's mighty Christian of you, Miz...?"

"Farraday."

"Well, thank you, Miz Farraday."

"You're sure welcome. There's no other roomers in the house tonight and the Bible says to love the sojourner."

"We're much beholden," said Garnick. "You wouldn't also happen to have a bottle of spirits on hand, would you? My lady's had a right shock and I could stand a toddy, myself." He patted Quinn's arm. "We're not used to such big-city scares over in Cedarburg."

"You poor dears. There's most of a bottle of apple brandy in the kitchen. Here's the room key. Number four. I'll bring the brandy to your room in a few minutes."

Garnick paid and Quinn trailed him down the hall. He turned the key in the lock and they stepped inside. The room was dark and cool and smelled of citronella. The bed looked as big as Cleopatra's barge.

"How did you know about this place? Have you been here before?"

211

"A few times after I was cut loose from Douglas before I got my cabin built. I looked worse then than I do now. No surprise Miz Farraday don't, doesn't remember me." He pulled off his gun belt, sat down in the corner chair, and stretched out his legs. "After Douglas, this place felt like the Garden of Eden."

Where fig leaves were the only cover, thought Quinn. She went to the basin and poured the entire pitcher of water over her hands. With the grit washed off, they didn't sting so much. She slathered on the calendula and waved her hands about, letting the oil soak in.

Mrs. Farraday brought the brandy on a brass salver with two glasses. Garnick took the tray and thanked her.

"Mind now, it's strong. My late husband detested weak brandy. He called this brew 'distilled lightning.' Well, I'll leave you to yourselves. Water closet's at the far end of the hall. I'd have given you a closer room, but I'm without help and haven't had time to clean. Use all the water you want. There's clean towels on the peg."

Garnick poured Quinn a tot of brandy and set it on the washstand. He took his drink across the room and lifted his glass. "To Paschal and Garnick's next criminal sortie."

Her hands were too slippery to hold the glass and she didn't trust herself drinking claret, much less distilled lightning. "How many hours do we have to wait before we leave?"

He drew the curtains. "Come see for yourself. It won't be full dark for another six hours."

"You really think we should wait so long? It'll take another hour to walk to Winthrop's office. Maybe we should leave sooner. If we don't leave soon, the horse-cars will stop running. Or maybe we should go back to the stable and get Leonidas and the rig."

"You needn't be uneasy, Quinn. You can have the bed. I'll catnap in the armchair. Like you asked, I'll keep my distance so as not to touch off any amatory excitation."

"You don't understand, Garnick."

"Not all, maybe, but some. It's not crazy to be worried about a lit fuse." He mussed his hair, which was already mussed. "If it's not plain as a steeple, I'm in love with you and have been from just about the first time I saw you. These last few days you've given me cause to hope you're of a similar persuasion."

Yes seemed an altogether inadequate response. She nodded, at a loss for words.

"I know your last sally into matrimony didn't pan out, I'm thinking for more reasons than you've let on. I'd like to change your mind, but we can live however you want, Quinn. What you need to know is, I'm in this partnership till death do us part." He downed his brandy and frowned. "Should that be till death *does* us part?"

She laughed and her heart swelled so big it hurt. "You're becoming a grammarian, Garnick."

"Whatever's the proper way to say it, I'm serious."

"Well, then." She took a nip of the distilled lightning, which made her eyes water enough to disguise the tears. "I suppose it's time we find out what's going to happen when the spark from that fuse reaches the powder. I'm going to wash off the muck of the riverbank and make myself pretty. When I come back, I shall expect to be kissed comprehensively."

"Yes ma'am. Happy to be of service."

She picked up her reticule with her comb and indispensables and walked down the hall to the water closet. The boat-shaped wooden bathtub extended almost the length of the narrow room, which was dank and dark except for a shaft of light that filtered through a small, jalousied window near the ceiling. There was no stove to heat the water, but she had no desire for heat on a day like today and according to the hydropaths, cold baths alleviated congestion of the brain. She set her reticule on a low shelf, slipped out of her clothes, and folded them on top. Folding

213

a dress this soiled and shabby was pointless, but with a thorough brushing maybe she could salvage it for one more wearing.

She turned on the faucet and waited for the tub to fill, a tinge apprehensive after seeing the revolting river water. But this water came out of the spigot clear and colorless, piped as was now the norm from two miles out in Lake Michigan. When the tub was full, she climbed in and immersed herself to the neck in the cool water. It was pure bliss. There was even a fresh cake of lavender soap.

She lathered all over and laid her head against the back of the tub. Memories of her parents' marriage floated through her mind. Her mother had been the most loving of wives. Quinn had once asked her how she could love a man who treated her with such contempt. "Why, I couldn't live without him," she'd said. A week after his murder, she moved in with a defrocked priest. For all Quinn knew, she now believed she couldn't live without *him*. Maybe love was just another invention, whomever you wanted at any given time, like Victoria Woodhull believed.

A sound like a door closing somewhere down the hall caught her attention and she looked up and noticed the bathroom latch hanging loose. Where was her mind? She should get up and lock the door, but there was no one else in the house but Garnick and Mrs. Farraday. She ran the sponge along her neck, down her arms and across her breasts. The bath was deliciously soothing. The congestion in her brain dissipated, her tired limbs relaxed, and she closed her eyes.

When she was seventeen, beaten blue by her father and turned out of his house, she'd run to Thom for refuge. Now she was homeless again, but a lot smarter and more resourceful than the girl she used to be. She didn't need a man to take care of her. She didn't need refuge. She needed Garnick. The word she'd been unable to think of came into her mind like a comet. Essential. Garnick was essential.

A mild draft fluttered across her face. She half-turned as a pair of rough hands seized her shoulders and plunged her underwater. She couldn't breathe, couldn't scream, couldn't see, couldn't think. She clawed at the hands, but they held fast. Wild with fear, she bent her knees and slid on her back toward the faucet. The move must have overbalanced the owner of the hands. They let go. She sat up, coughing, and gulped a lungful of air.

Through a curtain of wet hair, she saw Jack Stram. She hit and scratched and tried to scream, but his iron fingers closed around her skull and pushed her under again. She thrashed and kicked and mourned her death. To be found naked and shriveled in the bath, caught unawares by a creeper she should have expected and barred the door against, infuriated her. Josabeth Allbright's artless little dig came back to her with a vengeance. *Being a woman detective must be frightfully venturesome, is it not?*

She summoned one last invention. With his hands holding her under, she relaxed. Against every instinct, she lay limp and still while second by second, saint by saint, she entreated them all – Patrick, Peter, Christopher, Jude, the archangel Gabriel, his dozing namesake down the hall. No help came. Her lungs felt as if they would explode. She would die and Fen Megarian would pen her obituary in salacious detail and congratulate himself on his poetic sensibility. Absurd that this would be her last thought.

The hands lifted. She held her breath one impossible second longer, praying that Stram had bought her act and backed away. Whether he had or not, she couldn't wait. She sprang up, heaved herself over the rim of the tub and flopped onto the floor.

Gasping for air, she wiped her hair out of her eyes and saw his boots, crusted with river mud, moving toward her. He bent to lift her, but she hooked both arms around a knee and jerked. His legs flew out from under him and he went down hard on his backside.

They were both floundering. He grabbed at her arms, but she was too soapy to hold onto and scooched out of reach. He got to his knees and, holding to the side of the tub, pushed himself to his feet. She dived for the shelf where she'd stowed her things. He caught her arm and she pivoted, jabbing her elbow back into his Adam's apple. He wheezed and struggled for breath. Half-blind, she grabbed for her purse.

She raked her sopping hair out of her eyes and dug in the reticule for the derringer. Her hands were wet and clumsy and the stupid pouch was suddenly a web of snarled threads. Stram was wheezing and coughing. She wrapped her fingers around the gun but couldn't pull it free.

"Bitch," croaked Stram. "I warned you not to mess with me." He lunged and slammed her against the wall.

She was still fighting for air, still grappling for the gun, but somehow she forced a strangled scream. His hands closed around her throat. The gun was hopelessly enmeshed. Fumbling blind, she jammed the barrel against his chest and her finger curled around the trigger. She fired point-blank. He staggered backward, eyes glazed in surprise, and collapsed into the pool of water beside the tub. The hole in his chest made a gurgling noise, as if the wound was sucking in air and leaking it out.

Her windpipe ached. Air came in convulsive gulps. She turned off the water and watched in a daze as the pool at her feet turned red.

Garnick kicked open the door, gun drawn. He took in the scene, flicked a towel off the peg and handed it to her. "Did he hurt you?"

His voice seemed to come from far away. Her head might as well be still underwater. She couldn't speak.

"Quinn? Are you hurt?"

"I'm all right."

He knelt, loosened Stram's red kerchief and pressed his fingers against his neck. "He's alive, just barely." He closed

216

Stram's staring eyes, gathered up her shoes, her wet clothes, and the derringer, and led her out into the hall. Her bare feet left bloody tracks on the wooden floor.

Mrs. Farraday gawped from the other end of the hall.

Garnick put his hand on Quinn's shoulder and propelled her inside their room. "Miz Farraday, there's been a shooting. Lock yourself in your quarters and stay there. I'll go for the police soon as I tend to my missus."

He followed Quinn into the room and locked the door. She was still clutching the towel against her nakedness and shivering. He ripped the cover off the bed and wrapped it around her. Her hair was dripping and formed a puddle on the floor. He walked her to the washstand where she'd left her brandy and held the glass to her lips. "Drink this."

She took a sip but pushed it away. She couldn't stop trembling. She was cold and scared and speechless, but her heart was still beating. She was alive.

Garnick hugged her tight. She folded her arms around his neck and kissed him like there was no tomorrow. The bedcover fell off. He lifted her onto the bed. It was a tending to like no other. Incredible, she thought, how potent an aphrodisiac survival could be.

CHAPTER 26

When Stram had come calling at Mrs. Mills' boarding house, Quinn airily told him he wouldn't be the first man she'd shot. That boast sounded obscene to her now. During the war, a death was lamented with the saying "somebody's darling." Quinn didn't have to guess whose darling Stram was. He was Rhetta's darling, a father-to-be. There would be no happy family reunion now. Jacques Stram lay dead in a Police Department wagon and all his secrets under the shroud with him. Quinn tried to convince herself she'd had no choice, but had she? When he was down on the floor wheezing, before he got up and tackled her, maybe she could have run out the door. Or if she'd screamed sooner and louder, Garnick could have gotten there quicker. Ifs were as thick as snow in January.

"I can't understand how a beast like that got into my house," said Mrs. Farraday, "or what he thought he would find. He must've been crazy."

Quinn poured her a second glass of brandy. She almost poured herself a third, but she needed her wits about her when Chesterton finished with Garnick and came to interrogate her. "When the police are done with their investigation, Mr. Garnick and I will help you clean up the blood, Mrs. Farraday. I'm so sorry about the damage to your house."

"It's not your fault, dearie. I'm just amazed you had your husband's pistol with you in the bath. You must have had a presentiment, like a forewarning."

"If I'd had common sense, let alone a presentiment, I would've set the latch. I wouldn't have let myself be half-drowned."

"It's a crying shame is what it is. A crying shame."

Quinn was too mad to cry. Mad at herself, mad at Stram. How could she and Garnick have missed him at the reaper works? He was obviously watching them and despite their precipitous route back to the street, he managed to follow them. Why? Why had he come out of hiding? He'd wanted to disappear and yet he risked coming out in the open to try and kill her. What did he think she knew that could cause him trouble? His death had certainly caused her trouble. If the police disbelieved her claim of self-defense, she could be charged with murder. And whatever secrets Stram had known died with him. She might never find out who killed the Kadingers and burned her office.

She worked the comb through her matted hair, easing out the tangles, trying not to see Stram's face, trying not to worry she'd gotten herself in the family way like poor Rhetta. That cathartic mingling of limbs with Garnick had awakened a sensuality she didn't know she possessed. But even in her elation, she was conscious how vulnerable such feelings made her.

A knock sounded at the door. She smoothed the wrinkles in the dress she'd borrowed from Mrs. Farraday and went to answer.

Garnick was alone.

"Where's Sergeant Chesterton?"

"He decided you've had enough for one day." He gave Mrs. Farraday a meaningful look.

"Murderation! Well of course she has. I need to get on with cleaning up and leave you people to recuperate."

"The police took care of most of the mess," said Garnick. "You oughta try and get some rest yourself, Miz Farraday. This has been one catawampusly chewed-up day."

"I do believe a little respite would do me good." She cast a wistful look at the brandy.

Quinn handed her the bottle. "Mr. Garnick and I have had plenty."

"If you're sure." She toddled out and left them alone.

"Did Chesterton believe my story?" asked Quinn.

"He was a mite suspicious seeing Stram had nothing but a sawbuck in his wallet."

"I'm glad you thought to search him before the police arrived. Where do you suppose he got all that money?"

"Hard to say. Four hundred's a lot of spondulicks to be carrying around in a bad neighborhood. Could be he stole it."

"Or was paid to kill me."

Garnick blanched under his tan. "He had a revolver and a bowie knife on him."

"Then I guess I'm lucky he decided to drown me."

"How are you holding up?"

"Steadier now. My neck hurts and my knees are bruised. I keep playing what happened over and over in my mind trying to think what I could've done differently."

"You'll never quit rehashing how it could've gone or should've gone. From now on I'll be rehashing how I let him trail us here and why I didn't hear the melee and get there in time to shoot him, myself."

"I can't imagine why he thought he had to kill me, but with him dead, it's all the more important to dig out the secrets cached in Winthrop's office files."

"You can't still be contemplating burglary?"

"What else can we do, Garnick? If we don't finish what we started, the devil will win. All these murders, all this evildoing will go unpunished."

"With a woman as single-minded as you, I give the devil low odds." He looked at his watch. "It's after midnight. If you're bound and determined, we'd best get moving."

Quinn pinned up her still-damp hair and reviewed the contents of her shredded reticule. Her watch was still running, albeit minus its crystal. The card with Elfie's new bank account number had been lightly toasted by the gunshot but remained legible. The same with her Widow's Certificate. Her vial of hand cream was cracked and leaking and her little purse mirror in smithereens. More bad luck. Superstition held that she could nullify the curse by burying the pieces under a full moon. Bad luck had come calling irrespective of mirrors. She threw the bits in the wastebasket.

What was this? Curlicues of gold wire caught in the snarled threads. She worked it loose. The remains of Delphine's ring! She'd forgotten about it. It wouldn't be much use now. No jeweler could envisage what it had looked like originally except maybe...with her fingernail she winkled the fractured ivory centerpiece out of the tangle. The carved angel was in two pieces, but beautifully defined. It was worth holding on to.

The borrowed dress had no pockets and she gave the salvageable articles to Garnick to keep.

He reloaded the derringer, which stank of gunpowder, and said, "I guess we're ready. Chesterton's coppers did a pretty decent job of swabbing out the water closet. I don't reckon we need to come back here after we're done at Winthrop's office. I'll take you back to Madam Lou's if you're sure that's where you want to go."

"I should pay Mrs. Farraday for the clothes."

He pulled out his money clip. "How much would you estimate a getup like that is worth?"

Quinn stood in front of the cheval mirror and considered the pillowy, outdated green skirt with its rows of flounces and the floppy, funnel sleeves bagging from the elbow. "It was all she had that came close to fitting."

He laid a bill on the dressing table. "Let's call it a dollar and let's clear out. I don't see a reason to wake her up to say goodbye."

"She's been awfully kind. We drank at least half of her brandy, there's blood on one of her towels and she'll have the vapors for a week after this fright."

"Five then, but if she had no more rooms to rent, she should've locked up for the night and Stram would've had to bust in the front door. I'd have heard him coming and he'd never have got to you."

"No more rehashing, Garnick. What's done is done."

They set out along Rush Street, black-dark and quiet but for the creaking wheels of a soil cart as it stopped and started and stopped again. The heavy air weighed down on them, almost too thick and sultry to breathe. Quinn wished for Leonidas and the carriage, but there had been no safe place to park near the McCormick factory. They had stabled the rig and taken the horse-car. She would have rejoiced at the sight of a horse-car now, but they had ceased running hours ago. Winthrop's office seemed forever away, over two miles to the south after they crossed the bridge. Her wet shoes rubbed a blister, Mrs. Farraday's dress scratched as if it had been starched, and the wide funnel sleeves flapped against her skirt. She felt like a crippled bat.

As they drew closer to the city center, more people caroused about the streets but the detectives navigated around them. By the time they turned onto Clark, the noise had died away except for the distant bray of a foghorn. Winthrop's office was in the middle of the block, halfway between two gaslights. Quinn and Garnick walked up and down the block. The businesses on either side of the office, a milliner's shop and a bookbindery, were dark. When they had satisfied themselves no one was out shopping for hats or books, they stole into the alley behind.

223

Garnick held a lit match to the backdoor lock and examined it. "We should've remembered to bring a jimmy."

"Drat! How could I have been so slapdash?"

"You've had a lot on your mind. We both have."

The match flamed out and he struck another. "We can try to smash it and he'll know he's had visitors, or we can wait till tomorrow night and come prepared. It's a new Yale. Even with the right tool, it could take an hour or more to pick it and the damage would prob'ly show."

If she'd been less physically uncomfortable or less impatient to get this larceny over with, she would have put it off until morning. She could contrive some excuse to lure Winthrop across town and finesse her way into the office. Maybe one of his neighbors had the key in case of fire. Maybe the lock wasn't as hard to pick as Garnick thought. But she had gathered too much momentum. She said, "Let's break the plate glass window in front."

"I don't know, Quinn. There's a lot of businesses on Clark and a fair number of private homes. Anybody passing by could send up a hue and cry."

"We're far enough away from the gaslights and we didn't see anybody."

"True, but once we get inside, we'll have to light a lamp. Another thing we should've remembered is a blanket to cover the window. No way to do a proper ransacking without light."

"If anyone sees, they'll just think the lawyer's working late. But we'll keep the lamp low and be out before anyone notices."

The waxing three-quarter moon shined its light on Garnick's lowered brows and downturned mouth. "We've come good through more than one close shave already today. If the sound of breaking glass doesn't draw a copper, a well-lit pair of burglars poking around behind a broke window just might. Don't you think we're pushing our luck?"

"We have to if we're going to solve this case."

"If we end up shot or jailed, we won't solve beans."

"We won't end up shot. Should I look for a rock or a brick or something?"

"I reckon the butt of my revolver will do."

They walked around to the front, rotating their heads like owls. Moonlight glinted on the glass window with its painted gold sign heralding "MICAH WINTHROP, Attorney at Law." With no one in sight, Garnick wound a handkerchief around his knuckles and pulled out his revolver. "Stand back."

He lined up the gun handle against the "O" in WINTHROP, made two practice swings that stopped short, then drew his arm back and rammed the butt against the glass.

It sounded like the dome of heaven crashing. She tensed for a blaze of lights and a scream of sirens. Surely the whole street would come alive with vigilantes. Garnick beat out the corner fragments, stepped over the wall into the interior, and unlocked the front door for her.

It was pitch dark. He struck a match and they located a lamp on Winthrop's desk. Quinn lifted off the frosted glass shade and twisted off the chimney. She held her funnel sleeves out of the way as Garnick lit the wick. He replaced the chimney, but not the shade.

"Set it on the floor behind the desk," she said. "Better not make things too bright."

They spotted a second lamp. When it was lit, Quinn looked around.

"You search the desk," she said. "I'll take the pie safe."

She set her lamp on the floor. Its wavering light lent an ethereal cast to the photographs on display – the older woman with the haughty mien, the elderly gentleman with the knee-high children. The other photograph, the one of the young woman in the tiara, had been removed. A dark thought occurred. Quinn had assumed she was the actress

225

who played Medea, but what if she was the flirtatious Delphine Kadinger? What if Winthrop was the suitor she spurned?

"If you find the likeness of a girl in a tiara in his desk, I want it," she said.

"If a tiara is some kind of a crinkum-crankum headdress, I'm looking at it now."

She crammed the awful implications into a recess of her brain for later reflection and pulled open the tin doors of the pie safe. Inside, folders had been stacked on three shelves. She flipped through the labels and extracted the one marked "Handish." She took out the only page and bent close to the lamp to read.

10 July – Ned Handish, wanted for murder in Cairo since January. Denies killing his wife. Claims he knows who did it and has come to Chicago to obtain the man's confession. He has business associates in Cairo who owe him money and he wants to clear his name and go back. If he is innocent as he insists, I advised him to return and stand trial. He has the ludicrous idea that a lawyer can write a letter to the authorities in Cairo and make the charges go away simply by certifying that this Merkerson person has confessed.

"Wouldja looky here!"

Quinn flattened against the wall. It was a husky voice, not loud but belligerent. The man sounded close enough to reach out and touch her. She extinguished her lamp and darted a look at Garnick. He wasn't there. A halo of light where he'd been hovered above the desk like a spirit manifestation.

"Lotsa broke glass 'n higgledy letters," answered a disembodied, mumbling voice. "M, C, N, P. Whas that spell, Shep?"

"Shh. Somebody's movin' around in there."

"I don't see nobody."

"In the back. There's a light."

226

Quinn looked. The halo above the desk was swinging around and around.

"Sa ghost," said the mumbler.

"Nah,'sa looter. Let's go see whas to loot."

"You go."

Neither of you go, prayed Quinn.

Boots clumped hard on the wooden floor. One of them had hopped the sill. His boots squeaked as they inched forward. She caught the strong whiff of rotgut liquor and pictured him, gun drawn and aimed at the looter behind the desk. Garnick would be anticipating him, revolver in hand. Quinn cringed. There would be a shooting after all. Her bull-headedness had once again endangered both her and Garnick.

A second clump. The other one was in.

Her mind recoiled. She couldn't bear another glut of blood. What to do, what to do? Her powers of invention had deserted her. She rubbed her throat, which still ached from Stram's hands, and opened her mouth to scream. Nothing came, not even a groan.

"It's about time you boys showed up," said Garnick, moving out from behind the desk. He swung the lantern in one hand and his revolver hung loose in the other. "We've been waiting here for two hours. Where's your brooms and pails? Where's the lanterns you were supposed to bring? Didn't the runner tell you we've had a robbery here? We need that glass picked up and plywood nailed across that window by morning."

"Wha–?" The first man stumbled back toward the window. "We ain't here for no goddamn cleanup."

Quinn got back her crust. She stood up and stepped forward. "Then please explain why you *are* here."

The intruders were bleary-eyed, discombobulated, and mercifully unarmed. Squeaky boots said, "The window's broke out. We came to inquisitate."

"You sure you didn't come looking to steal something?" demanded Garnick.

"No such a-thing," mumbled the second. "We was gonna stop the looters."

"Well, you're too late. The coppers are here already, gathering evidence out in the alley. You'd best get out before I call them in to bag you. Go on now, beat feet!"

With an agility rarely seen in the inebriated, they hurdled the windowsill and were halfway down the block by the time Quinn stuck her head out to check.

She said, "I'm sorry I put us in a pickle, Garnick. One of these days I'll learn. Thank you for saving us."

"I don't think those boys were much of a threat, but I'd feel a whole lot easier if we hoofed it before more 'inquisitators' show up. Grab an armful of everything you want to steal. There's no reason to be finicky about the mess at this point."

"Okay. Is there a bag or satchel lying around to carry the plunder?"

Chapter 27

By the time the burglars arrived at the Mansion, the outside lights had been doused and most of the customers had gone home. The only person still pottering about the place was Sissy. She was waving goodbye to her last client as Quinn and Garnick walked in. The departing man looked sprightly. Sissy looked tired. She tucked her earnings into her décolletage and greeted Quinn and Garnick with a weary smile.

"You want to see Jemelle again, Mr. Garnick?"

"Not now, Sissy. Miz Paschal's been staying here as Lou's guest. You remember her from the other day, don't you?"

Sissy regarded Quinn's sea-weedy hair and ill-fitting, bat-winged dress. "She don't look the same."

Quinn said, "It's been a really hard day, Sissy. Is it all right if I go up to Lou's room now? I'll be careful not to wake her."

"Lou's got company tonight. The mayor, I think. She took a bottle of French champagne upstairs with her and left orders she wasn't to be disturbed till noon."

"Oh."

"Is there another room she can use?" asked Garnick.

"Just her?" Sissy's eyes slid back and forth between them as if she divined exactly what they had been up to, and how recently.

"Just me," said Quinn. Even if all they did was sleep, she wouldn't go to bed with Garnick in a brothel.

Sissy gave her a pitying look. "I guess you can share mine if you don't mind sleeping double."

"I don't mind. And I really appreciate it."

Garnick ran a hand through his hair. "Have you got a bed for me somewhere? Doesn't have to be a bed. I can bivouac in the piano room, on the couch if that's all right."

"'Cept for Lou's special friends, it's against the rules for a man to stay overnight, Mr. Garnick. You know that."

"We've got an important meeting here in the morning with one of His Honor's colleagues. In fact, Mayor Rice may want to sit in."

"Then I guess it's okay, seeing as how it's you and all."

"You're a peach, Sissy."

"I'll go and fetch you a sheet, but you'll have to spread it up yourself and square accounts with Lou tomorrow."

Quinn didn't turn a hair. A brothel was a moneymaking enterprise and the man she loved had been a valued customer until late last year. It was a fact she wished she didn't know, but she couldn't feel resentment. If anything, she felt grateful. Garnick might have kept his nightmares at bay by drinking himself into a stupor, or dulled his mind with morphine like so many veterans had done. Instead he came here and Minnie had broken the house rules to let him stay all night and give what comfort she could. The brothel joggled Quinn's moral compass. On the night the office burned, when she straggled in friendless and needy, these so-called "fallen" women showed more charity than she could have expected from any of the so-called "virtuous" women of her acquaintance. She said as much to Garnick.

"I reckon they've got about the same mix of virtues and vices as the rest of us." He sounded defensive.

230

"I don't mean to be backhanded or snide, Garnick. I sincerely appreciate their...humanity."

"There's more to them than what they do to get by. They've got their own angles and pursuits, places they're from, places they'll go soon as they can fix on something better."

Quinn didn't think Minnie's ambition to open her own brothel constituted "something better," but where vice was concerned, it had lately become difficult to keep her interpretations consistent.

Sissy returned with a sheet and feather pillow for Garnick. He and Quinn said goodnight and, yawning, she followed her new roommate down into the bowels of the place, along a passageway of closed doors and complicated lives.

Sissy's room was small and dreary and the musk of her last client hung the air. With the briskness of a nurse, she yanked off the used sheet and replaced it with a clean new one. At least Quinn hoped it was clean. The horsehair mattress atop the low, cast-iron bed felt extra firm and sturdy, no doubt for occupational reasons. Quinn wouldn't have cared if it were made of pea shucks. She was dead on her feet.

The washstand was supplied with soap, tooth powder, and water. She performed a cursory toilette, cleaned her teeth with her fingers, and dropped onto the bed in nothing but her chemise and pantalettes. Her eyes closed. A few minutes later she felt the mattress give as Sissy snuggled down on the other side. A subversive thought scratched at the periphery of her consciousness. Had Garnick ever taken comfort in this bed?

Brothel nights under the bridge, she decided. This would be the last one. She would wall off the past and concentrate on the future. She put the pillow over her face. After that, black nothing.

She slept the sleep of the innocent. No pangs of guilt interrupted her slumber. No nightmares about the past, no worries about the future. At dawn, a spear of sunlight pierced the transom above a shaded window and woke her. Somewhere in the distance a rooster crowed. She opened her eyes and sketched out the day ahead. Winthrop's files, the meeting with Tench, finding a new boarding house.

A decadent, fatty smell affected her like an astringent. She sat up and saw a jar of beard oil on the table next to her, no doubt left behind by the last person to occupy this side of the bed. She rubbed her eyes. There was something leveling about waking up in a brothel. Whatever fate had brought you there, you couldn't feel self-righteous or superior.

Sissy was still fast asleep. Very quietly, Quinn slipped out of bed and dressed. Her watch had died during the night, but the clock on the dressing table said eight o'clock. In two hours, if all went as planned, Alderman Tench and Fen Megarian would be here. A fortuitous appearance by Mayor John B. Rice would add a measure of suspense to the meeting. Her intuition told her his all-night visit with Lou was no coincidence. She and Garnick had a lot of reading to do in a short time.

She gave her hair a vigorous brushing, picked up Winthrop's satchel, and started for the kitchen. Garnick was sitting at the table counting Stram's greenbacks like he was dealing a deck of cards, inspecting each bill front and back.

"Is it counterfeit?"

"Looks legal." His smile was intimate, his hair endearingly tousled. "How'd you sleep?"

"Like a baby. A baby on laudanum."

"No bad dreams?"

"No."

He got up and took a pan off the stove. "I made a stack of johnnycakes. Are you hungry?"

"Ravenous."

"Good. I found a crock of cane syrup. Let's eat."

Quinn set the table and Garnick served their plates and poured the coffee. They sat down to breakfast like normal people. It seemed so ordinary, yet so unreal. She could scarcely assimilate the events of the past two days – whipsawed between happiness and horror. She should have had bad dreams, should be haunted by Stram's staring eyes and gurgling chest wound. But it was like something that happened to somebody else, a story she'd heard secondhand a long time ago. Her mind was anesthetized. Maybe the anesthesia wouldn't last, but in the meantime the cakes were good and her appetite was hearty.

"I didn't know you could cook, Garnick."

"You're enjoying the full repertoire, though I have been known to fry an egg or a pork chop if there's any on hand."

She wondered if breakfast together like this would become routine, whether it would be boring without the pulse-quickening ingredients of death and danger. When they finished eating, she cleared the table while Garnick covered the leftovers for the next people into the kitchen. In passing, their arms touched and she felt a frisson. A kiss ensued. Again, she thought how vulnerable she'd become, not just to the passions and predilections of another person, but to her own desire. Only a few days ago she'd been rational – sexually curious to be sure, but in control of her life. She concealed her doubts with a quip. "If this keeps up, I shall have to start calling you by your Christian name."

"Like as not it'd slip your mind in a crisis."

"I don't think it would, but no more canoodling, Garnick. We've a lot of reading to do and not much time before our first interview of the day."

"Nobody could accuse you of going moony on me." He pocketed the stack of bills he'd taken off Stram and poured a second round of strong coffee. "What is it we're looking for, Quinn? We know the government's a-wallow in graft. We know Tench was paying Kadinger for something Kadinger didn't want his clerk asking questions about. We know from Verner that Tench was Delphine's paramour. And we know Winthrop's played us for saps."

That last item made Quinn's blood boil. Winthrop must be sniggering up his sleeve at them, or he would be until he discovered his empty file cabinet this morning. He couldn't be sure they were the thieves, but it was dead certain he'd be asking all over town where she could be found and wondering who else would have cause to burgle his files.

"I don't know exactly what we're looking for, Garnick. Anything that ties Stram to Winthrop or to any of the other people in this imbroglio. Who he worked for, what he was doing at the Kadinger home besides seducing Rhetta, why he broke cover to come after me? Anything."

She emptied the booty from Winthrop's satchel onto the table. The tiara rolled out on top. Ornately carved coral spikes studded with pearls, it looked like something from another century, or part of a costume worn by an actress portraying a woman from another century, another country. Maybe Quinn's first guess had been correct and it really was Adelaide Ristori in the photograph. She fanned out the rest of the loot across the table. The picture was there, still in its frame. "You did find her, Garnick!"

"Who is she?"

"I'm not sure, but wouldn't it be an eye-opener if it were Delphine?"

"You think the lady had both Winthrop and Tench on her string?"

"Maybe. I wish we had a magnifying glass." She held the photo close and studied the hands. The woman wore a large ring, but it was impossible to make out the design. "Do you have the center stone from that ring I gave you?"

He fished it out of his pocket and they compared the cupids on the woman's bracelets to what Quinn had first thought was an angel on the ring.

"They look the same to me," said Garnick. "Leastwise they both have wings."

234

"Josabeth told us the unnamed suitor demanded Delphine give back the jewelry he'd given her. Whoever gave her the bracelet must also have given her the ring. The bracelet may have been destroyed in the fire. If Rhetta hadn't borrowed the ring, it would probably have burned, too."

"It's possible Winthrop was holding these baubles for somebody else."

"But not a photograph," said Quinn. "And Winthrop would be beside himself if a woman failed to appreciate his extraordinary attributes."

"Tench can tell us whether or not it's Delphine. Meanwhile, let's get started on the files." Garnick grabbed a thick one marked *City Business* and dug in.

Quinn started with the Handish file, some of which she'd read the night before, and reread what Winthrop had written about Handish. *He has the ludicrous idea that a lawyer can write a letter to the authorities in Cairo and make the charges go away simply by certifying that this Merkerson person has confessed.*

"Listen to this, Garnick." She read the sentence out loud. "Does it sound like Handish believed it was somebody named Merkerson who killed his wife?"

"Handish sure sounded hell-bent, beg pardon, on beating a confession out of Stram. Hard to fake that much hate."

"The feeling could have been genuine if he was thinking Merkerson when he said Stram." She rethought her assumptions. "At first I thought Handish came to us of his own volition, but what if Winthrop sent him?"

"That would explain how he came by our business card," said Garnick. "You gave the shyster a packet a few months back with the idea he'd hand 'em out to anybody who came to him with an absconded wife or a suspected embezzler at the till."

"Clearly that was wishful thinking on my part. But suppose Winthrop or one of his other clients wanted Stram found, but couldn't afford to be seen in the low places Stram hung about? Suppose he sent Handish to sic us on Stram."

"Makes sense. Handish must have memorized that description of Stram. I remember you had to pull the words out of him."

"Do you think Handish was completely in the dark about Winthrop's trickery?"

"Like as not. If we're talking brain power, Handish appeared to be pulling a light wagon."

"I don't know. He was smart enough to keep out of prison for all this time. If he hadn't been so bent on proving he didn't kill Florrie, he might have lived a long life and never served a day. The fact he was killed on the other side of Lou's hedge must mean he came here for a reason. There are too many other brothels in town for it to be coincidence."

"Jemelle gave me the feeling she's holding out on us a jot," said Garnick.

"More than a jot. She's a prevaricator of the first order. Handish was never looking for Stram. He didn't give Stram money to pay her to lie about Elfie, but somebody did and that somebody made sure she worked Handish's name into her statement. We'll definitely have to have another session with Jemelle Clary." Quinn recalled that cornered animal look in her eyes. "Do you think she'll cut and run if she feels pressured?"

"I'd be surprised if she stuck around for Elfie's trial."

"That's the day after tomorrow," said Quinn.

"Then I reckon we'd best corral her this morning after we've talked to Tench."

They each went back to their reading. After a few minutes Garnick slid the *City Business* file across to her. "Have a gander at this. Hiz Honor's interest in prostitution started before he graced us with his presence here in Chicago."

Quinn pulled out a yellowed newspaper clipping, a review of a play, *The London Merchant,* in which the young John Rice had acted. He had toured the East Coast performing in the tragedy about a young apprentice seduced and corrupted by a prostitute. She read aloud. "*To supply the deceitful fille de joie with money, he robbed his kindly master and murdered his wealthy uncle. Tortured by guilt, he repented all and his uncle forgave him with his dying breath. The woman remained remorseless. Like the impious harlot Jezebel, she declared herself doomed before the world began.*"

Garnick said, "Reminds me a little of Megarian's style."

Quinn folded the piece back into the folder. "There must be a journalist's manual on how to write about women."

There was another clipping about a fire that broke out at a theater Rice owned after he moved to Chicago. He had taken to the stage and commanded the audience to remain seated, which they did until flames started licking at their ears. She sighed. "Winthrop may have learned something about Rice's past and was blackmailing him, but it's not apparent from what's here."

"Keep reading. There's several pages on each alderman. I can guess some of the abbreviations, AS, Annie Stafford. CH, Cap Hyman. But the numbers could be anything – bribes, money extortion, votes. All creation, it could be donations to the widows and orphans society for all we know." He got up and refilled their coffee cups.

Quinn had already drunk enough coffee to galvanize a stuffed bird but felt as if they were on the verge of a major discovery somewhere in this mishmash. She perused the file page by page. Winthrop's precisely slanted Spencerian penmanship was as clear as her thoughts were messy. On the page headed *Tench,* a double column of initials and numbers might as well have been hieroglyphics. In frustration, she sandwiched the papers back together, stood the folder on end, and rapped it against the table.

An old envelope fell out, one engraved with a picture of a Union soldier saluting the Stars and Stripes. It was addressed to Winthrop in a cramped, untidy hand. She opened it and read the note. *Who is Jack Stram? Imperative! JBR says find at all cost.* Enclosed with the note was Megarian's article about Gentle Annie horsewhipping "a mangy, no-account jasper named Jack Stram" after he punched one of her girls. It brought Quinn up short. Had Winthrop gone looking for Stram, himself? Had he talked to Jemelle before she did?

"Caught red handed!"

Her heart jumped into her throat.

A mountainous man in a black wool suit strutted into the room like a monarch. His white beard jutted over his black string tie, his watch chain stretched across his magisterial paunch, and his probing eyes heralded power. "I should have you arrested."

Garnick stood. "Good day to you, Mr. Mayor. Would you care to sit and discuss the charges over a cup of coffee?"

"Murder's the charge. My police informant tells me you killed a man last night."

Quinn collected herself and went to stand beside Garnick. "He attacked me and I shot him. If you are of a mind to make common cause with us and pool information, perhaps together we can fill in a few of the blanks in the life of Jack Stram."

Rice puffed his chest like a pouter pigeon and took hold of his lapels. "The meeting you requested is being held earlier than planned. Tench will be here soon. Regrettably, Mr. Megarian has been detained."

CHAPTER 28

Madam Lou, crapulous after her evening of champagne, watched from the back door as the mayor and his party assembled around the bench under the gazebo. Her eyes skipped from face to face. Probably wondering which bodies would have to be dragged into the alley when the conference was finished, thought Quinn. The mayor's scowling police bodyguard stood like a totem pole watching from the far corner of the hedge. He had a sloping forehead, a protruding jaw, and the physical attitude of a man primed for assault. She'd feel a lot less nervous if the lunk hadn't disarmed Garnick. Did he still have the derringer she'd given him in his pocket?

Rice seated himself first and occupied more space than the others put together. When not bounded by walls, his girth seemed to expand. His gestures appeared broader and more commanding as he bade Quinn and Garnick to take their places opposite him.

Henry Tench, a gangling man of about fifty with pomaded black hair, squeezed in beside the mayor and opened the meeting with a double-fisted, table-rattling whap. "What's your game? That runt of a news hound you sent to chum the waters says you want to play dirty." He had a pointy nose that tipped up sharply on the end as if it wanted nothing to do with the sinister mouth below.

"They're de-*tec*-tives," said Rice, each syllable rich with disdain. "Mr. Winthrop hired them to investigate the murder of Rolf and Delphine Kadinger. And with a minor deception, to find Mr. Stram. They found him last night and as Sergeant Chesterton tells it, Stram fared ill."

"That's right," said Garnick. "Your attorney keeps more irons in the fire than a cavalry smithy. Seems he can't turn away a single client, strings 'em all along with a morsel of hope. Ned Handish, Elfie Jackson, Verner Kadinger, my partner. As we've gotten forrader down the road with Mr. Winthrop, he's proven a mite too treacherous to keep on with. Has that been y'all's experience?"

The mayor nodded toward Winthrop's files. "Let's begin with an explanation of where you got those documents."

"Let's begin," said Quinn, "with what you've done with Mr. Megarian."

He cut his eyes at her. "There are times when a saucy comeback from a pretty woman can be charming. Now is not one of them. Where did you get these documents?"

Garnick grinned. "We stole them."

Tench's mouth quirked toward his right ear.

His Honor's eyebrows climbed higher.

"Did you think your legal eagle gave 'em to us voluntarily?"

"If he had," said Rice, "it would seriously alter my opinion of his professionalism."

With an unconcerned, almost lazy manner, Garnick paged through the city business file. "There's some choice reading here. I knew you boys had your hooks into Annie and Cap and a few of the big bugs, but this is an impressive record, Mr. Mayor. I surmise the lawyer keeps track of who's paid up and who's holding out?"

"He handles, shall we say, certain ticklish matters as they arise. Now quit the jousting and come to the point. Why have you poked into our business? What is it you're after?"

"Besides the individual who murdered the Kadingers, you mean?"

Rice glared.

Bolstered by Garnick's audacity, Quinn said, "Why did you want to find Jack Stram? Was that the ticklish matter Winthrop was taking care of for you?"

"Did I not make myself clear, madam? I'm the one asking the questions. Defy me at your peril." His voice rang with a theatrical resonance.

Quinn could see him treading the boards upon a stage, matching his face to the role, his voice to the script of the play. How much of his performance this morning was theater? The mayor of Chicago might engage in a little graft on the side, but he couldn't afford to inflict actual bodily harm on any of his constituents. She said, "What did Stram have on you and your crony Mr. Tench that makes you so fearful?"

Tench came off the bench, murder in his eyes.

Garnick's right arm shot out and clapped him hard in the chest with the heel of his hand. Madam Lou yelped and the bodyguard rushed forward.

"Down!" ordered Rice in a peremptory voice. "Stand down, all of you."

Tench sat and the bodyguard backed away.

"Lou, my sweet." The mayor seemed to notice her for the first time. "Go back inside. I wouldn't allow anything unpleasant to happen in your charming garden."

Lou didn't look convinced.

"Do as I say. When we're finished here, I'll stop in to say goodbye."

She hesitated for an instant, but apparently thought better and retreated.

Garnick closed the file. "What say we call a truce, gents, see if we can't help each other out? Miz Paschal is fierce to find out why Stram tried to kill her and who it was burned down our office."

Rice shrugged. "Hard luck. But as you will have deduced from Winthrop's note, we know less about Stram than you except that he made himself a fixture in the Kadinger house."

"You saw him there?"

"Mr. Tench saw him."

Quinn pulled the framed photograph of Delphine out of the satchel. "Do you know this woman?" she asked Tench.

"Sure I know her. It's Delphine Kadinger."

"Her brother says you were her lover."

"Then he's a dunce."

"What would cause him to think such a thing? Did you buy her jewelry?"

"In a pig's eye. Maybe he saw her cooing and fawning. She carried on like that with every man who walked in the door."

"So you did visit Delphine?"

"I went to the Kadinger's house plenty, but not to see her. The city had business with Rolf Kadinger."

Garnick skewered Tench with an accusatory stare. "What kind of business was costing the city a thousand a month?"

Tench tweaked his nose, then an earlobe, then his nose again. "Private business."

Quinn took for granted he was hiding some kind of hanky-panky, but she had to admit it was a stretch to picture this fiftyish, peaky-nosed alderman pitching woo to a girl like Delphine. "While you were conducting your business with Mr. Kadinger, did you have occasion to talk with Jack Stram?"

"Nah. I saw him mooching around, all eyes and ears, like he was looking for something to blab or to filch. I asked the maid who he was and she gave me his name."

Rice said, "We asked Kadinger about Stram, where he lived and what he did when he wasn't dallying with his maid, but Kadinger knew little or nothing about the men who came and went in that house." He assayed the photograph from under hooded eyes. "She was made for the part of the temptress, the lady of pleasure who lures the innocent young man to commit theft and even murder."

Quinn dared ask another question. "How did Winthrop know where to look for Stram?"

"After Annie Stafford whipped him in the street and got his name in the paper, we knew the sorts of places he frequented. Winthrop questioned the girls Stram liked, but his efforts came to nothing."

Garnick took the city file out of the satchel and spread it out across the table. "Did Stram stumble onto something jeopardous to you, Mr. Mayor? Is that why you were so het-up to find him?"

Rice inhaled prodigiously, which lifted his shoulders and expanded his chest. "I fail to see how any details regarding the city's business with Mr. Kadinger can help you. More importantly, you haven't suggested how it is you can help us." He executed a smile perfectly calibrated between cordiality and menace. "That being the upshot of this meeting, we will relieve you of Mr. Winthrop's files and be on our way. You can expect the police to follow up with questions in a less congenial setting."

Quinn reassessed the situation. Garnick had regarded Chesterton as a friend until this morning. She had trusted him enough to tell him about this meeting. But he'd known that Rice and Tench wanted Stram found and he'd gone to them immediately last night without the least concern for Garnick & Paschal. She glanced at the uniformed bodyguard, idly slapping a truncheon against one palm. The mayor might not soil his own hands with violence, but his police minions could do his bidding anonymously at a time and place of their choosing.

Tench reached for the satchel and started to replace the file, but Garnick caught his arm. "No call to be hard-barked about it, Mr. Mayor. In case you don't know it, this lady's by-name aside, she's the widow of Thomas Sinclair, of *the* Sinclairs. And while I may not look what you'd say well-connected, Edmund Allbright of the Merchants Bank is a friend of mine. His daughter Josabeth has entertained Mrs. Sinclair and me in her drawing room. An uncongenial follow-up would consternate more upstanding citizens than I reckon you want to cross."

Rice's gaze was locked on Garnick and Garnick's on Tench. The bodyguard held his truncheon poised in mid-air.

Garnick let go of Tench's arm and focused on Rice. "I hope you haven't been too uncongenial to Mr. Megarian, but he's not the only scribbler in town and there's parts of your lawyer's files we could repeat from memory like the lines of a play."

"You mis-reckon my capacity to eradicate obstacles in my way, Mr. Garnick." Rice's gray eyes stared back, implacable as a meat fork.

The back of Quinn's neck prickled. Either Rice was a very good actor or Garnick had seriously mis-reckoned. They both had. She wanted to kick Garnick under the table, tell him to hand over the files and promise not to throw up any obstacles.

"I won't ask," said Rice," what impelled you to go beyond the task Winthrop set for you or why this alleged *lady* has chosen to slum with prostitutes. A pair of down-and-out snoopers who consort with strumpets and involve themselves in shooting frays? Come now. You over-value your importance. No person of standing would sully his name to defend you or believe your allegations against me or the city. But for the sake of argument, what would it take to scrape the two of you off the soles of our shoes?"

Garnick's expression tautened, but he remained cool. "What did you pay Kadinger's employees to do for you?"

"His employees?" Rice frowned.

"Laborers," said Garnick. "Don't palter. His clerk gave us the crux."

"We had no use for Kadinger's workers. His clerk doesn't know what he's talking about." The mayor's eyes narrowed, then widened, as if something had begun to fall into place in his mind. "If I were to give you your answer, what would you do with it?"

"Not a damn thing unless it led to the Kadingers' deaths, or the dumping of Confederate corpses in the lake, or it turns out you tried to scupper our investigation by burning our office."

"The woman who killed the Kadingers is in jail," said Rice. "Winthrop will be lucky if he keeps her from the gallows. Your investigation has been of no avail."

"It isn't finished," protested Quinn. "She's innocent and we'll prove it yet."

With a roll of his eyes Rice relegated her to insignificance. "What is your arrangement with Megarian?"

"We've promised to give him the inside story on what happened to the Kadingers, if we uncover it."

Rice stroked his beard. "Tell the man what he wants to know, Henry."

"Are you crazy? They'll double-cross us. We'll be outed in tomorrow's *Tribune*."

"The paper can't afford to print an unsubstantiated rumor."

Quinn smothered a laugh. Megarian was having a field day with an ancient myth.

"Nothing they say can hurt us," said Rice. "Mrs. Sinclair dispatched the one person who might have caused us problems. Go on, tell them, Henry."

Tench's upper lip curled over his teeth. "We paid Kadinger under the table to put it about to his wealthy investor friends that the city would default on the water-works bonds. We mopped up when the dupes started selling at a loss."

"The rumor spread with remarkable speed," added Rice. "We advanced the funds for Kadinger and certain other friends to buy back the discounted bonds for our account. At the same time they acquired as many as they could for themselves."

"Is Edmund Allbright one of your friends?" asked Garnick.

"He was Kadinger's friend," said Rice, "and too credulous for his own good or that of his clients. The city was never in danger of defaulting. Each bond is worth its coupon value of a thousand dollars, redeemable on the due date at seven percent interest. Unfortunate if some early investors got cold feet and sold for less. We've denied the rumor from the beginning."

"Bonds!" The sheer banality of their malfeasance jogged Quinn out of her funk.

She couldn't believe it. And Rolf Kadinger was complicit in the swindle. "With all the other laws you break, that everybody knows you break, you're fiddling bonds, too?"

"A five-hundred-thousand-dollar public work," said Rice, "yields a higher return than our modest take from the brothels. Henry and I plan to stand for re-election in sixty-nine, which is why Mr. Megarian was disinvited. To quell any unwelcome disclosure, we need to know who Jack Stram worked for. Whether during his visits to the Kadinger home he pilfered evidence of our payments to Rolf and whether *you*..." the mayor inserted a dramatic pause, "removed any such evidence from Mr. Stram's person after his untimely demise."

"No," said Quinn.

"I took four hundred dollars off him," added Garnick. "Later on we'll pass it to the woman he was friendly with, but for now we're keeping hold of it. We never found out whose payroll he was on, nor even what he was paid to do."

"He was afraid of the man who hired him," said Quinn. "I think because that man murdered the Kadingers. Stram called him the 'man upstream,' obviously meaning someone in a position of power. Someone like you, Mr. Tench. I'm still not sure it wasn't you."

Tench leaned in, mouth working, but Rice held up his hand and Tench's jaws shut with a pop. Rice said, "With such a figurative turn of mind, you would be better suited to a career as a novelist than a detective, Mrs. Sinclair. But I can assure you neither Henry nor I desired the death of Rolf and Delphine Kadinger. Quite the contrary. And if you are looking for the grave robbers who are trying to scuttle the water-works by dumping corpses in the lake, Mr. Garnick, I suggest you concentrate your search on those individuals who bet against the project. And now, if you will hand over Mr. Winthrop's files..."

"Will you return them?" asked Quinn. "Elfie Jackson's trial is coming up. There's a signed statement he'll need."

"You had no thought of that when you robbed him." Rice sorted through the files, found Jemelle's statement and laughed. "If Winthrop thinks the affidavit of a naughty-house wench can persuade a jury, he shall certainly have it. Now. This meeting is adjourned."

They left abruptly. The mayor didn't linger to tell Lou goodbye and his bodyguard didn't return Garnick's gun.

Quinn saw them exit through the hedge and continued to stew. "Do you think I have too figurative a turn of mind, Garnick?"

"It's your imagination that makes you a good detective, but maybe Stram was more literal than you thought." He pulled out the roll of greenbacks and smoothed a Lady Liberty twenty open on the table. Someone had drawn a crude map in black ink over part of the bill. "If I'm not mistaken, that's the area upstream of the South Branch of the Chicago. A lot of lumber docks on that stretch of the river."

"Kadinger's company?"

"About where the X is. Now under the management of Mr. Burk Bayer."

CHAPTER 29

Jemelle was gone, spirited away before sunup in the white and gold barouche with the purple doors. Marcel, Lou's regally accoutered coachman, burnished the ornamental brass trappings with the tenderness of a lover. He had a long face, a shiny bald pate, and his long, stick-thin limbs reminded Quinn of a daddy long-legs.

"Where did you take her?" she asked.

He viewed the detectives with a jaundiced eye. "I drive the gals where they say to drive them. I don't notify the other gals where that is."

Quinn hated his assumption that she was one of Lou's "gals," but why would he think otherwise? After these last few days why would anyone? "Please, Marcel." She put her hands together in a prayerful gesture. "Jemelle's due in court the day after tomorrow. A woman's life depends on her testimony."

"I don't know that gal. I know Miss Jemelle."

"How well?" asked Garnick, all wide-eyed innocence. "She hasn't been at the Mansion for long."

"What are you getting at?"

"Do you know she's wanted by the law?" Garnick's expression was grave.

"The law?"

"She could go to jail if she fails to appear in court," said Quinn, having no idea if that was true. "You could land in jail yourself as an accessory."

"What's an accessory?"

"A person who aids a fugitive to escape," said Quinn, inventing again. "Did she have a valise with her when she left?"

"She had two." He drew himself up straight and proud, straining the brass buttons on his livery. "I don't care if she was a fugitive. Those that run got reasons. Only a rat would send the law after a scared woman."

"Was Miss Jemelle scared this morning?" asked Garnick.

"She looked over her shoulder a few times, nervy like."

Quinn tamped down her alarm. Jemelle knew she was in danger and she was smart enough to run. The only hitch, she might not be running from the right man. "Did she have any visitors last night?"

"Marking visitors ain't my job."

"Marcel, Jemelle has gotten herself involved in a murder. She's right to be scared, but she may not know which direction the danger's coming from. Please tell us where she's gone. We don't want to arrest her. We want to warn her."

"Miss Jemelle's had a hard life. Big Annie's place was a sty, no place for a human. I hope she don't get kidnapped back there."

"If you're worried," said Garnick, "you can ride along with us to make sure she stays safe. In fact, we've no way to travel unless you drive us."

Quinn could see Marcel's reluctance begin to wane. "Think how terrible you'd feel if something happened to her and you hadn't done what you could to warn her."

After an interval of silent reflection, he said, "I took her to the rail station."

"Did she say where she was going?" asked Garnick.

"St. Louis, but the next train ain't till noon. I can get us there. Let's make time!"

Quinn and Garnick boarded the garish contraption and Marcel barreled away from the Mansion, switching the horses' backs like a Pony Express rider. Quinn held onto the door to keep from bouncing all over the seat. Garnick sat on the facing seat and braced his legs against the floorboard.

She said, "You talked so tough with Rice and Tench. I wish you'd demanded your gun back from that bodyguard."

"That copper's the kind of thug who'd beat a man to death whether the mayor approved or not. I'd as soon err on the side of caution and scavenge a replacement. I'm still packing your derringer. You got a pouch to carry it?"

"I borrowed a purse from Sissy, but I don't want to touch that gun. I don't think I could ever shoot any gun again."

"You could if you had to."

She rubbed her neck, which was still sore. Glad as she was to be alive, she was pretty sure she'd fired a weapon at another human being for the last time. She couldn't decipher Garnick's speculative look. Anyway, the ride was too rough and noisy to talk.

The barouche slowed in a clog of traffic and a man on the sidewalk hooted at her and made an obscene gesture. She shrank against the seat back, fixed her gaze on her lap, and entertained the idea of appropriating Stram's cash and running away with Jemelle to St. Louis. Marcel unleashed a string of less than genteel observations regarding the paternity of the heckler, the bovine stupidity of the other drivers, and the almighty bumbling of the pie eaters from Peoria who didn't know how to cross a city street. The blockage cleared and the Mansion's scandalous conveyance jerked forward, leaving an outcry of curses and epithets in its wake.

"Water off a duck's back," said Quinn.

"Uh huh."

"Really."

The traffic around the rail station made progress impassable. Marcel's shouts and imprecations had no effect. Stalled, Garnick and Quinn hopped out and began to push through the throng of pedestrians.

"Wait up," called Marcel. "I got to park proper. I can't leave Madam's barouche in the middle of the street."

Quinn secretly hoped never to see the purple horror again. "I'm sorry, Marcel. We're really grateful for your help, but it's half past eleven. We've no time to waste."

Marcel shouted a parting prediction about the destination of their souls as they rushed on toward the station house. Inside, a mob of departing and arriving travelers and heavy-laden porters shouldered this way and that. The St. Louis train was waiting on the tracks. Jemelle was nowhere to be seen.

"She must have boarded already," said Garnick.

They hurried to the train, but a conductor stopped them and asked for their tickets.

"We're not traveling," said Quinn. She pulled out of her purse a small bottle of hand cream she'd borrowed from Sissy's washstand, keeping her fingers over the label. "Our sister forgot her medicine. She has heart dropsy."

"All right but make it fast. We're due to leave at noon on the dot."

They climbed aboard and started making their way through the cars.

Garnick said, "I hope you've got a line of persuasive patter in your bag of tricks in case Jemelle refuses to cancel her plans and come along peacefully."

"I should have told the conductor she'd escaped from the lunatic asylum and you were a keeper come to retrieve her."

They spotted her at the back of the fourth car, sitting alone with her luggage in the seat beside her. She saw them at once and the animosity in her eyes did not augur peace.

Quinn threw herself into the facing seat. "You can't leave before Elfie's trial, Jemelle."

"The lawyer won't call me to testify. That piece in the *Tribune* gave him cold feet."

"He's changed his mind," said Quinn.

"Can't you badgerers leave me alone? You've got my signed statement." Her bruises had faded and a new front tooth had been deftly wired into the hole left by the old. The red lip salve was gone, her brown hair was rolled at the nape of her neck and encased in a simple silk net, and her sinuous figure looked austere and standoffish in a dark navy traveling dress. She looked like an ordinary woman, making an ordinary journey, perhaps to visit an ailing relative or take up teaching school in a prairie town. Only her eyes gave her away. They had seen too many Jack Strams. She said, "I want nothing more to do with Elfie's troubles. She brought them on herself."

"Oh, you helped a little," said Quinn. "We've been thinking about your statement, wondering if you might like to correct some falsehoods."

"How many times you think I'm gonna change my story? You want a correction, make it up your own self."

Garnick stepped out of the aisle to let passengers through to the next car. He propped his elbows on the back of Quinn's seat. "Could be you just misrecollected where some of your information came from, Jemelle. For instance, the way you learned the name Handish."

"I told you. Stram said Handish gave him the money he paid me."

"The problem," said Quinn, "is that Stram didn't know about Handish. He never heard of him."

"Have it your way. I don't know who gave Stram the money. He's the one paid me to lie about Elfie. You badgered me to take back that story and I did, so go rattle your hocks."

"How did you come to hear about Handish?" persisted Quinn.

253

"He looked me up a couple of days after Stram socked me. I don't know how he found me so don't ask. He said Stram was trying to pin a murder on him, some gal down in Cairo. He meant to set him straight and did I know where he was staying. I didn't, but I saw a chance to make more money in a day than I'd made the last six months in this crummy town with Annie skimming half my take. I told Handish the last I heard tell Stram was living in a boat down by the reaper works. I figured if he didn't find him, it wouldn't be on me. He could've moved on, which I guess he did."

"To perdition," said Quinn. "He's dead."

"Music to *my* ears."

A cacophony of squawks filled the car as a man wrestled a large wooden crate of chickens down the aisle. Jemelle pulled her suitcases in closer and stared out the window.

Quinn waited until the squawking passed into the next car. "What did you think when the man found dead in the alley behind Lou's place was identified as Handish?"

"What do you think? That he was dead. That he'd found Stram and Stram shot first."

"But you never saw his body, did you?"

"No."

"Then it must've given you quite a turn when you saw him walking around alive."

She licked her lips and twisted her gloves.

"All aboard for St. Louis! All aboard!"

Garnick tapped his watch. "Quinn?"

"Yes, yes. But you did see Handish again, didn't you, Jemelle? Isn't that why you're on the run?"

"You're a glutton for punishment, ain't you, long as you ain't the one getting punished?" She pulled one of her bags into her lap like a barricade.

"Leastways give us a description of the man you say called himself Handish," urged Garnick.

"Light hair and eyebrows, expensive clothes, kind of a dandy. A real spieler."

"Winthrop," grumbled Garnick. "He used Handish like a puppet when he was alive and he's still using his name."

"When was the next time you saw him?" asked Quinn.

"The day I gave you my statement. He showed up late that night wanting to know what else you'd asked, what else I'd said about him. Wore his hat low and his collar high like he'd rather be dead in a ditch than spotted in a whorehouse. He said I'd be wise, his word, to leave town before Elfie's trial. He showed up again around midnight last night to remind me. I didn't like the odds he was offering if you know what I mean. He gave me money to vamoose and that's what I'm doing. You ain't dragging me off this train."

"All aboard! Last call for St. Louis!"

"You heard the lady, Quinn. No use persisting." Garnick stepped into the aisle. "Let's skedaddle."

She got to her feet but turned to make a last appeal. "Please, Jemelle. We won't let him hurt you and Elfie needs you."

"Can't you get it through your heads? Elfie matters like Deuteronomy to me."

Garnick made a more-in-sorrow-than-in-anger face. "Did you used to go to church or did somebody happen to mention Deuteronomy's the part of the Good Book that warns against bearing false witness?"

"You go to bla—"

The high-pitched whistle blared. The train chugged and began to move.

"Come on!" Garnick grabbed Quinn's arm and pulled her into the gangway at the end of the car. He hopped onto the bottom step, still holding her hand. "I've got you. Jump."

The train chugged and swayed and the sight of the tracks passing underneath made Quinn swimmy headed. She pulled back and tried to free her hand from his grip. "I can't."

255

The tracks raced under her, faster and faster. The whistle trumpeted.

"Now!" With a force that nearly ripped her arm out of its socket, he yanked her down the steps, wrapped his arm around her waist, and made a leg-pumping, hair-raising leap. They came to a running stop well clear of the tracks.

When Quinn got her wind back, she leaned against him to steady herself. "I don't know what got into me. The motion of the tracks made me dizzy."

Garnick gave her a hug and laughed. "No honeymoon train to Niagara for us. Let's go on a lake cruise."

"Don't get ahead of yourself, Garnick." She laughed, kissed him on the cheek, and put the momentary weakness behind her. As the train gathered speed down the tracks, she said, "I'm sorry Winthrop won't have to face Jemelle in court. If she'd felt safe, she might have unloaded the whole truth."

"I suspicion Jemelle had more to be scared of than Winthrop."

"What do you mean?"

He took Quinn's arm and steered her toward the row of hackneys. "She's away clean now. It can wait. Anyways, I'm of two minds whether the whole truth would do Miss Elfie as much good as you think it would. Showing her lawyer up as a first-class finagler during the trial would prob'ly make the jurors all the more wrathy. As he ain't the one they're called to render a verdict on, I expect they'd take out their displeasure on his client."

CHAPTER 30

Garnick deposited Stram's money in the Garnick & Paschal bank account for safekeeping. He withdrew twenty dollars of his own money and bailed Leonidas and the rig out of the stable. After a quick mid-day snack, he and Quinn went shopping for a dress for Elfie to wear to trial and one for Quinn to replace the ill-fitting outfit she'd borrowed from Mrs. Farraday. Quinn had heard of a seamstress on Alcott Street who often had ready-made dresses for sale and they began there. They were in luck to find the shop open and the dressmaker at her Singer machine stitching up a storm. She had three pre-made dresses on display, one in a size Quinn thought would fit Elfie. It was cut modestly enough. Quinn held it up and considered its possible effect on the jurors. Its sunflower bright hues might be construed as too gay and gladdening for a woman accused of murder and she hung it back on the dress form.

A tawny colored, sack-like dress lay across the ironing board. It could be taken in with a few darts and made to fit, but it fell on the frumpy side of the scale. Elfie had to look pretty, but not pert. Quinn and Garnick continued shopping.

In a ladies apparel shop on Pine, Quinn stopped in front of a gray-green walking dress with a single flounce garlanded with an embroidery of mountain green leaves. It was soft, quiet, and appealingly chaste. It practically radiated innocence.

"What do you think of this one, Garnick?"

"I'd say the girl who wore it to a box social would get more than a few bids from the gents."

"Perfect." Quinn had the proprietress box it along with a new petticoat and green velvet hair net. In the same shop, a Berlin blue cotton frock with not too many buttons and a trim skirt cried out to Quinn. The seamstress altered it to fit and Quinn wore it out of the shop feeling like a new woman. She and Garnick spent the rest of the afternoon canvassing for a respectable boarding house that would accept her without a letter of recommendation. Grateful as she was to Lou and the people at the brothel, she couldn't spend another night there. Could not go on being mistaken for "one of the gals." She had no idea what to expect at tomorrow's trial, but if Winthrop called her to the stand and asked her where she lived, her answer would not be Lou's Mansion.

So far, three boarding houses had turned her away, notwithstanding her fresh blue dress and semi-true story of a fire that destroyed her previous residence. It was getting late and Garnick, who had different ideas about where and how she should pass the night, was starting to grow restive.

"We can spend the night at my cabin and nobody's gonna know. Winthrop's not going to call either one of us to testify. He'll be too worried we might let the cat out of the bag about him and Delphine."

"It's already out of the bag. Did you see the way Rice looked at that photograph? It was news to him that his attorney had been involved with the 'temptress.'"

"Winthrop must have met with her father a few times," said Garnick, "to communicate His Honor's suggestions on how to sow doubts amongst the bondholders. If Tench was telling the truth about the lady's overfriendly bent, I expect she flirted with Winthrop and he got carried away."

"Yes, but he didn't want Rice or Tench to find out they were lovers."

"I reckon Winthrop thought a dalliance with Kadinger's daughter would dint his respectable image or maybe cause the mayor to question his judgment and discretion. He dang sure didn't want her pa to know. That might've queered Kadinger's willingness to promote the bond hoax."

Quinn recalled Delphine's teasing eyes and ambiguous, self-amused smile in the photograph. "She must have enjoyed the intrigue. I can just hear her regaling Josabeth with hints about her secret suitor and mocking Verner by telling him Alderman Henry Tench was another name on her roster of conquests. In some ways she was the ideal girl for Micah. Rich and beautiful, with a respectable veneer and a heart as hard as hickory. He must have been incensed when she chose an ex-sawmill worker like Bayer over him."

"Could be he just felt relieved," said Garnick, drawing Leonidas up in front of another boarding house sign.

"I don't know." Quinn smoothed the skirt of her new dress and brushed a tendril of loose hair out of her eyes. "He may have really loved her. He took a big chance displaying her picture in his office, especially when Verner came in."

"Well, you don't want to take a chance displaying me to a would-be landlady, so I'll pull around the corner and wait out of sight."

She tried to ignore his undertone, but the significance hung in the air. She felt her independence slipping away as his expectations grew. "Thank you," she said and went to inquire at MRS. SOSEBY'S REZIDENSE FOR SINGLE LADYS.

As it developed, seeing Quinn in the company of a man wouldn't have mattered to Mrs. Soseby. She was a round, squat woman with a mass of wispy white hair that spiraled around her head like a giant cobweb. She had a vacancy and she wasn't choosy about letters of recommendation. Moreover the room had a private back entrance.

"You want to have a look?"

"No." Quinn wasn't choosy either. "I'm sure it's fine."

"Fine's as may be, but it's clean. Come and go as you please so long as you're quiet. Breakfast's at six and dinner's at six, come in at the front and turn left to the kitchen. Five dollars for the week. In advance. Laundry's extra."

Quinn gave her the money. "I'm afraid I'll miss dinner this evening. I have to be somewhere."

"I figured. Looked like that mister you drove up with didn't cotton to you sending him off." She dug in her apron pocket. "Here's the key. Room's around the side. If the fella ends up winning the argument, be sure you leave it behind when you go."

***

Quinn and Garnick arrived at the jail just after six o'clock. They entered the gloomy hallway and marched toward the office where they'd first met Chesterton. Quinn hoped he wasn't the officer on duty. She wasn't sure how he and Garnick would get along in the aftermath of Chesterton's duplicity. They were standing in front of the door, Garnick's fist raised to knock, when Chesterton walked up behind.

"Here to turn yourselves in for another bout of criminal mischief?"

"We've come to see Elfie Jackson," said Quinn. "We brought her a dress to wear to her trial tomorrow." She held out the box for him to inspect. "I presume you won't drag the poor woman into court looking like she's been brutalized in a dungeon."

He looked daggers and kicked open the door. "Bring it in."

She set it on the desk. He lifted the lid, pawed about, and shoved it back at her.

"You carrying iron, Garnick?"

"I left it in the city's care, Chez. It's for the best. Wouldn't trust myself with a loaded gun. I'm so disregardful of late I'm apt to mistake a good buddy for a backstabbing snitch."

"If I was out to do you over, Garnick, I'd have locked you and your mouthy she-partner up for homicide." His glare conferred a bounty of contempt. "You still got that derringer or you just take it with you to the bath?"

"Cut the claptrap," said Garnick. "We're on terms with the mayor now so you don't have to give us a bad time. Give your gums a rest and chaperone us through your fine clinker to Miss Jackson's cell."

Chesterton picked up the key. "The lawyer's been here already. Prisoners don't generally get more than one visitor a day. Consider this visit a gift, Garnick. Over and above what's required or deserved."

"Any Greek in your blood line?" twitted Garnick, but if Chesterton got the allusion, he ignored it and turned a cold shoulder.

Elfie was on her feet, peering through the bars. When she saw them, she smiled and the effect transformed her whole being. "You came!"

"As promised," said Quinn.

Chesterton unlocked the cell and she and Garnick stepped inside. As the gate clanked shut behind them, Quinn felt a lurch in the pit of her stomach. Had they walked into a trap?

"One hour," said Chesterton.

"You're too good to us," answered Garnick with a grin, but he must have worried that his backstabbing buddy could leave them caged for as long he pleased.

Chesterton clomped off, rattling the keys like the warning of a snake.

Elfie reached out for the box. "You brought me a new dress!" Her hair had been combed and the look of despair displaced by euphoria. Her eyes positively shone. She

261

dropped the box on the cot, swept the dress into her arms, and hugged it to her body. "It's gorgeous."

"I hope it fits," said Quinn, bewildered by the change.

"It will. May I keep it after the trial?"

"Yes, of course."

Garnick said, "You've chirked up a lot since I was last here. Somebody must've brought good news."

"Mr. Winthrop says the trial will be over in little more than an hour and by noon tomorrow I'll be free."

"He sounds more confident than he led me to believe." Quinn didn't know how to break the news that her alibi witness had vamoosed at her lawyer's instigation.

"He's found a witness who'll swear I was with her at the time of the fire. As soon as she testifies, the judge will dismiss the case."

"What?" Quinn was stunned. "Jemelle left town and you didn't name anyone else who might vouch for you."

"I didn't know there was anyone else. Mr. Winthrop is a miracle worker." She slipped the green velvet net over her hair and spun around holding the dress. "Burk will love the circlet of leaves. Green is his favorite color."

Quinn's thoughts reeled. The woman was insane.

"Tell us who Mr. Winthrop has lined up to give you the alibi." Garnick spoke calmly and evenly. "Did one of Annie's girls have a sudden revival of memory?"

"Nobody would believe a prostitute. They wouldn't have believed Jemelle even if she cut the sass and swore on the Bible. No, it's the lady who runs that chophouse on Roy. I must have forgotten about her. There were days after Burk left when I walked for miles, not knowing or caring where I was."

Quinn couldn't decide if Elfie was remembering or repeating what she'd been told to say. "However did Mr. Winthrop discover this lady?"

"He happened to take his supper there the other night and she told him I'd been in the place for hours on the night of the fire. I was crying and she tried to comfort me. She gave me a bowl of soup and asked me my name. She remembers hearing the fire wagons go by while I was sitting there. I stayed until she closed the kitchen then she put me in a hackney and paid the driver out of her own pocket."

"That *is* miraculous," said Quinn. "And yet this good Samaritan has remained silent for weeks as the newspapers pilloried you."

Elfie's euphoria vanished. "I thought you'd be happy that my suffering is about to end."

"I am happy, Elfie. We both are. It's only that we're puzzled by the way Mr. Winthrop happened into that chophouse, how he happened to strike up a conversation about a criminal trial with the cook who happens to remember serving you soup on the night of the fire."

"You're not my friends! You're trying to keep me here!"

"That's not so," said Garnick. "We've always been on your side."

"You're not or you wouldn't say such things."

Quinn contended with a constellation of misgivings. About the change in Elfie's demeanor. About the miracle of the witness. About green being Burk's favorite color. "I didn't mean to upset you, Elfie. I'm glad Mr. Winthrop found an alibi witness, but you really shouldn't try to make contact with Burk. If he attends the trial, which I doubt, any sign from you that you're still ob...that you still care for him may deepen suspicion in the minds of the jurors."

"But I love him. He's my husband. Anyway, it's all worked out and we'll be together again the way it used to be." She must have seen the look in Quinn's eyes, which did not reflect the same outcome. Her face fell. "Go away!"

Garnick checked his watch. "I reckon you'll have to bear with us a while longer, Miss Elfie. We're penned up together till the man with the keys comes back."

"You can call the guard." She tried to hide the dress behind her back. "I don't want you here! Leave me alone! Guard! Guard! Guard!"

The cry was taken up by a male voice farther down the row of cells, but no guard came. Elfie backed into the corner and sat sulking on the end of the cot. Quinn perched on the other end. She said, "There's no way Chesterton didn't hear."

"He's making a point," said Garnick. He settled on the cot between the two women and made himself comfortable. "Time will tell how sharp a point."

Quinn looked behind her at the bars and a chill went through her. "Do you think Chesterton means to keep us locked up all night?"

"Too soon to get in a swivet. It hasn't been an hour."

Quinn looked across Garnick at a stone-faced Elfie and brooded. Had Winthrop gone out and recruited a witness to lie for her? A victory in an important case would enhance his legal reputation, but did he have another reason to make sure she went free?

Winthrop was an enigma. He had supported the mayor's bond scheme, secretly romanced Delphine Kadinger, posed as Handish to worm Stram's whereabouts out of Jemelle, then scared her out of town before the start of the trial so she wouldn't learn his true identity. He had visited the Mansion, but even if he'd chanced upon Handish, she could conceive of no motive for Winthrop to kill him. Nor could she think why he would kill the Kadingers. Delphine rejected him, but no one knew about their affair so there was no loss of face and Micah had too high an opinion of himself to pine for long.

Quinn felt as if she'd been pining forever. The shadows lancing across the cell floor from the high barred window above had lengthened as her patience shortened. Things that hadn't bothered her before began to make her twitchy. The veins of grayish-black mold creeping along the gray walls, the stagnant air tinged with the smell of ammonia, the forced inactivity. She watched a cockroach dawdle across the gray floor as if it had all the time in the world. An awful sense of being shut up in this concrete box overnight made her want to gnash her teeth and scream.

"What time is it, Garnick?"

"Close on eight o'clock. Sun will soon be going down."

"Two hours," said Quinn. "I hate Chesterton."

"I reckon this is a demonstration of the 'uncongenial' setting the mayor was suggesting if we set ourselves against him and the city."

"But we told him, you told him we weren't going to make trouble about the bonds."

"Did *you* believe me?"

"Yes. You looked him dead in the eye and said all we want is the murderer and the man who burned our office. You sounded entirely honest and straightforward."

"Thank you, detective. Rice didn't believe me either."

"Call that shiftless guard again," said Elfie. "Guard! Guard! Take them away!"

No one came. After a few more bootless cries, she went silent again and Quinn resumed her brooding. There was something out of kilter about the way she'd been thinking. Something about Elfie. Something in the echo of that Medea myth.

The shadows crawled slowly across the floor. She felt as if she'd been buried alive in this sarcophagus of a cell for eternity. A howl was building at the back of her throat. It felt imminent, wild to break free. She pushed it down with all her might. "I'd rather be hanged than locked up like a monkey in a zoo, even if I did commit homicide."

"Homicide?" Elfie was suddenly curious. "Who did you kill?"

"Jack Stram," said Quinn. "The man you saw at Annie's place, the man who offered Jemelle money to lie about you. Did you ever hear his name?"

She didn't answer. Quinn leaned forward and looked into her face. "You know the name?"

"No."

"Did Burk know your friend Jemelle's husband had left her and that she was doing the naughty at Annie Stafford's place?"

Even in shadow, Quinn saw the dawn of doubt spread across her face. "Did you tell anyone else?"

"Who else would I tell?"

"Elfie, I think Burk sent Stram to bribe Jemelle. He wanted you convicted of the murders."

"Shut your mouth, you! You don't know the first thing about love." She flung the new dress onto the floor and went to huddle in the corner, face against the wall.

"I'm sorry, Elfie."

In a voice like cracking ice she said, "You and your dead man's ring to protect you! You deserve to be alone."

Quinn picked up the dress and folded it back inside the box. She said, "If after the trial you need a place to stay for a few days, you're welcome to share my room at Mrs. Soseby's on Pine Street. You may not have to share if I'm still locked up in here."

"You won't be," said Chesterton as he approached from down the corridor, keys rattling noisily. "Not this time." He discharged a loud, malevolent laugh.

Quinn held her breath as the key clicked in the lock and the gate screaked open. She had to contain herself to keep from running. Only when she and Garnick were well clear of the jail did she breathe again. "Do you suppose that chophouse is open? I could eat a steak, and a glass of wine is absolutely vital."

CHAPTER 31

The chophouse was closed and shuttered and the detectives settled for sausages and beer in the German saloon where they'd eaten before. Elfie's bizarre behavior had stirred doubts and Quinn would've liked to see this alibi witness she didn't remember. It seemed more likely that Winthrop had bribed the woman to remember Elfie. If that was so, it meant that Mayor Rice and Alderman Tench had instructed him to make Elfie's case go away, which by their calculation, meant Paschal and Garnick would go away.

Garnick was philosophical about Chesterton. "He's got his job to think about. As between going along with the mayor's chicanery and being a pal, he's had to walk a narrow line. He went out on a limb when he didn't pat me down. I could've been lying about not having a gun. In fact, I was. I'm still carrying your derringer."

Quinn pushed the sausage around on her plate and sipped her beer without enthusiasm. "Have I been a fool to set so much store on Elfie's innocence? She said she'd do anything Burk asked her to do. What if he asked her to set the fire while he was off in Rock Island dickering over lumber with Mr. Jigamaree. What was his name?"

"Harrell Paulson, Second Street. I wired a fella I know lives down there. He's a right good judge of character. He talked to Paulson and Paulson corroborated Bayer's alibi."

"I figured Bayer would be too smart to make up something that couldn't be verified." She gave a self-deprecating smile. "You don't assume things the way I do. I'm glad you followed up with Paulson. You acted like a real detective."

"Just filling in a hole."

"Just keeping us professional, you mean, while I run around making Elfie the personification of trampled womanhood."

"She's taken more than her share of abuse. It's natural she'd play on your heartstrings."

"I don't know. Winthrop fooled me. It would really sour my mood if she's fooled me, too. That Medea myth keeps nibbling away at my confidence."

"Like you told Megarian, you can't mix up a real person with a myth."

"Yes, but I've been defending Elfie because I don't believe she would have killed Delphine out of jealousy or to punish Burk for leaving her. But what if she killed her because that's what Burk wanted her to do? Or because she thought it's what he wanted her to do? Medea killed her own brother to help Jason and threw his parts in the sea."

"It'll be interesting to see how the trial plays out," said Garnick. "I expect Burk will be in the gallery along with Verner and Megarian and half the city council. Could be some of Chicago's most bodacious madams show up for the entertainment. Wouldn't surprise me if there's fireworks."

***

Quinn spent a fraught night in her room at Mrs. Soseby's thinking about the fireworks to come and rehearsing in her imagination the ways, short of shooting Winthrop dead, she might contribute to the spectacle. He was so underhanded, so intent on keeping his precious respectability. She would tell him in no uncertain terms what she thought of his deception and his ethics and his witness intimidation and if he gave her any grief about stealing his files, she'd tell him to go to Halifax. She half-wished she'd burned the Sinclair v. Sinclair file, wished she could chuck the ashes down his bespoke trousers.

What had she said in that note to Winthrop? Rhetta gave me a distinctive ring given to Delphine by her lover. I'm sure it can be traced. I'm hiding it in my office. In our *undetectable* secret safe. Had that little professional exaggeration made burglary seem futile and arson the expedient remedy?

She pictured Winthrop arriving early to pick her up for dinner. She pictured him sneaking into the alley and casually dropping a bag of oily rags into the trash barrel. Perhaps he loitered for a few minutes, pretending to smoke a cigar. When he was sure no one was looking, he tossed the smoldering butt into the barrel and came around to the front door, a smile on his face and a boutonniere in his lapel. All the while he plied her with wine and threw cold water on her investigation, he was reveling in the secret knowledge that fire was consuming the evidence that could link him to Delphine Kadinger. Her fingers fairly ached to feel that derringer in her hands again.

Sleep eluded her until the small hours. Garnick's wake-up knocks at seven o'clock startled her out of the bed like the popping of rockets. She dressed in a hurry and over the breakfast of bread and cheese he'd brought, told him the theory she'd worked out about Winthrop.

"If that's how it was, it's high time for a reckoning with the counselor."

"Do you think he'll go to his office this morning before the trial?"

"Let's find out."

They didn't talk on the drive. The only thought searing through Quinn's mind was that reckoning. Winthrop owed her and one way or another she meant to make him pay.

Garnick was as much a victim, or almost as much, but he gave no outward indication of anger. That could be a good sign or a bad. As they pulled up in front of Winthrop's office, it crossed her mind neither of them should be carrying that derringer.

The broken window had been boarded up and there was no indication what kind of business went on inside. Garnick gave the door a series of noisy kicks. "You in there Winthrop? Open up or I'll batter my way in."

"Be careful," said Quinn. "He may have a gun."

"If he does, he better know how to use it."

The door opened. "I could have you arrested for the damage you've done," said Winthrop. He was attired, as usual, in a crisp white shirt and smartly tailored suit, but his sleep-deprived eyes had lost their presumption of authority. He looked worried. "What do you want?"

Quinn brushed past him into the office. His files lay in a confused pile atop his desk. She shuffled through them and held up the framed photograph of Delphine. "Your assignment to us omitted a relevant fact, Mr. Winthrop."

"Several," said Garnick. "When you get down to the marrow."

"She gave me the picture. An innocent souvenir of our acquaintance."

"If the acquaintance was so innocent," said Quinn, "why sneak around like a criminal?"

"As I explained to the mayor, the lady and I agreed our relationship should remain private."

"To protect her reputation or yours?" Quinn asked.

"Both."

Garnick sat down behind Winthrop's desk and put his feet up. "Rice had you feeding her pa a script about the water works bonds, how to mislead his friends who'd bought high into selling cheap. He must've seen you come and go. Did the old sinner not care that you were tupping his daughter?"

"It's no surprise to hear such vulgarity from your mouth, Garnick. But you don't know what you're talking about."

"What a hypocrite you are," said Quinn. "You ensnared Rolf Kadinger into your scheme and you seduced his daughter. When she gave you the mitten and married Burk Bayer, did you kill her out of spite?"

"No." The red blotches that broke out when she'd proposed investigating Tench broke out again. "I didn't set that fire. And if anyone was seduced, it was me. Delphine was a predatory piece of work, self-willed, no respect for boundaries of any kind. And Kadinger? He was greedy to the bone."

"A kindred spirit," cracked Garnick. "With all the angles you play and the clients you diddle, you must be sitting on a tall stash of green. Enough to buy your lady friend some splendiferous trinkets. I never saw anything to beat that tiara."

"Perhaps the ring," said Quinn, thrusting the photograph into Winthrop's midsection, "but I'll get back to that. Did Delphine know about the conspiracy to defraud the water bond holders?"

"Hardly. Her father didn't trust her with anything more substantive than the choice of which gowns to buy. When I first met him in the mayor's office, he warned us all, should we have occasion to call upon him at his home, we were not to discuss business in the hearing of his daughter. 'A dear little thing, but a bit of a flibbertigibbet,' he said. He didn't know the half. Listening to her prattle about the skeletons in her own family's closet, her brother's embarrassing scrapes and her late mother's addiction to laudanum, I understood very well she wasn't to be trusted."

"You didn't tell her the rumors about the bonds were false? Not even to impress her with the fortune you'd be making off the hoax? Not during the interludes when the two of you were engaged in horizontal refreshment? You didn't drop a hint while you were billing and cooing and promising her the moon?"

The red blotches darkened. "Clearly Garnick has dragged your mind into the gutter, madam."

"And you, sir, are supremely qualified to speak about the gutter." She walked up and down, aligning her thoughts. "Are you saying Delphine couldn't have told her new husband the bonds were a safe investment?"

"She knew nothing about them one way or the other. And regardless what Kadinger was telling other people, he wouldn't have questioned their safety to Bayer."

"Why's that?" asked Garnick.

"Before you disseminate doubt, you have to disseminate confidence. You have to sell the bonds. Kadinger sold Bayer two at a thousand dollars apiece."

"When was this?" followed Garnick.

"Last March at the grand opening of the water works. A regiment of Zouaves in their French fez caps and red sashes served as Honor Guard to the procession. Bayer had apparently served with the Zouaves during the war and was invited to march. Somewhere along the parade route, he flashed his saber and a suggestive look at Delphine. After the mayor gave his speech extolling the new project as the Eighth Wonder of the World, she sought Bayer out and introduced him to her father. I watched Kadinger steer Bayer to the council table where bonds were being sold and later asked Tench. He said Bayer wrote a check on the spot. The casual expenditure naturally whetted Delphine's interest."

"More pearl earrings and gold filigree rings," said Quinn, but her attention had wandered to someone who wore a round kepi cap like a fez and a red kerchief that might once have been a sash. She stopped pacing and looked Winthrop in the eye. "You have deceived me in every possible way. I want honest answers from you now or I

272

swear I'll make it my life's mission to make yours miserable."

"Don't be ridiculous. You can't threaten me. I'll have you arrested as a nuisance."

Without turning, she said, "Garnick, would you shoot a man for me?"

"I reckon if he was a thoroughgoing rotter I would."

"He is."

Garnick left the desk and came to stand at her side. "Just say the word."

Winthrop's arrogance withered as Garnick drew the derringer. "What is it you want to know?"

"You sent Ned Handish to us under false pretenses to help you track down Jack Stram. Did you tell Handish to fire a shot at us to make sure we took the case seriously?"

"No."

"Did you kill Handish when he ran into you at the Mansion?"

"I never saw Handish at the Mansion. I've no idea who—"

"You used Handish's name when you talked to Jemelle. What did she tell you about Stram?"

"Only that he was a mean drunk. She'd been seeing him for a few weeks when he showed up with money and demanded she make up a story about Elfie. She didn't know why he'd be spending time at the Kadingers. She thought he'd been living in a boat near the reaper works, but if he was I never found him."

"Did she know if he'd fought in the war?"

"No. That's all. Whatever else you may think of my character or my methods, I believe Elfie Jackson is innocent and I'm trying to prevent a terrible miscarriage of justice."

"Yes, the miracle witness." Quinn wasn't finished probing the sinkhole of the lawyer's character. "One last question. Is Thom Sinclair's name really missing from that property deed?"

Garnick held the gun against his temple. "The truth."

"It's there."

"And you cut a deal with Geneva Sinclair to simply delay until I gave up?"

"She was never going to relent. You knew that."

"I'll put a lead pill down his gullet right now," said Garnick.

"Wait," said Quinn. "I'm tallying up the money Mr. Winthrop owes us. What would you estimate a hundred acres in DuPage County would sell for?"

"Nearabout two thousand," said Garnick. "Round her up."

"Plus the cost of our office, which he burned to the ground."

"It'll run upwards of five hundred to rebuild or reimburse the owner."

"Plus the value of my personal possessions, which this rotter destroyed to keep the world from finding out he was Delphine Kadinger's jilted lover." She smiled. "By the way, Micah, I forgot to leave Delphine's ring in the office that night. I still have it. But fire wouldn't have destroyed it. The ivory may have been charred, but the gold wouldn't have melted. How could someone as brilliant as you not know that?"

Garnick dug the barrel of the gun deeper into Winthrop's temple. "How much money do you have, counselor, in cash and bonds?"

Quinn raised her hand and pushed the gun down. "I believe we can trust Mr. Winthrop to do the right thing, Garnick. That is, if he wants his reputation and his license to practice law to remain intact. I believe we can rely on Mayor Rice to make sure his attorney pays his debts and stays out of trouble until after the next mayoral election. Meanwhile I'm looking forward to an awesome performance at Elfie's trial. A win can only bring more business his way and keep money pouring into Mr. Winthrop's coffers."

CHAPTER 32

Quinn and Garnick arrived at the courthouse an hour before the trial was scheduled to begin. The street in front and the streets in all directions bustled with citizens zealous for justice, the kind meted out in a matinee melodrama. The mayor's luxurious monogrammed vehicle, pulled by two sleek gray steppers, parked in front of the main entrance. Rice waved magisterially to the crowd as he climbed the stairs. Around the corner Annie's bouncer directed traffic around her Landau carriage, which he had parked catty-cornered so that it impeded travel in both directions. A piratical figure with long, unkempt locks and a face like chipped granite handed Annie out.

"Cap Hyman, himself," said Garnick, drawing alongside. "Afternoon, Cap, Miss Annie. What's brought y'all here to the show?"

Annie debouched from the carriage door like an immense yellow waterfall, yards of silk spilling over a bluff. She set her overfilled pumps firmly on the ground and planted her hands on her hips. "You know damn well what brought us, Garnick. Is any dirt gonna come out about Henry Tench or did you promise what you can't deliver?"

"The show's yet to unfold, Annie." He guided Leonidas around the Landau and parked the rig.

"I hope she doesn't hold it against us when the city continues to put the bite on their establishments," said Quinn.

"Not much she can do long as we keep clear of Hairtrigger Block."

Quinn was less sanguine about what anyone could and couldn't get away with, but she marched up the courthouse steps fairly bursting with curiosity and residual anger.

Mayor Rice, Winthrop, and a heavyset man with mutton-chop whiskers and a thick sheaf of documents conferred beneath the judge's bench. Quinn guessed that Muttonchops was the prosecutor. Their heads turned as Annie and Cap promenaded down the center aisle and installed themselves in the front row. Garnick and Quinn took the seats behind and to the side in order to see around the yellow wall that was Annie. Winthrop eyed Quinn with something like trepidation. She hoped the look of unalloyed loathing she threw back at him confirmed his worst fears.

The judge presented an impassive countenance. His round, appraising eyes ranged over the assemblage as if sorting the sheep from the goats. Black-robed and nearly neckless, he reminded Quinn of a crow. At the only other trial she'd attended, the judge entered last and everyone stood. She wondered if the mayor's august presence had muddled the rules.

The defendant sat alone at the defense table – head bowed, hair primly netted, gloved hands folded in her lap. A dour and forbidding Sergeant Chesterton stood behind her chair, presumably to prevent any attempt at escape, and next to him a beefy policeman with one hand resting on the butt of his gun kept a beady-eyed surveillance on the growing crowd.

"That's Fogerty," said Garnick. "The guard Elfie knifed. And here comes our friend Tench and a few of his profiteering chums."

276

Quinn watched them slide into the pew across the aisle. Tench parked himself at the end of the row closest to her. He wore a black look and stretched his right arm as if to show that he could reach out and clout her if she caused trouble.

She surveyed the rest of the spectators. Behind Tench a middle-aged woman wearing round pince-nez spectacles observed the crowd from behind a wicker hand fan. Was she the alibi witness who was supposed to end Elfie's ordeal or was it the raw-boned woman in gingham to Garnick's right? The woman's head was bent over her knitting so she couldn't see anything in front of her but Annie.

A spleeny Verner Kadinger sat cheek by jowl with a well-dressed, self-important looking man, Caleb Cranston, or some other lawyer. She recognized two women from the Opera House ladies room whispering in the ears of their gentlemen companions.

Quinn turned to check out the late arrivals. "Moses' horns!"

"What?" Garnick followed her eyes. "I figured he'd turn up."

"Yes, but I can't believe he brought Josabeth. If Elfie sees them together, she'll have a fit of hysterics."

Bayer escorted Josabeth into a pew several rows behind the defense table. Elfie would have to about-face to see them. Burk saw Quinn staring and showed her his seductive half-smile. She thought she understood now why he'd placed Jack Stram in the Kadinger house and why he'd paid him to set the fire.

A flash of light scared the bejabbers out of her. She looked toward the source and saw Fen Megarian holding up his tray of smoking chemicals. He appeared to have suffered no harm at the hands of the city fathers.

"Get a bead on that mug," said Garnick. "He's like an old mouser after a snort of catnip. His Honor must have granted him permission to cover the trial."

Quinn hadn't forgiven him for what he wrote about her, but she had decided to supply him with the story of what happened to the Kadingers. She would hold herself strictly to the facts. Megarian would no doubt supply the poetry. She looked back over her shoulder. The first time she'd met Stram he said the man who hired him would be one "crazed zu-zu" if he learned that Stram was still in town. She'd assumed zu-zu was a drunken stammer or an obscenity she didn't know. Now she thought she understood. "Garnick, did the Zouave soldiers go by the nickname Zu-Zu?"

"I've heard 'em called that."

She said, "I'm going to go talk to Bayer."

"If you're fixing to stir the possum, I'd better come with you."

"If by that you mean confront him about Jack Stram, that's for after the trial. I just want to make sure he stays out of Elfie's line of sight."

"Don't goad him, Quinn."

"I won't." She picked her way through the crowd still jockeying for good seats until she reached Bayer. In a low voice, she said, "You shouldn't be here, not with Josabeth. What if Elfie turns around and sees you?"

Josabeth clouded up. "My goodness, I've never heard such effrontery."

"Don't take offense on my account, Miss Allbright," said Bayer. "Detective Paschal and I have a rapport." He showed Quinn his half-smile. "Miss Allbright insists I go out in public and not be deterred by all the foofaraw surrounding the trial."

"As if he had something to hide," sniped Miss Allbright, her ringlets bobbing.

Quinn glanced toward the defense table and the broad backs of Chesterton and Fogerty. The bailiff led the jurors into the box. A few of the men wore work clothes and dusty boots, but they all appeared sober. The mayor took his front row seat opposite Annie and Cap and nodded at the judge.

The judge banged the gavel and Winthrop and the prosecutor withdrew to their separate tables.

A tingle of indefinable dread passed through Quinn. "Elfie's under a lot of stress. You'd better take Miss Allbright out for a walk and give Elfie a wide berth."

Bayer rose. "I beg your pardon, Miss Albright. The detective and I need to clear up a misunderstanding. I'll return momentarily. Follow the action so you can tell me what I've missed." He took Quinn's arm and led her out and down the hall a way. He stopped in front of a closed door.

She said, "There's no misunderstanding. I've told you what I think. Don't flaunt your new lady friend in front of Elfie."

"You have a different look about you, detective. A gleam in your eye. I can't tell whether it's because you've solved your murder case or your romantic quandary. Either way, the change becomes you. What's put those stars in your eyes?"

His glib charm infuriated her. "I've finally figured out how you murdered your wife."

"Indeed? We must discuss your hypothesis."

"The trial will begin any minute. Mr. Garnick and I will pay you a visit later."

"I think we should talk now." He opened the door and maneuvered her inside. It was some kind of library, empty and windowless but lit by sconces interspersed among the shelves. Bayer closed the door and leaned his back against it. "So you've got the goods on me. Do please elaborate."

She had backed herself into this corner, without a partner, without a gun, and without a plan. She shouldn't let him bait her, but that self-satisfied half-smile – as if nothing could touch him – set her off. "It was Jack Stram who started the fire that killed Delphine and her father, but he did it on your orders."

"Now how can that be? I only saw the man when he called on Rhetta. We didn't speak more than a dozen words."

"That's a lie. You and Stram fought together in the war in one of the Zouave regiments. However it came about, you met again here in Chicago. Stram seemed like the kind who would tap a well-off friend for money and you needed a henchman. You arranged for him to meet Rhetta and you paid him to keep company with her in order to spy on your father-in-law."

"My father-in-law treated me like a son even before I married Delphine. Why would I want to spy on him?"

"You thought he was making bad investments, buying worthless water bonds, and losing money you considered your own. You didn't know he was in cahoots with members of the city council to spread doubt about the bonds, start a panic, then buy them back cheap from desperate sellers."

Bayer laughed. "Why, the sly old dog. He should have told me."

"Would that have saved his life?"

"There was plenty of money. Why would I want him dead?"

"Because like Jason, you wanted it all. With Kadinger out of the way and Verner disinherited, you could control the company, the investments, everything that came with the Kadinger name. I wouldn't be surprised if you inveigled Delphine to help plot her father's murder. She couldn't have guessed you'd commissioned hers as well."

His handsome features knitted into a parody of innocence. "It's true I asked Jack to keep an eye on the Kadingers for me, to watch where Rolf hid his papers and alert me if Delphine strayed back into the arms of one of her old lovers. But Jack was injured in the war. He wasn't right in the head. He stayed drunk half the time and often acted irrationally. If he misinterpreted his *commission*, as you so cynically put it, then he needs to be arrested and tried."

"He's dead."

That wiped the cavalier smile off his face. "When? How?"

"I shot him. He was trying to kill me. Was that also on your orders?"

"Is that what he told you?"

She wavered. Would a suggestion that Stram made a dying admission wring a confession out of Bayer? "Yes. He said you paid him four hundred to do the job."

Bayer let out a nickering laugh. She'd muffed it.

"Jack saw enemies behind every rock. If he thought he was being pursued, he'd have gone after you. He told me he'd gone after you when Garnick first began asking questions about him at Cap Hyman's. Jack was an excellent sniper. You're lucky to be alive. And you dodged a second attempt. Congratulations, detective." The smile returned. "There's no denying Jack was a menace."

"A menace to you. Weren't you afraid he'd peach on you?"

"Jack wouldn't have betrayed a brother Zouave, not if you'd cut off his hands and feet."

Quinn's stomach roiled. Burk Bayer was going to get away with murder and he knew it. He was laughing at her. "You're a monster, a manipulating devil without an ounce of human feeling."

"Yours is a lone voice, detective. I'm popularly regarded as a kind and generous soul."

She wanted to lash out at him, but he was beyond shame. "Did you pay Stram to dump dead bodies into the lake?"

"I thought old Rolf would see the error of his bond buying if the water pumping into Chicago's kitchens couldn't be kept free of human remains. Jack removed a couple of corpses from the cemetery excavation project, but he dumped them too far from shore. They didn't wash up near the intake crib as soon as I'd expected. It was wasted effort."

"I bet you didn't trust poor, not-right-in-the-head Jack to accomplish a successful arson. I bet you prepared the tinder and kerosene and placed it in just the right spot under the upstairs bedrooms before you left for Rock Island. All he had to do was drop his cigarette into your nest of flammables and hightail it."

"Even if happened as you say, you have no proof."

"Maybe there is proof. Stram was afraid of you. He called you a pit viper. He knew how cold-blooded you are and he was the only one who could link you to the fire. Maybe he left an insurance policy with Jemelle or Rhetta or Sue in case you decided to eliminate him as a risk. Maybe he hid a confession in one of those boats at the reaper works. If he did, I'll find it."

Bayer gave her a long measuring look, then leaned down, put his mouth close to her ear and whispered. "Listen to me, Quinn. You need to stop speaking these slanders. No one will believe you. I was in Rock Island. Whatever you think, it's all conjecture." His breath was hot and silky.

She shoved him away with both hands. "It's the truth though, isn't it? It all went according to your plan. You lied when you said you'd learned where Jemelle was working by reading the newspaper. Elfie told you her old friend had fallen on hard times and gone to hook at Annie Stafford's. You sent Stram to get acquainted and report back to you how she could be manipulated. Elfie knows you paid Jemelle to fit her up for the murders. I don't think you can rely on her absolute love anymore."

He gave her a pitying look. "You still don't understand, do you?"

The door bumped open against his back and he moved out of the way as Garnick pushed inside, a worried expression on his face. "Everything okay in here?"

Josabeth hustled in behind him, ringlets bouncing. "Mr. Bayer. You mustn't let these people monopolize you. You've helped them in every way possible."

"You're right, Miss Allbright. Let's return to our seats. The trial is probably well underway by now." He took her arm and walked her back toward the courtroom.

"Damn it, Quinn." Garnick shook his head in exasperation.

"I didn't mean for it to happen." Her nerves were still vibrating. "I'll fill you in later. What's happening in court?"

"Elfie's on the stand. Let's go."

The judge frowned as they entered a few steps behind Bayer and Josabeth. He apologized to the jurors and instructed the bailiff to bar the door against any more latecomers. Elfie answered Winthrop's question in a meek but clear voice. She had been Mr. Bayer's housekeeper, but couldn't help but hope he would someday marry her. She had behaved badly when he first dismissed her, haranguing him at the Tremont and trespassing upon the good will of his fiancée and her father at their home. She was deeply embarrassed and contrite, but she didn't set the fire. She cast a beseeching gaze at the jury and touched a lace hanky to her nose. The prosecutor declined to cross-examine.

The judge thanked her and Winthrop called Mrs. Arnetta Crowley to the stand. The woman with the pince-nez came forward and swore on the Bible to tell the whole truth and nothing but the truth. Yes, she was sure the defendant had spent the entire evening in her restaurant on the night of the fire. The poor girl had been brokenhearted and disconsolate but made no threats of any kind and there was no possibility she could have been anywhere near the Kadinger residence. The prosecutor again declined to cross-examine.

"I detect the intercession of a Higher Power," said Garnick. "I reckon His Honor figures closing out Elfie's case

283

the way we wanted will scrape us off his shoes once and for all."

The judge charged the jury with the duty to bring back an honest verdict on the basis of the testimony they'd heard and sent them out with the bailiff. He looked at the clock, nodded at the mayor, and remained seated. So did everyone else. In the quiet that followed, Quinn remembered a footnote in the book Miss Nearest had lent her. It described how at the end of a tragedy a god hoisted the actors up on a machine – the deus ex machina. The god explained all the bad things that had happened and restored order out of chaos. Quinn saw no deus ex machina, although the mayor seemed to have taken on the role of god. The judge's nod looked sure as a promise.

Across the aisle, Henry Tench scratched his nose and tapped his feet. The spectators shifted in their seats and whispered among themselves. The judge drummed his fingers on the bench. The minute hand on the clock ticked. Megarian's head stayed buried under the black cloth of his camera, waiting for his perfect shot.

The jurors were out for less than five minutes. They trooped in and the swarthy young foreman announced, "Not guilty."

Elfie leapt up and a wild cry broke from her throat. Megarian's camera flashed and banged and everyone was up and talking at the same time.

"Bugger all," growled Annie in a voice that carried above the noise.

The corruption of the trial left Quinn feeling hollow. For all the risks and losses taken by Garnick & Paschal, for all their efforts and energies, nothing they had done made a difference in the end. It was Winthrop's contrivance that freed Elfie and even though Quinn knew to a certainty who'd killed the Kadingers, there was no way to prove it. Bayer's self-satisfied smile, which was a tacit admission, would be deviling her for the rest of her days.

284

The mayor's imposing head rose above the crowd in the distance. Elfie had disappeared in the crush of the mob. Megarian, too short to be seen, was probably already pressing her for quotes. Quinn thought about waiting for her and offering her a ride to Mrs. Soseby's Rezidense for Single Ladys, but she'd told her where it was. It was up to her. Maybe she'd go straight to the bank, take the money Burk had left her, and go back to Rock Island. Quinn turned and her eyes met Bayer's as he waited for Josabeth to precede him into the aisle. He said, "No hard feelings, detectives. It's good to see your faith in Elfie's innocence rewarded."

Quinn took Garnick's hand. "Let's go somewhere. Anywhere."

They threaded their way through the crowd and down the courthouse steps into the afternoon heat. Quinn was at loose ends. She had no idea what she wanted next, nor even which way to turn.

"Burk!"

Quinn looked up and saw Elfie at the top of the steps.

"Burk! Thank you so much for the money."

Burk and Josabeth stopped mid-way on the steps and looked back at her. Elfie bounded down the steps, holding the skirt of her pretty dress with both hands, a radiant smile on her face.

"No," said Quinn, that tingle of dread returning. "No, no, no."

Burk's back was to her, his auburn hair shining in the sun. She couldn't see Elfie standing in front of him, but they seemed to be having a friendly exchange. Burk was laughing. Suddenly Josabeth shrieked and jumped away. Quinn started up, but Garnick held her.

The air went still, all sound and movement suspended. Slowly, Burk twisted around, a rictus of shock and pain on his face. He stared straight ahead into empty space, then his body jackknifed and he tumbled head over heels down the concrete steps. He landed at Quinn's feet, the hilt of a butcher's knife projecting from his chest.

The world lurched back to life with a piercing shriek and kept on shrieking. Men shouted and from somewhere above came a flash and a bang and a sharp chemical smell. Quinn looked up as Chesterton and Fogerty forced Elfie's arms behind her back and led her away. Her face was serene as a shriven martyr.

CHAPTER 33

Quinn turned over a queen, two tens and two threes. "Do I win?"

"Not this time." Garnick pushed three deuces across the table.

"But my cards have a higher count than yours."

"Your mind must've been elsewhere when I explained about pairs and triples."

She sighed. "He acted as if none of their lives mattered."

Garnick knew where her mind was. Transitions were unnecessary. They were spending the evening after the trial in her room at Mrs. Soseby's where, to allay the trauma and tensions of the day, he had half-heartedly suggested teaching her to play poker.

"All that tormented soul talk he threw out when we first met him at the Allbrights' house was guff. He had no heart, felt no guilt. Rolf, Delphine, Elfie, Stram, they were all expendable in furtherance of his interests." She had recounted her conversation with Bayer three times and each time she lighted on another shade of meaning. "You were a soldier, Garnick. You had your loyalties. But what kind of hold would a man have on another to make him do murder for him?"

"The army conditions men to carry out orders. Could be Bayer was Stram's commanding officer and Stram got used to doing whatever Bayer told him to do. Maybe that spent cartridge Stram carried with him came from a round Bayer took for him or saved him from. Or it could be Stram was just a blighter who'd do anything for money, same as Bayer."

She massaged her forehead as if she could rearrange the contours of her brain. "Tell me again what that copper told you. How did she get the knife?"

"They're not sure. She had breakfast in her cell with Winthrop under the supervision of a guard. Winthrop asked and received dispensation for her to clean up and dress for trial in the hotel across the street. She must've hoodwinked the guard to let her go to the kitchen for something. He turns his head and presto, she's got the knife. Leastways that's their story. Wouldn't have been hard for her to hide it under her skirt."

"Do you think what I said to her about Burk wanting her to be convicted is the reason she did it?"

"You can't know why another person commits murder, Quinn. Elfie had an abundance of grievances to choose from. I think she lied when she said she didn't recognize Stram's name. She may never have met him in the flesh, but I'd guess Bayer told war stories about his old Zouave buddies."

Quinn remembered Josabeth telling them about the 'spellbinding' stories he'd told her. Poor girl. She must be shattered and no one would ever convince her she'd had a lucky escape. A speech Medea made near the beginning of the play stuck in Quinn's mind. *Men's designs are deceptive, their vows though made by the gods, come loose.*

"We were right from the beginning about Bayer. Next time we get a case where the main suspect has an unshakable alibi, remind me to ignore it."

"We know Bayer used Stram as his cat's-paw," said Garnick, "but there's one killing I'm less inclined to ascribe to him."

"Handish?"

"Right. The thing I never got around to telling you was about what I saw on Handish's shirt collar."

"I remember. Some kind of wax, you said."

"It was lip wax. Pert nigh the same color as Jemelle's lip wax. I don't say she killed him, but she kissed him at some time or another. And that big roll of cash he had on him was never found."

Quinn thought again about the complicated and dangerous lives of the hookers and the thin line of defense that separated them from disaster. "If Jemelle did kill him and take the money, it should set her up comfortably in St. Louis.

"I reckon. If she's not arrested for passing counterfeit bills."

"True. It wouldn't surprise me if Marcel knows what happened to Handish and accepted a small gratuity for his help. Maybe even Lou."

"Especially Lou," said Garnick. "But maybe the spate of bad publicity for the ladies of the night will slow down now. Megarian's gripper happened in the city's most elite precinct and no soiled doves involved."

"I can't wait to read his poetic masterpiece." She got up and stretched her back. "I suppose Verner will inherit the Kadinger estate now."

"Unless Bayer has a long lost brother or a deserted bride comes out of the woodwork."

"Moses' horns!"

Garnick laughed. "There's no prophesying. Anything can happen." He picked up his jacket and threw it over his shoulder. "I'll be heading home tonight."

"Home?" She drew a blank.

"My cabin."

"Oh."

"Haven't been around much. Things to take care of."

"But it's early yet."

"It's a corduroy road. Not safe to drive over after dark. Don't want Leonidas to step in a hole. You need anything before I go?"

Quinn vacillated. She had a long list of criteria for how this relationship with Garnick should progress. There were rights and priorities and expectations to be negotiated. There were professional and personal obligations to iron out, financial responsibilities, the decision to marry or not to marry. If they didn't marry, how would they live? How would they present themselves to other people? Holy Mother of God, there was the dilemma of sex and the unintended consequences of sex.

Garnick's eyes crinkled at the corners. "I'd be pleased if you want to ride along."

She took a deep breath. There was no prophesying. "I'll just drop off Mrs. Soseby's key."

CHAPTER 34

CHICAGO TRIBUNE

This city was shocked anew yesterday by a specimen of murder transcending in its atrocity any previously recorded in this publication. Mere minutes after being reprieved from the gallows for causing the conflagration that killed Mr. Rolf Kadinger and his fair, young and accomplished daughter, Mrs. Burk Bayer, the murderess Elfie Jackson struck again with the savagery of a tigress.

Mr. Burk Bayer, whom a kind Providence had spared from the Kadinger catastrophe, was walking down the courthouse steps with Miss Josabeth Allbright, a familiar figure in society, when Elfie flew at them with knife upraised. With a pitiless countenance, she drove her weapon to the hilt through Bayer's heart. Seated around our family hearths in the gentle company of loving wives and mothers, we can scarcely comprehend so freakish an aberration of gender. This reporter has earlier observed the similarities to the fictional Medea. Yesterday, Elfie Jackson was her barbarous incarnation. She slew the innocent object of her sexual delusions and scattered mayhem through the crowd of spectators in attendance at her trial. As the villainess was led away, she showed no remorse.

An investigation has been launched. Readers may rely upon this reporter to discover why the jury acquitted and how the police could have allowed such a debacle to occur.

About the Author

Jeanne Matthews graduated from the University of Georgia with a degree in Journalism and has worked as a copywriter, a high school English and Drama teacher, and a paralegal. An avid traveler and crime fiction reader, she is the author of the Dinah Pelerin international mystery series. She currently lives in Washington State with her husband, who is a law professor, and a Norwich terrier named Jack Reacher.

Other Exquisite Fiction from
D. X. Varos, Ltd.

Chad Bordes:	THE RUINATION OF DYLAN FORBES
S. W. Capps:	RUNAWAY TRAIN *(coming in Oct.)*
Courtney Davis:	A WEREWOLF IN WOMEN'S CLOTHES *(coming in Aug.)*
Therese Doucet:	THE PRISONER OF THE CASTLE OF ENLIGHTENMENT
Samuel Ebeid:	THE HEIRESS OF EGYPT THE QUEEN OF EGYPT
G. P. Gottlieb:	BATTERED SMOTHERED
Phillip Otts:	A STORM BEFORE THE WAR THE SOUL OF A STRANGER THE PRICE OF BETRAYAL *(coming in Oct.)*
Erika Rummel:	THE INQUISITOR'S NIECE THE ROAD TO GESUALDO
J. M. Stephen:	NOD INTO THE FAIRY FOREST RISE OF THE HIDDEN PRINCE
Jessica Stilling:	THE WEARY GOD OF ANCIENT TRAVELERS
Claryn Vaile:	GHOST TOUR
Felicia Watson:	WHERE THE ALLEGHENY MEETS THE MONONGAHELA WE HAVE MET THE ENEMY SPOOKY ACTION AT A DISTANCE THE RISKS OF DEAD RECKONING
Daniel A. Willis:	IMMORTAL BETRAYAL IMMORTAL DUPLICITY IMMORTAL REVELATION PROPHECY OF THE AWAKENING FARHI AND THE CRYSTAL DOME VICTORIA II
Joyce Yarrow:	SANDSTORM

CPSIA information can be obtained
at www.ICGtesting.com
Printed in the USA
LVHW090441120721
692445LV00001B/16